Caligatha
By Matt Spire

Thank you:

Matthew Dabson for being the kind of lifelong friend everyone should have and the first person to read this book.

***

JD Saris for the millions of shared schemes and debates. It would be terribly insufficient to say my thinking and writing are better for them. I think I owe you a drink or two.

***

Steven Neal for the incredibly insightful suggestions that made this a much, much better book.

For my lovely wife Amanda, who believes in me more than is reasonable, has at least as much talent, and brought the cat into my life who really wrote this whole damn thing.

1

Tomb

After a sleepless night communing with his dead wife, Eric watches the world pass from the backseat with heavy eyes.

He'd sneaked out and borrowed this very truck, driven for an hour to the mausoleum, and unsealed Sofia's visage from the nutrient vat within her marble obelisk.

And for what? He wasted precious time. Every second spent awake brings her nervous system further beyond repair.

Eric jolts as Crane abruptly swings the dilapidated pickup into a small parking space, a perfect cube cut out of the pristine white walls of a loft. The exterior seems unaffected by time, save a broken front door and excess foliage draping through the bedroom's shattered glass window. A single tendril reaches past the balcony railing and sways in the breeze just above their windshield.

Crane gave them nothing. No directions, allowed little gear. The only radio is in Crane's ear.

Eric traveled to tell Sofia that Crane had become obsessed with these unexplained missions, but she sensed his despair before he uttered a word.

Another year, Sofia had said, struggling to part her cracked lips. *Just keep paying the jackals. One more year.*

So he'd spent the time lying instead. He told Sofia how close Crane was to having a cure, how he was saving enough money to buy the mausoleum from the jackals, until she'd lost the energy to listen. He resealed the obelisk while she slept, leaving her to an even deeper sleep, and stepped into the graveyard, passing the more peaceful dead to meet the dawn with a heavy heart.

One more year.

He forces himself to dispel the memory of her hairless scalp and gaunt face.

Pay attention.

He scans the loft. Eric has been through hundreds of these abandoned homes. Here, there are no stinging nettles or jumping cholla planted along the pathway to deter unwelcome guests, just an interior full of robust flora. No one is squatting inside.

In the backseat by Eric, Mae slips a flashlight attachment onto her rifle.

Eric grips the shotgun on his lap, watching the back of Crane's head. Already strapped to Crane's back is a flattened bag. A flashlight is holstered to his hip. Otherwise, he's empty.

"No one's home," Eric breathes.

Crane doesn't take the bait, doesn't mutter a syllable about what's inside.

He'd called this a typical sweep. More of the same bullshit.

Before, Eric intercepted shipments of medicine or performed solitary reconnaissance, at least pocketing whatever currency he found to pay the jackals.

There was nothing here. These modern lofts were the disemboweled remnants of urban convenience. Looters passed through decades ago like a swarm of ants, picking every bit of human gristle in mere days and leaving flimsy architectural bones for a more patient earth to digest.

One more year.

Crane presses his fingers to the radio in his ear. "Go," he says, and the three head to the front door.

The doorknob is missing, and the door shudders against the light breeze, groaning on its loose hinges. Without warning, Crane throws it open and steps into the dark.

Eric clenches his jaw at the reckless entry, but he and Mae follow, stumbling over the twisted remains of a screen door that's made its way indoors. Mae stifles a curse and turns on her light.

Inside, the loft is like every other abandoned home. Overturned, rotting furniture awakens in their beams, spindly shadows stalking them step by step on the yellow, water-stained walls. To their left, open kitchen cabinets and broken bottles. The skeletons of what might have been a family of possums draped across an island countertop. To the right, a face-down bookcase and the sunken frame of a sofa. The floor is plastered with so much old paper it's formed a brittle second layer over the hardwood.

Crane pulls out his own flashlight and paces the kitchen, a shell of paper cracking under his boots.

Mae's light stops beside him. A giant, warped painting rests against the wall beside a hearth. The fireplace and surrounding floor is blackened with soot. Another possum skeleton rests in ashes.

"Well done," she says. "Yum."

Crane roots through the cabinets as Mae heads deeper into the living area, towards a staircase.

Eric stares at the painting. The sunken canvas looks like an ancient map, the sort cartographers designed before explorers dared venture beyond the four corners filled with admonitions of darkness and monsters, but perhaps the continents had decayed on the canvas into shapeless, earthy brown froth after years of ruin. It was fitting enough. Darkness and monsters now pushed back against the torches.

"The stairs are good," Mae says, and they ascend to the second floor.

The bedroom is much brighter, covered in leaves and tendrils and the floor itself appears to have turned into a mossy soil. Vines have crept from window-to-window along the ceiling, spilling halfway onto a rotted bed, the only furniture other than another bookcase and a desk.

A breeze flows through the windows, weighted by a caustic stench.

Crane and Mae examine the bed and bookcase as Eric walks to the bathroom.

On the door is a partial handprint in dried blood. No patterns. Gloved.

"Mae," he calls.

Eric presses his body against the door, leaning in slowly, shotgun to the ceiling. Rotten air pours out, and broken shards of mirror glint from the sink basin.

Legs are draped over the bathtub.

"Mae," he says again, and her light shines into the bathroom from behind.

The man in the tub is a drifter with ragged clothes and one soleless shoe. From the looks of his blistered skin, he's been here a few days. The left arm is missing, but bandaged; he must've been dealing with that for a while. His head, a mess of beard and congealed blood, hangs at an impossible angle, cut deep at the throat all the way to the vertebra. Around him a porcelain halo shines black-red.

"He was killed in the tub," Mae says. "Not much blood on the floor."

"Surveyors," Eric tells her. "That's the work of a cutlass. He spooked 'em, pissed 'em off."

A cigarette butt rests upright on his chest, and around it a hole burned through his shirt.

"Yeah, Surveyors," Mae spits. "Steady enough to use the blade of their gun, vile enough turn him into an ashtray."

They backtrack into the bedroom, where Crane is holding a leather-bound book.

"I hope you found what you're looking for," Eric tells him. "The Guard sent—"

"Surveyors two days ago, yes. Look what they missed."

He hands them the book, its pages unsoiled and crisp.

***

If you're reading this, I am sorry.

The likelihood of your existence is exceeded by the probability of any one particular human sperm successfully reaching its mate. Or at least that's how Jericho explained things. His eyes glazed, fork suspended midair, forgetting the unchewed watercress in his mouth.

Don't bet on that baby, he slurred.

I'd said something about only one, any one, needing to survive to create life. Jericho rolls his eyes in this memory. He says something about the only thing certain is getting fucked.

"A big, sloppy..." and he stared at his fork as though he'd forgotten a word. "Mess. Miracle of life."

I am sorry. Even then, I was not thinking of you. I did not think of you until this final moment.

If nothing else, I owe you an explanation—how all this lifeless ruin is due to one man, a man so wrecked on guilt and drugs and sleepless nights he may well be insane. Why we've left you behind. But I don't know where to begin.

I owe my life to Jericho, twice over, but we never agreed on much. Never those fundamental questions of human destiny. The whys of life.

I remember all of it. There's not a detail I've forgotten. I keep piecing the conversations together, again and again, expecting a pattern to emerge.

Sometimes I believe there is nothing more human than forgetting. In a man's last hour, his memories may swell with the fragrance of his fondest lover. He may remember the shape of the moon on the night he professed his love. But when he tries to place the date, or even his age at the time, the only number that comes to him is a decades-old PIN, embossed on his cerebrum like square digits on a banking card or the LED of an alarm clock.

They say the devil is in the details, so I search those minutiae, line by line, hollow incantations that summon nothing but guilt and pain.

I wish there were things I'd forgotten. The rest choose what to forget and don't realize the choice is made until the memory slips away. But there are so many memories in this head. The old world is a boulder, and all that remains is an endless hill. It's a big responsibility, carrying it alone.

Maybe, then, I owe you this first confession: I'm only writing to convince myself this will be read.

2

Fugue

Jericho pushes two tablets across his desk.
Back and forth. Into each other. Away from each other.
There's every reason *not* to put the tablets in his mouth, *not* to take it one step further and chew them.
It's been a good day.
He sloshes a gulp of water around his bitter mouth, stares at the glass.
There are no good days.
He closes his eyes and waits. Half an hour until he leaves Blue Coral Inn.
Soon he feels it. The walls sink below his weightless body, his blood warms, thoughts fall into a languid mist—and in walks Maggie.
Had it already been thirty minutes? Just as time had begun to dissipate, the open door is like a violent injection of black ink in water. All serenity spins toward the open hole.
Her mouth moves in slow-motion. Drifting through the breaking waves of bliss and saying something he can't hear.
She settles into a chair.
Jericho stares at her lips, at the ballpoint pen digging into the corner of her mouth. His desk radio rolls in soft grey waves, a purring, frothing alien water.
"What?"
He realizes the radio's lost reception, fumbles with the volume dial. The waves recede. Everything fluid is gone from the room.

Solid edges, broken silences.

He studies her face, but can't really see it.

Here we go.

She smirks, the pen inching in, and he envisions black ink being sucked down her throat, encasing her skull, twisting from her eyes like blind snakes.

Tempt the ghosts and they will come.

With enough focus, the snakes disappear. He knows they're not real.

She leans in, laughing now, and he forces himself to stare at the details. The real details. Creamy skin, pearly teeth.

"You are *so* spacey," her eyes say, green wildfires scanning him over. The thin feathery lines above them narrow into a squint. Then, throatily, "Let's go to Paseka's tonight."

How long had she been talking?

Feel something.

"Yeah." He drags the dull ends of his chewed up nails across the desk, embracing the uneven texture, the wooden veins. They rise like roots under his fingertips. The walls begin to slant.

Shit. Pull it together.

He pushes his chair back and reaches to turn the radio fully off, but hits the volume dial and static ether rushes back over the room.

"No. Exhausted. Didn't get very good sleep...sleep last night. Tomorrow." It all rolls out fast, sloppy, disjointed.

She says nothing, exhaling loudly. Right away he remembers—she won't be here tomorrow night.

That level of focus takes too much effort. He's high, and the ghosts are seizing on this weakened state, banging on his mind's peripheral windowpanes.

He swallows hard to prepare for a full sentence. "To be honest I might just stay in one of the vacant rooms."

"Okay," *you fuck up*, "nothing new." *Just the same bastard you were yesterday.* "But you know I'll be out of town the next few days." *And I know you don't care.*

"We'll do something then."

He hates his indifference. But now he wants her to be gone. She wasn't supposed to come in, he was just supposed to get high and coast through the next few hours, sleep, wake up, repeat. But here she is, interrupting the plan. And the ghosts came with her, as though to say *you can't hide from us with your silly little pills.*

"On a Tuesday," she murmurs. "I'll be back in Caligatha on Tuesday."

"I know."

"That's not what I meant." She stands, straightens the name tag on her navy blue dress. "Look, I'll call you tomorrow."

He walks her to the door, dizzy. She's talking, but all his attention is spent on standing balanced with even weight on each foot.

With the salty breeze slipping in his panic recedes. The ghosts are already gone, everything is steady and in place. No more visions he can't control, no slanting walls or veins rippling out of his desk.

But no high either. That suspended feeling has inverted into a thousand tons. So much weight on each foot.

"I'm not going to..." She stares at him, probably looking for any sign of his attention. "Just take care of yourself."

He goes to say something without knowing what, but she kisses the corner of his mouth, that same spot the pen was drilling into her lip. Then she's gone.

Blotting the back of his hand on his forehead, he realizes how cold he is.

God damn it.

He waits for her to be far enough away, a slow ten-count. Then he rushes to the radio and turns it off in vindication. He resists staring in disbelief at the clock on his desk telling him it's been ninety minutes since he swallowed the pills, just palms the light switch hard on his way out and slams the door.

The breeze now prickling his skin, he sits on a bench behind his office. It's a short walk from the pier, but he endures the clamor and soon curls up against the wall, watching drums and crates make their way inland through bustling crowds in the distance. A few scattered groups walk by him, and a young couple stops a few feet away for no apparent reason, laughing at each other's attempts to wrangle their mouths around heaping ice cream cones.

Chittering like mindless, feeding insects. He imagines their stupid faces drowning on the melted goo.

His own imagination is pure irritability, never as vivid as what the ghosts conjure up. And the ghosts don't care about Maggie or nameless couples on the shore—no, they exist to torture him. Only him.

Today the ghosts came and left much quicker than usual. A brief reminder of his tenuous grip on sanity.

There's a pain between his eyes, a flowering bruise. It bleeds with patience into a familiar yellow-white flash lingering in his vision.

He covers his face and breathes. It's not so bad. He needs to rest, wait out the terrible inverted high.

In half an hour or an hour, he finds himself at ease, then jerking back awake from a falling dream.

His eyelid twitches, occasional voices boom in the distance, and an invisible gull or two grumble somewhere nearby.

His irritability has waned. The smaller, disparate crowds don't bother him anymore.

He props himself up.

A new billboard a block away stares back at him, a woman in a bikini leering over her dipped sunglasses. They must have put it up this morning. A faceless man, cut off at the ear by the edge of the sign, has his arm around her. *GET LOST*, it tells him. Strangers laugh in the background, some holding martinis, but the message seems personal. Her eyes are cold. She's not smiling.

I try, I really do.

He forces himself to think of Maggie, and how he pushed her away. He shouldn't have panicked and let her ruin his high, shouldn't blame her for it. But that only leads to how he doesn't care.

But she's right. Or the angry words he imagined simmering in her head were right, anyway.

There was nothing wrong with *her*, just how she had come into his life unannounced, like an insect into his bed.

You asshole. How can you compare her to a louse?

The gulls sound closer, and like they're arguing.

I don't mean it like that though.

"Shut up," he says to himself.

He sits, and after his blood redistributes, locks the office door and leaves.

It's a gray day, hard to tell the sky from the clouds from the water, but the sun will soon set. He's fallen asleep a few times on the bench or in his office, and the walk home along a black sea transforms everything into an empty fishbowl, all loneliness and mirrors.

An obsidian plane of sea foam is the stuff ghosts are made of, but none would materialize. Once a day is usually it.

And they aren't real ghosts, anyway. He doesn't think so.

He looks back at Blue Coral Inn.

Sleep tight.

***

Back in his apartment, Jericho rolls a cigarette by the open window. It's only about seven, but the sky is a glow of light pollution, a blacklight in the darkness.

He debates drinking coffee or scotch. Scotch wins out over the remaining week-old wet cement mold of coffee grinds.

A group of young men, no doubt away on a late holiday, shout at each other. Though he lives in a quiet area, it rests between the beach to the west and the nightlife in the southwest, so drunks are always crossing through.

The scotch will soon be gone; he'd fallen asleep clutching the bottle last night and not remembered how much he imbibed. Maybe he could call Reuben, see if he wanted to grab a drink.

No, damn it, he'd want to go to Paseka's.

Besides, he's not sure he can tolerate Reuben now anyway.

He takes a sip and decides to call Maggie.

"Jericho," she says.

"How are you?"

She doesn't respond for a moment, then, "All right. I just got to my parents' house."

"Oh. Why did you leave early?" But he doesn't want to hear the answer, cuts her off. "Do you need to go?"

There's a half-breath, half-laugh. It's always amazing how people put more meaning into precise little sounds than the words that follow. What's the point of language, anyway? To let these sighs mull around in the mouth, transforming the *huffs* and *tsks* into something more deceptive?

"No. But I told you I would call tomorrow."

"I've been thinking about you," he lies, regretting it as he speaks.

"Oh yeah?"

He stares at the window pane, into his own eyes.

Nothing. Why even call?

"We're not really dating, you know?" he says.

"Jesus. Thanks for the phone call."

And that's it.

He stares at the phone and wonders what he meant. It was something of a fact—had they ever used the word *dating?*—but stating it made it an even truer fact. Now he'd lost her for sure.

That would be okay because it was nearing autumn and the owner of Blue Coral would be gone until spring. The slow season had begun, and at least half of the forty-eight rooms at Blue Coral would be vacant until April. The kitchen staff of the adjacent Tombolo's Restaurant, he needed. Blue Coral's housekeeping he couldn't afford to lose. A front desk manager like Maggie would not be so necessary; he could check in the lonely winter wanderers on business trips, coordinate meetings in the banquet room with the kitchen. There was a night receptionist, so he wouldn't have to work nights. And no one this season would give a damn about the nightlife, so he wouldn't need to be knowledgeable about the concerts and fairs and theater productions that didn't happen in the winter anyway.

But none of it makes him feel any better for developing an immediate disinterest in her.

Everyone is just a fucking hole.

He takes out his last two pills.

Shaped like no one.

Two pills. Too many, too soon.

One to stop thinking about Maggie. With a mouthful of warm scotch, he swallows, calling Reuben.

One to deal with Reuben. He swallows again and walks to his bed.

Reuben answers after three rings.

"What's up, my man?"

"What're you doing?" Jericho mutters.

"Thinkin' of goin' to Paseka's with Fern, grab a few once the sitter's here. The lady got her cast off today. Celebration time, right? Sound good?"

This will not be a transaction, is what this means. For as badly as he treats Fern, he never gives Jericho drugs around her or their twin girls, Alana and Stacey.

"Not really. Maggie wanted to go there."

He does feel a tinge of guilt—Fern's arm had been in a cast ever since he and Reuben started talking again a couple months ago. She'd tripped on one of Alana's toys and fallen down the stairs. Jericho couldn't imagine what hell it must be, chasing after those girls with a broken arm. But he knows this celebration thing is just an excuse for Reuben to drink too much.

"Oh," Reuben laughs, "Maggie. Hah. Don't wanna ruin your depression with gettin' laid?"

"Something like that. I turned her down. She might be there."

"You're crazy, man, you should be all over that."

But he never was. She was the one who insisted on "getting to know him", on having drinks at the hotel bar, on staying in a room because it was too late and she was too drunk to drive home.

"Sometimes it feels like... we're just our relationships with other people."

"I thought you weren't dating, she was only on your back?"

That was true. They didn't have a relationship. She'd flirted and followed him about for a couple months, or a little longer.

But they'd never slept together again. Or maybe they had once, or twice. Surely she would give up soon. She would come back from visiting her family having realized what an asshole he was, snuffed of all desire.

"That's not what I mean."

"What?"

Jericho pauses. "Nevermind." He knows better than to be so nebulous with Reuben.

But Reuben says nothing, so he continues. "We are what we are...or aren't...for other people. We define ourselves... by our loneliness, by our unavailability, by... I don't know."

"Not even been a minute since I picked this phone up and you're already gettin' me down. What's that even gotta do with bein' with Maggie?"

"I don't know."

"I swear, you had more game when you were a damn scientist. How you even *manage* to bag a girl anymore—I'll tell you—*that's* a goddam miracle."

It's hard to remember. But in the snippets he sees of himself, he's going along with her every whim, offering elusive responses, standing disoriented in the doorway. Being pulled onto the bed. A willing prop with a truant mind.

Nobody's fault. Things happen.

Reuben is laughing. "No, no, see, let me explain something. That's how *you* define yourself. Relationships, whatever type, they're give-in-order-to-take situations."

"Marriage?" he bites, wondering why he even called.

Because there's no one else. We're just our relationships with other people.

These conversations always turn into lectures about how he needs to take "it" easy. As though the whole universe and everything he's endured could fit into a little two-letter word, three lines and a dot, and be flicked away.

No, he didn't call for this conversation. He called for drugs.

"Everyone uses each other for fun, fuckin', help, love, work, whatever."

If Reuben wrote a self-help book, it would be four letters long: beer. Or maybe three: sex.

What's that feeling? Hypocrisy? Jealousy?

"Lovely," Jericho says, resolving to end the call.

"Hey, hey," Reuben laughs, "don't go gettin' critical on the damn phone with me, man."

"Can I buy?" Jericho sighs.

"Tomorrow. Now, listen. Your life ain't what it used to be, I know, I know." *Rehearsed sympathy.* "You gotta let go, give in to shit like this. You're gonna eat every pill on the planet. Maggie, *Maggie*—I mean you *have*, you know, seen her? That ass is *therapy*."

"Nevermind."

"Man, if I had your money I wouldn't be tryin' to keep busy. I'd buy a girl or two like that, go to one of those islands, drink champagne off—"

"Thanks," Jericho interrupts.

Voice of a bigger asshole heard. Objective complete.

"Hey, look, just tell the girl you're done and move on, and don't sleep with one of your managers again, dumbass."

"I'd rather not talk about it anymore."

"Great. Believe it or not I don't give a shit about your soap opera. Keep padding my pockets, babe. But hey, I'm gonna go." There's a muffled thump followed by the sound of an engine revving and Fern's voice in the background. "I'll see you tonight if you can man up and come downtown."

"Are you driving?"

"Don't lecture me, dopehead. I'll have my license back soon." *Dopehead.* Knowing Fern heard stings.

"Right. Well, can we meet for lunch tomorrow then?"

"Uh, yeah. I'll have the girl cover me at the shop a little longer tomorrow. Man, I've got some stories with her."

"Thanks."

"You gotta get outta your stale apartment somehow, buddy."

"I was thinking of Tombolo's."

"*The hotel bar?* Christ on a stick," Reuben says, laughing as he hangs up.

As the line disconnects, it occurs to him he *could go*. Maggie wouldn't be at Paseka's because she's miles away at her parents'—he *just* called her. This lapse in memory should frighten him, but he's getting used to it.

Life itself is the only thing keeping score.

Oh well. It's hard to see Reuben and his wife together these days, although he couldn't deal with Reuben alone.

What a piece of shit.

He turns to the wall. A crayon drawing of fish talking on two cans and a string is taped by the side of his bed. He keeps little else on the walls, but Alana's drawing makes him smile from time to time.

Sometimes he can be happy when he sees little Stacey and Alana, little remnants of temporary innocence, if he ignores Reuben and Fern speaking in couples' tongue.

"Daddy, daddy!" a three-year old Alana chanted at Reuben once, excited feet stomping and knees bending, "How can fish talk on their phones without getting eletera-cuted?"

"Fish don't talk on the phone, babe," Reuben had said. "They write letters. They're old-fashioned like that."

"Oh. Okay!" And she ran off never doubting him.

Where Reuben was quick on his feet, Jericho had laughed long and hard. His laughing must have made an impression on her, because she'd rushed back minutes later with the drawing and in a shy whisper asked Reuben to give it to him.

He can't smile this time. Guilt tickles his throat. Staring at the crude and innocent fish makes him wonder what he would tell his own little girl.

Autumn...

He stares at the ceiling, the tickle becoming a tight ball.

She has no face.

The morphine is alive, its anesthetic fingers slithering up his face and wrapping around him. The last thing he thinks about is Fern's cold, stern face staring down at him in that hospital bed months ago.

Sorry.
He lets go.

***

Jericho doesn't dream the way he used to, where every fear of inadequacy is stark nakedness or decaying teeth. The surrealist connect-the-dots of dreaming only smacks him with terrible scenes and vivid memories. More and more, he's able to direct the dreams, feel a *part* of them. Eyelids twitching, enamel gnashing, twisting a full-body tourniquet of sticky sheets—for a reason unknown, he hastens along string after string of associations, entangled at every hyperbolic scene—can he change things? Alter the past? It doesn't matter. Soon the web breaks and he falls into the painful acid bath of reality, either birthed kicking and screaming or curled fetal, the helpless dead skin shed by a mysterious animal of dream.

Quarter to three, he awakens haunted by some phantasmically-connected string of faces, a centipede of eyes and mouths and melted wax skin, veins, sinew. Beautiful, sorrowful brown eyes.

Yellow glow fills the walls of his room, and he turns to stare at the desk clock's blinding light.

2:46, 2:46, 2:46.

He repeats the numbers in his head to drown out their sad whispers. "*Don't go, don't go...*"

The faces became more and more featureless as he passed them, dissolving dolls. At some point he realized he hadn't begun at the very start, hadn't seen the first face. Who was this person, melting in pain? This panicked him, and the faces panicked too, moaning and howling, "*Don't go, don't go...*" until they were mouthless little heaps, sounds of pain escaping in defeated pockets of air.

"Fuck," he says out loud, wiping his face and neck as though the vision was a tangible slime.

He didn't see her in the dream, but it must have been her. She's always in the furthest recess of his dreams. Laying in bed, feverish, beads of sweat collecting on her brow and huge belly, halfway through the third trimester.

He murmurs a plea for something reassuring, some nostalgic comfort, something that feels like home.

There's never anything.

The ghosts come and go, manipulate his visions, taunt him with lunacy, but when they come in dreams they're different. Tortured.

Frail arms of light are searching the uneven brick walls of his room, while a gangly spider hurries against a draft by the window to pluck together residence.

Only after nightmares, he longs for Maggie in his bed, a breathing talisman.

Something, anything, to fill the void he'd become.

He disentangles from the damp sheet, heads to the bottle of scotch. In the window's glow a silhouetted moth is suspended in the glass.

"Bastard," he says, tilting it. "Lucky bastard." Noticing wings flinch, he feels bad and puts the cap on, shakes it into a quick death.

He's out of pills too, but he's been excessive. He knows what happened last time, and he doesn't want that. Not yet.

Pushing aside all the formal white shirts he wears to work, he pulls a jacket out of his closet. The nights will soon grow cold; it's already a bit chilly in his room.

He stares at the wedding dress, wrapped in protective muslin like a corpse. His fingertips graze the surface before he gingerly pushes the collared shirts back, covering it.

***

Caligatha's streets are wet, stirring the feeling he's always trailing behind something. Silence nearly overtakes the whispering drip of trees and occasional splashing tires in the distance.

The long-dead cocoons of Victorian architecture never raise his spirits, but after dark the town seems to bow its giant head, commiserating. Jericho feels as ancient after his thirty years. These cluttered buildings, Industrial Age fever dreams of Gothic windows and trusses and scrollwork and turrets, stand despite infinite beatings from coastal storms, having lost but a few shingles or cobblestones to time.

They almost seem to take the abuse for lack of any other option; change would destroy the invented narrative, the charm of an idealized history. Everyone wants to live in tomorrow and vacation in yesterday.

Jericho's days, too, are designed to be at once transient and eternal, an endless and unevolving pattern of disposable experience. The roulette of faces at Blue Coral, the sleepless nights, the nightmares when he does sleep, the pills, the night walks. A fixed set of variables.

His memories become weaker and weaker; only the ones that repeat stick.

Three blocks from his apartment, he passes Reuben's new employer, Eden's Vineyard, tomblike in its solemn terra cotta. An eroding mural hangs between thin rectangular windows like a stray fingerprint, an Art Nouveau Eve clad in lush foliage. She appears to blow something from the palm of her hand, but whatever it was faded.

He's still mad at Reuben. *Dopehead.* He deserves that. But Fern—he can't stand for her to hear.

He peers into the black windows of Eden's Vineyard, wanting to uncover a private understanding, but he's unable to see past his own dim reflection.

How does Reuben treat the people inside? Does he greet everyone and smile? Does he make advances on the women? Does he bother to make advances on Fern anymore?

He walks away from the window with an eerie sense that someone might be watching from inside.

How do some people do what they do? Reuben frequented the places that fired him, soaked up the company of those he fucked over.

He's never been more disdainful than this past summer. After Reuben lost his bartending job at Paseka's by sneaking too much of the liquor into his belly, he managed the front desk of Blue Coral for a brief stint. Everything seemed fine until he didn't show up one busy June morning, leaving arrivals stranded. Half of the reservations were refunded, and a business meeting planned for the banquet room ended short of a fistfight between Jericho's frazzled chef and a locked-out group of realtors. After the chef and morning bartender walked, Jericho realized it wasn't an isolated incident.

Jericho didn't know. He took such great pains to *not know*. And with Reuben smoothing things over with the owner—well, he was always picking up Jericho's slack recently, at a price.

The real disappointment, however, was in finding Reuben. Casual and reckless—his name was on the front desk's computer, assigned to a room. He must've left his card key at home, and been too drunk to realize he could use the housekeeper's card, booking himself a damned room like an idiot.

Jericho swiped his own card, expecting anything. Reuben was sprawled unconscious on a twiglike vacationing student he'd picked up at one of the trashy tourist bars. One of Tombolo's whiskey bottles at the foot of the bed, plastic pourer still in the neck.

Jericho took him into his office and sat in tensed quiet.

Why are you such an asshole?, his mind screamed, *Pissing in your cozy little domestic bed! What happened? Why did you even marry Fern? Because you wanted what I had? Well now it's gone! You still have Stacey and Alana!*

But the two men's agreement was sealed in near-silence.

As they left Jericho's office, Fern walked up with their two little girls, kissed her husband's cheek. He could tell Reuben's blood was running cold, but somehow he tugged on one of her curly brown tresses and kissed her lips. Jericho choked on his nausea imagining the student's dried sweat moving from Reuben's to Fern's mouth.

"Good morning!" Stacey hollered as she clung to Reuben's leg. "Momma said we can have *bumblebee* pancakes for breakfast!"

Jericho tried to feel relief in the levity of her indecipherable demand, but everything once adorable now just seemed vulnerable.

"Why do you keep giving my man so many overnight shifts?" Fern said with a half-smile. Jericho studied her pouty lips for signs of a sad knowing. "You try handling these twin devils alone."

"I don't know," he told her, watching them walk off. Her arm around Reuben's waist. Reuben's sex-crusted hand running through Alana's hair.

"I don't know," he told the student as he helped her gather her things when she asked where Reuben was, snatching up a polaroid they'd taken at the bar to crush it in his fist.

"I don't know," he told Maggie, the night receptionist at the time, when she asked why everyone from the morning shift was so upset.

"You're a nice guy," she said, breaking the narrative. Pen drilling into her lip. "I'm sure it was nothing."

"I don't know. Are you free afterward?"

Is that what happened? Is that how they'd started?

"After one in the morning?"

"I'd like to talk. Can I meet you at the bar?"

She paused, uncertain, her lips poised like Fern's.

Sad, smiling, pouty, playful, confused.

What's the fucking difference anyway?

"Of course."

It's begun to rain again, and Jericho dives under Mila Ristorante's canopy, surprised to find he's walked fifteen blocks.

His memory has become like a winter tree. It grew out of his head long ago. All the facts dried up and fell away, and soon he'll just be following his own footsteps, circles in the snow.

Maybe everything with Maggie *was* his idea. Or maybe he just wanted her to take Reuben's job as front desk manager. He can't be sure.

So many *I don't know*'s. He wishes all women could be like little Alana. "Oh! Okay!" Running off. Realizing he was full of shit years later. In her head, some whimsical white lie, a fish at a typewriter, not a polaroid of a strange woman kissing her father.

Fuck you, Reuben.

But for what? Being his own honest reflection?

He pulls out a spare cigarette.

It's wet. He wishes he'd talked Reuben into giving him more pills instead.

He tries to think of innocence, of something Alana would say, but his own inner voice calls back in somber rhyme.

Circles in the snow, round and round we go.

3

Glyphs

Eric looks up from the leatherbound book.
"What the fuck is this," Mae asks. "Someone's journal?"
But now Crane shines his light into a footlocker he's placed on the bed.
"It's all here," he tells them, rooting through unblemished papers. "Look."
He hands them a clipping from a magazine. Mae takes it, and Eric is tempted to feel the texture against his fingers. Many years have passed since he felt such clean glossy paper, let alone one from a magazine. However banal, it is a strange artifact from another time.
Mae narrows her eyes at the print. "Gozip? What the hell is this?"

Gozip: Is it true that Jericho held wild parties on your property?
Melendez (former landlord): I knew there was drugs—like, pills—passing through sometimes, but you couldn't ask for a more quiet tenant.
Gozip: We've heard these parties were within weeks of the death. Can you confirm that?
Melendez: Oh, I don't know, Mr. Amano, he seemed very depressed, you know. He didn't move here until months later.
Gozip: Sounds like a pretty lavish lifestyle for an undergraduate drop-out, doesn't it? Expensive women, drugs?
Melendez: Mr. Amano rented the efficiency. No oven, mini-fridge.
Gozip: What about the women?

Melendez: He wasn't living on my property during the trial but if he had women around, I never seen them.

Gozip: What about reports of strange, ongoing experiments? Is it true he likes to lure these women to his home and cut them open with scalpels?

Melendez: When police came, when he overdosed, that apartment was empty, man, just like a mattress and a computer.

Gozip: No, maybe, bloodied panties or strange tupperware containers in the fridge?

Melendez: Man, I tell you, Mr. Amano didn't even have a pair of scissors.

Gozip: Disturbing.

"No," Eric says, "*That* Jericho? You're kidding me."

"Keep reading," Crane says, motioning to the book.

***

I didn't realize I'd been obsessively collecting articles about Jericho until I'd amassed five shoeboxes full.

It began when I stole the first article about the death from him. Jericho offered that I move in until I got on my own feet, but I figured he really needed someone to look after him.

That was when Jericho only made it into little newspaper articles, back when newspapers were still a thing. The Los Angeles Times. Other articles followed as the bizarre nature of the death caught on. Then the trial. The verdict of innocence. All the grisly details laid bare over the span of eighteen months, but he only saved the worst: the death.

I stole it, I suppose, because I was trying to steal the obsession from him. He'd read the clipping so many times, passing out on oxycontin or morphine and drink, that not a letter was unsmudged, the paper worn thin and soft. He tortured himself with it.

When I stole it, I didn't know there was video footage of the death. Like many others, I didn't see the video until it was admitted into evidence at the trial.

The video just tears your heart to shreds. The newspaper clipping became so meaningless in comparison.

Only he must have watched the entire video in the courtroom. I can't say what happened in that frozen moment, where anyone dared to stare in that room full of turning stomachs, but I had to draw my own eyes. Before the video even turned grotesque, as soon as I saw her, all vitality drained in her last days.

His recorded voice echoed through the court, asking if she was certain, and she begged. For the sake of their unborn child, for the sake of little Autumn. The brightest soul of my class, begging. I had to look somewhere, anywhere else, and by chance I caught his face. I watched him, in a state of misery beyond expression. Unflinching. Dante's nightmares could not devise a more horrifying punishment than Jericho endured at that moment.

When time thawed, I became aware of the commotion: several in the room had fainted. There was the rankness of vomit. But Jericho was still.

He'd been broken. No newspaper article mattered, no verdict mattered.

Not long after, his partner from University and only other friend committed suicide. Jericho tried to reach out to his family, to his widowed wife and two little girls, but they refused contact.

That's when the drugs started for him, and the articles for me.

I'd become obsessed with keeping those articles, the written transformation of a man. The slow rise from a nobody to a devil to a god.

I guess that's when it all started.

All those articles, and how much did I read between the lines?

***

"I barely remember this stuff," Eric says. "I was a kid when anyone last talked about it."

"We all were." Crane nods, solemn. "Now, I believe there's more to be found here than just an accomplice's confession."

4

Lydia

It's early, but the air is awake with earthy rain and coffee, the buttery aroma of the bakery, and there's something discernibly wintry about the air. Even the faint, fishy stench of the far away fresh market adds a richness to the morning bloom.

Lydia sets her book down and stretches. It's too dark for reading, especially under the table umbrella.

A car door shuts around the alley, and she jumps.

"Oh hun, look at you." It's Florence, owner of The Sandy Sparrow, rushing and fumbling with bags and an umbrella.

"Do you need me to move?"

"Move inside, you silly thing." Lydia takes the umbrella and bags as Florence unlocks the door. "Thank you. Now, what are you doing in this crazy weather? You're lucky someone forgot to put up the chairs."

"Woke up early. I thought I'd wait, it's really not too bad."

"I can't believe no one saw you." They step inside the dark cafe. "Is anyone even here?"

"I'm sure. It's been smelling wonderful."

Florence calls to her employees as she disappears into the kitchen, turning on the overhead lights.

Lydia sets Florence's things down and walks back to the entrance. "Would you like me to lock it?" she calls out.

"No. I'm late, hun, didn't you notice?"

She hadn't noticed, really. Nor, until seeing her reflection in the door, had she noticed how wet she'd become. Her dark chestnut hair is drenched black, its short wet clumps ridiculously plastered to her oval face.

"I'm an otter," she says aloud, shaking her head until it has some messy semblance of volume.

"You're a what?"

Lydia smiles and walks along the wall. Florence has hung new art. They're watercolors of ocean scenes in gorgeous detail, but each substitutes humans with fish or dolphins on beach towels and in life preservers. Under each is a title and price.

"Don't judge me," Florence says from behind the counter. "You know that's what everyone wants to see."

"This one says 'Shell Life.'" She taps a painting of a starfish tanning on a beach chair, and fakes a frown. "That's not a pun on *still life*, is it?"

"I don't make them, dear, I just sell them. We'll be ready to go in a moment."

The door swings open and Lydia locks gazes with a familiar-looking man. Shortish, about her height, and like a shadow, all brown and black with sad blue eyes. For a brief moment, he seems to recognize her too, and she can almost feel his gaze moving across her like fingers on braille. Then he jerks away and marches for the counter.

They've almost passed a few times in the street, she thinks. Late at night when she can't sleep.

She sits and watches Florence and the man talk. He asks if they have coffee, and Lydia snickers. She notices him fidget, looking around nervously, and lowers her head.

After a while, he sits a few tables away with a steaming cup, drawing circles on the table with his finger and stealing glances at her.

Florence brings her usual banana-nut muffin with a chai to the table and asks if she's reading a self-help book.

"Oh, no," Lydia laughs, flipping the cover over.

"Accounting?"

"Some light reading for the store."

"Aw." Florence flashes a patronizing smile, but then she asks how her father's doing.

"There's still some good days in there."

Really, they're all the same, but people like to hear about "good days." No one wants to hear, "*This is the nine-hundred and first day in a row to be worse than the last.*"

"Well, you should bring him down sometime if he's up to it."

"Sure. He's a recluse now. A big, fat, brown recluse."

Florence giggles. "Oh, we need to fix that." Then to lighten the mood she raises a brow and nods to the man, rolling her eyes, and Lydia wonders what he must've said after she tuned him out. Florence walks away, leaving her curious.

That stubbly, pensive, square face and nervous glance evoke something hard to place, like an aging memory of a faint dream. She picks apart more food than she eats and leafs halfheartedly through the book–in part because she has already learned many of its lessons on her own, but mostly because she finds herself distracted by the strange man.

Florence returns, and Lydia places her money on the table.

"It's almost Fall," Florence says.

"Do you like Fall?"

Florence squints. "Are you going to school this year?"

"Next year, maybe."

"You're a bright girl, Lydia."

She sips the last of her chai, deepens to a passive, self-assured voice. "I know. I'm waiting for the professors to catch up."

Florence snickers and collects the money. Walking away, she says, "This town's one big service industry, hun. Nothing is real here."

Lydia stands, looks to the windows. The sun is breaking.

The man is looking outside, too. She feels strangely brave.

"Have I seen you somewhere?" she asks, trying to sound as polite and unbothersome as she can.

"I don't know," he says before turning. It doesn't seem true, even though he's answering for her.

"Oh, well, small town." He reacts to her smile by staring back at the table. "Well, have a nice day."

The invisible fingers of his eyes trace her back again, and she can't tell if she likes the flustered sensation it stirs.

***

Back at Eden's Vineyard, Lydia plans her day. She writes "call restaurants" in her notebook, and stares at the next empty line.

With any luck, the emerged sunshine will continue, and vacationing couples will stroll in to complete their night with a merlot or malbec or champagne, their security deposit towards romance.

But she can't rely on that.

She yawns, regretting the mild chai. Nothing would feel better than her soft bed, the cool draft of her window.

Around her stand narrow aisles brimming with the dull glimmer of bottles. Nothing to restock, and these modest sales would diminish in the coming months.

She spends a few minutes chalking up a description of a new fall beaujolais on their blackboard, even drawing the berries and pomegranates. They look like a horrible pile of severed eyeballs or little white olives and onions, so she redoes them in purple and red chalk. Remembering it's Saturday, she adds an apple brut cava, and the word "TASTING" in huge letters at the top. Careful to avoid anywhere it might get wet if the rain returns, she places the sign outside under the giant mural.

She always feels strange putting silly drawings under the mural her father had commissioned, an enormous homage to the mother Lydia never knew. It faded prematurely, and was too stylized to resemble her mother in an eerie way, but it is vast and emotionally dense.

In the kitchen she grabs a tonic water and mouses up the loud wooden staircase. Her father Claudio is resting, silver hair matted to his pillow, but opens his eyes and grunts when the door creaks too much.

"Good morning," she whispers.

"Is it?"

She sits in his wheelchair. "Good, or morning?"

He mixes a laugh and cough, pulling himself up. "Either. It can't be morning."

"Let's see. I ate breakfast. They delivered the paper. The sun's up. I'm sorry. No one's waiting on you."

"You should've woken me earlier."

"Oh, come on! Make up your mind, old man!"

She understands what he means. Ever since she was little, he woke up at dawn to unload cargo at the docks until he had enough money to open Eden's Vineyard. Old habits die hard even when they can't be practiced.

"Bah." He motions to his bedside table. "I smell rain."

She takes his pills from the drawer, dragging the wheelchair closer with her feet, and stops.

The bottle is so light in her palm. That isn't right at all—no, it should be nearly full.

Digging for another bottle, the *right* bottle, she grits her teeth—*no, no, no*—tries to channel the energy into shaking her leg. But there are no other bottles and she knows it.

In the last couple months, father's been taking twice as many pills. And behind her back, too. Acting stoic.

"You're imagining things," she says of the rain. She's terse, but she can't help it. "It's a beautiful, sunny day. We should go for a walk." She hands him two pills and the tonic water.

She's tried to ignore it, hasn't checked in a few days but—she grips the hollow, weightless bottle—what were there?—fifteen, twenty? She can't ignore it anymore. More and more go missing.

Downstairs the door opens, and Reuben calls out.

Father takes his pills, swallowing hard. "It is late," he says. "Dust off my cobwebs and take me downstairs."

And down the longest eight steps in the world they go. Every day she can feel that miniscule difference, his weight dropping pound by pound, as she strains less and less to hold the chair—everyday it's easier, and everyday it's harder all the same.

"Your clothes are damp," he says halfway. "I might be a haggard troll, but I'm not blind."

"It's beautiful out!" she insists. "I fell in the fountain."

"What fountain?" she croaks, imitating his voice. "The one near the new church. What new church? The church near the bookstore they built twenty years ago. What new bookstore?"

"Oh, stop." But he coughs, which she guesses is a laugh.

She needs to keep talking, keep him laughing. Anything to cover the agonizingly slow *thump, thump, thump* of the wheels hitting each step, jarring his pained bones and pummeling his dignity.

Big, fat brown recluse. Not so much.

Reuben is filling the register when they emerge. "Gonna be a big one today."

"Good," her father says, "I can almost afford the concubines to push me around."

He insists on wheeling himself through the aisles, examining the stock, then settles in the corner, exhausted.

Lydia brings the daily mail. The paper is the only thing he'll invest himself in, his last connection to anything beyond these walls.

"Looks the same as yesterday," he says.

"We did pretty good, even for a Friday," she tells him. It's a half-truth, but it doesn't matter. He only pretends to keep track of business. "And I call the restaurants today to take their fall and winter orders."

He ruffles the paper. "Is Macbeth still at the theater?"

"I'll also host a tasting today for some of our new fall items."

"Nice drawing," Reuben says in a tone that's either condescending or flirting. She imagines he uses the same tone for both.

"Here, Caligatha Ensemble. Fridays at nine and Saturdays at seven this month. We missed last night."

"It's Saturday, Dad. We can't close."

He might seriously expect them to. She can never tell how confident he is of their financial stability. It had been a mystery beginning with her gradual inheritance of overdue bills and sloppy bookkeeping. She suspected whatever poor business skills he had only suffered as he shifted focus of all his fortitude onto the cancer.

"They're only performing Macbeth because of Halloween, I'm sure of it."

"Oh. Then it's settled. We'll close up at five so we have time to make our picket signs."

She would like to take him. A year ago, he stopped visiting his last spot in the outside world, the beach at dusk, where he stared out at the golden horizon as though witnessing the parting gates of heaven, waiting to join Lydia's long-gone mother. But now all sense of wonder is dry. Whatever meaning the play holds for him, she wants to believe it promises he still has vitality remaining, buried deep down.

"Reuben," she asks, "would you mind opening so we can run some errands?"

"Anything you want, babe. I was gonna ask if you'd cover me an extra half hour at lunch."

"I'm staying here," her father says.

Lydia frowns. "You could use the sunlight."

He shakes his paper. "I'm not a plant."

"Yes, you are."

"Then my ass is rooted right here."

Fine. At least she knows the longer she's gone, the longer he'll be stuck downstairs, forced to socialize with Reuben and the odd customer or two. There was no way he'd break his stoicism to ask Reuben for help up the stairs.

"Okay. I'll be back in time to cover you for an hour, Reuben, but could you try to find some missing stock while I'm gone?"

"What is it?"

"I left a list in the back last night. Just cheap stuff, but I can't find the receipts."

"Crazy," Reuben says. "I'll check it out."

***

Watching colorful multitudes pass on the way to the pharmacy, she tries not to dwell on Eden's Vineyard or her father, but she can't help it.

She's worn sunglasses even though she hates when people can't look in her eyes. There's a hard tightness in her throat and her sinuses swell.

Dr. Garrick is always kind when she hands over the prescription, asks how she's doing by name.

"Good," she chokes. She'd like to give some humorous anecdote, her big claim to fame, but it's not happening. Not today.

He adjusts his glasses and reads, though her father's prescription has only changed twice in three years.

"Still kickin'?" He grins. She's not sure exactly what the joke is. "I guess I'll have to wait until the next wedding anniversary to see old Claudio."

Lydia catches herself looking puzzled, then realizes he means visiting Eden's Vineyard, since father hasn't come into the pharmacy in so long. She's zoning out, staring at his ashen mustache and coat, hating the way he resembles all other doctors.

It always reminds her of the day she got the big sit-down. She was eighteen, but in memories she seems younger, and the doctor is huge, his white coat hanging above her like clouds of judgment. There were so many unfamiliar, heavy words, like being cursed at in a foreign language. *Stage three. Carcinoma. Renal cell. Metastatic.*

Now she understands all of them far too well.

The cancer spread through his body and into his bones like a tree endlessly thirsting for pain. It was the doctor, of course, who told her about pain. Since her father refused operation, he wanted to use another one of those words, what they called *immunomodulating* drugs, but her father wanted nothing to do with it, holding out even on painkillers at first.

She leaves the counter. Everything in this place is a horrible reminder of the terrible things now or the terrible things she can't remember because she was too little. The baby monitors, the pregnancy tests.

Cancer, childbirth, all this inside-out death.

Outside, there are so many couples. If it wasn't for that nearly empty pill bottle, she'd beam back at them, at the kids feeding birds. But now she's souring, staring at what looks to be a foreign student in Caligatha for summer work. Her strapless top, short skirt. Her beyond-stylized hair. Later tonight this girl will probably go to the club, enjoy loud music, drinks, sex. Carefree. All like soaking in sunshine. No consequences.

She goes back in to check on his prescription. It isn't ready, so she buys a pack of cigarettes, her first pack since the last time she came to the pharmacy.

Outside, she walks away from the crowds, finds empty tables in the nearby park and sits to smoke.

She feels ungrateful. She could've been just like that student. Her father worked hard, tried to save.

"God chose you for a reason," she used to hear when she was little. Greatness was to come from such tragedy.

She watches the student walk by. She can't be much older than eighteen. And really, the way she dresses, her mannerisms—that *was* Lydia three years ago.

There are so many just like this student. All those clones of the three-years-ago Lydia, now they're just the ebbing and flowing crowd. Back then, she could pick out a person here or there as a friend, but her friends moved away to study and she hadn't replaced them. There were acquaintances all across town, like Florence, but no one close, no confidants, no one she could bribe into taking her father to the theater. Unable to afford more employees, she was always at the shop or watching over her father or running errands for either of the two. She wasn't so sure she was the product of divine intervention, but whatever the intent, her reason for existing had become finding ways to pay rent. The glorious phoenix with clipped wings.

She crushes her cigarette on the table, glad she wore the sunglasses, and returns to the pharmacy. This time the medicine is ready.

She starts to ask if filling her father's next prescription early would be possible, but stops. She already knows the answer. They'll need to increase his dosage. Which means she needs her father to fess up to his increasing pain and go to the doctor.

Maybe Reuben can cover the store next Friday or Saturday so they could attend a showing at the theater. That might open him up a bit.

5

Necromancy

I should clarify that Jericho was never a monster. After all, he saved my life twice.

We first met at UCLA when he was still a graduate student, I about to be a retired professor of literature.

His was the rarest case of sheer brilliance, which following the shoeboxes full of glossy magazine cover articles scarcely needs further expounding. She was the most insightful, gifted student in our creative writing program, and his reason for living from the moment they met. Any of her tribulations became his own.

Perhaps it could not have been any other way. Someone gifted with his brilliance is often lacking in guidance. He needed that balance. She was his intuition, writing the maps as he lit the way.

Indeed, it was her parents that drove him toward immunology. She was, next to my own wife Emma, one of the strongest people I've had the gift of knowing, capable of channeling misery into superb memoirs reflecting a far greater scope of the human experience. Jericho, I'm afraid, in his limited capacity for the abstract arts and boundless desire to please her, saw only injustice and the lack of resolution.

Where those experiences gave her incredible resolve, Jericho heard the trumpets of war, the war on disease. Despite what anyone believes, despite what happened, he truly had the best intentions. He told me he wanted to "kill death," a statement no more foolish or brazen than that of any young genius with a new generation of technology at his fingertips.

When I tell this to Emma, she reminds me that countless spiritual leaders and mythological gods found inspiration in the same directive. This savior complex has resulted in the deaths of hundreds of millions more in the relentless hunt for infidels, witches, and evil spirits than have ever been saved. Which is probably zero.

But it was undeniable that Jericho had tipped those scales, I would tell her. Jericho has saved millions, and none have died in his own hands save the one he loved.

I should clarify that Jericho was never a monster, but I don't tell her that anymore.

No—anymore, I still believe in his heart and his brilliance, but I've awoken to Emma's consternation, catching off-handed remarks that rouse wonder about the hunt for invisible evils that Emma ascribed to saviors.

Something inexplicable, like muttering about ghosts.

***

Eric closes the book. It's impossible to remember. He knew the name, but–*Jericho Amano*–people hadn't really uttered it since he was a child.

Empirical knowledge of the time is gone, obliterated. These stories are forgotten legends.

Crane knows something he isn't willing to share.

He listens to Crane and Mae shuffle through the downstairs. If something is hidden in the loft, what could it be?

A small part of him wonders if Crane thinks he'll discover the cure hidden in another footlocker, or under the floorboards; they'd unearth original blueprints for the virus, and work backwards from there.

Hadn't they given up figuring out why everything went wrong?

He steps over to the rotting bed, to the open footlocker. It's filled with nothing but magazine and newspaper clippings. Most of them are brief and sensationalist articles about Jericho, but there's a few from scientific journals.

Immunology. Realm.

He picks a sheet with the smallest print.

Realm, Mental Health, and Safety Concerns in General Population Users, the heading declares, with a smaller note that reads *Leviathan-funded study*.

It's all a joke now, like reading about the science of alchemy.

***

Abstract:

Episodic Dissociative Projection (EDP), or colloquially "Ghosting", has been reported in a minority of users representing 0.02%. This figure is based on collected physician diagnoses and consumer reports in the controlled market of the State of California and may be higher.

EDP is characterized by infrequent feelings of disconnect from one's own body; not feeling in control of one's moods, thoughts, or actions; equilibrium disturbance; and rapid fluctuations in environmental perception. In extremely rare cases (two to date), vivid hallucinations and short-term memory loss and/or potential psychogenic fugue have been reported.

No evidence exists of symptoms persisting separate from or beyond cessation of Realm.

Because of the nature of Realm and relatively low incidence of EDP, it is difficult to discern whether these episodes are symptomatic of rare and idiosyncratic flaws in the consumer's unique adaptation to the experience; pre-existing and undiagnosed mental disorders independent of Realm; unadvised concurrent administration of psychoactive drugs; or as-yet undocumented flaws in the design architecture.

Given the low incidence rate, seemingly transitory nature of EPD, and lack of FDA interest to date, authors recommend uninterrupted operation and continued, long-term study.

6

Ghosts

Jericho sits at the receptionist's desk of Blue Coral Inn, watching a gull make its way up the stairs to the front balcony outside. A departing group sits on the benches, amazed, whispering to each other. He imagines it will continue up to the window, hop up and in, and peck at his skin. He itches at the thought.

By noon, all but four guests have checked out, and three of them are staying the weekend. One appears to be a glitch in the computer. He scans the monitor's long list of rooms, too anxious to focus. It's a jumbled grid of codes, NORES, OCCUP, CRLRM, TMBRT. His head begins to hurt.

No ghosts. Please.

He focuses on one occupied room. Room 114. The checkout date reads *00/00*.

He stares and stares at the numbers.

00/00.

He's out of touch with everything at Blue Coral.

He prints yesterday's records, restarts the computer and tells housekeeping to keep an eye on the front desk. His irritability is returning, and not wanting to hear a word from anyone else, he rushes past the idle bodies on the porch, stirring away the gull, and leaves.

Reuben is already at Paseka's, two beers in, chatting it up with a bartender Jericho's never seen. Her blonde hair is pulled back in a ponytail, her pink short shorts and legs crossed as she leans on the bar. Otherwise, it's dead empty.

Already he doesn't want to be here.

"My man," Reuben says. What a grating voice. A dumb bellow with a cocky inflection. "Grab this fine man a cider, babe."

"It's noon," he protests, but she brings him one anyway and tells Reuben she's going to smoke. Jericho wonders why she feels a need to tell the only patron where the fuck she's going. In fact, he doesn't understand how Reuben can even sit in this bar without a shred of humility less than half a year after being fired.

He watches the pink short shorts cross the bar.

Oh wait. I do.

After the door closes, Reuben sneers. "All right, Sober McGee, here's your drugs," and he throws a bag of twenty pills on the bar.

"Fuck you," he says, but pockets the item and tosses a wad of bills on the bar. "I'm not the one with problems."

"Don't make me laugh. Maybe you oughta take one now," Reuben fires back, unphased.

Jericho fondles the perspiring bottle in his hands, wondering what sound it would make hitting Reuben's thick skull.

Chill out.

He does want one now, but resists the urge.

"Sorry," he says, "didn't get much sleep last night."

"Surprise. Isn't Maggie outta town?"

"Yeah. Until Monday or Tuesday. I called her before you last night to break it off."

"That's a shame."

Jericho wonders what that means, or why he's even sitting here. He's got the drugs. He should just get up and go.

"Well, I didn't, I don't think. I don't know." Before Reuben can respond, "When do you have to go back?"

"Whenever," Reuben says. "But I'll be damned, was three accidents gettin' here."

"Weird." He goes to say something about Reuben being careful, with the drunken driving charge, but stops himself. Maybe it's because Reuben would get upset, or maybe he doesn't care anymore.

"Yeah, some guy—you know that one French cafe or whatever?—drove his car right through the goddam window. Be glad you're port-side, man, someone'll probably plow through the storefront and into my ass before the day's over."

"How is the wine store?"

Reuben laughs. "Easy money, just not enough of it. But you oughta come in sometime and check it out."

"Oh?"

"The owner, this old man, he's days from–" Reuben stops. "Eh, he's just really old. But the girl, his daughter, goddam. She's odd. Like, perky, all that fake smiling and in-charge stuff. And attached to the old guy. They live on the top floor. But damn, she'd be a hot little piece if she wasn't so weird."

"Oh." Jericho stares at the bar, waiting for Reuben to finish describing the girl's body.

As boorish as Reuben is, his one-sided conversation stirs something between envy and longing in Jericho, which makes him feel worse about Maggie. Watching Reuben wave around and shape his hands, he envisions her, but he isn't filled with lust.

Then he talks about his job, but Jericho's mind wanders to how annoyed Reuben is making him.

It's his own fault. Those self-pitying sleepless walks spent in miserable nostalgia, walking the great white topographic nothing in his head.

He begins to feel that pounding, weighing down his skull.

We're just our relationships with other people.

He thinks of the sign on the pier. *Get Lost.* The moth in the bottle.

Past futures and future pasts.

Something is awake and churns in his stomach.

God damned fucking chemicals.

The gray wash of the radio's lost reception.

The melting faces in his dream.

00/00.

The nausea swells. He stumbles off the barstool and hurriedly makes his way to the back of the bar through a blurred maze of stools, collapses on the bathroom door, catching his balance before hitting the tile.

Where are the pills?

He hoists himself up with shaking legs.

No, no, not the pills.

Leaning over the sink, he watches his face vibrate and expand. His fingers slide into the porcelain. The mirror shakes until he sees double, then an endless string of mirrors, an endless string of faces.

Don't go. Don't go.

He's being tossed around, turned inside out.

Then everything is black and weightless.

"Jericho?"

He jumps, grips the bar hard. It's not porcelain. It's not a sink. It's wood.

"What the fuck man?"

A cold sweat covers his body.

"What the fuck?"

"I'm okay," he manages.

"What's wrong with you?"

He looks around, unsteady. He's at the bar. The door is opening, and the bartender reenters, tossing a cigarette butt into the street behind her. Reuben is staring him dead in the face.

"You be goddam careful with that shit."

"With what?" he says, weak, and realizes Reuben is talking about the pills.

He pulls them out, counting in his shaking palm. There's eighteen.

"Yeah, that. Put those away. Did you just take some?"

He hears himself make an unintelligible noise.

"In the bathroom just now," Reuben says, firm, eyes wide and red.

"I have to go to work," he struggles to say. Forming the words is as clumsy and difficult as swallowing his own tongue.

He gets up, legs still shaking, and rushes past the bartender at the front door, holding himself and shivering. A block away, he darts into an alley between two buildings and vomits before he can reach the ground.

He rests his palms on the dirt and grass, spitting. His head pulses and rattles like a broken drum.

After a moment passes, a cool wave rests over his skin, and he notices the painful little pebbles digging into cramped hands, the rotten taste in his mouth, the burning of his lungs.

"Unnhhh," and he spits again.

His whole body shaking, he stands, leans against the brick wall, staring without thought at dead weeds under his shoe.

Afraid Reuben will turn down the alley any moment, worried and yelling, Jericho hides his face against the rough brick, gasping for air.

The ghosts have never been so violent.

***

In his apartment, Jericho stares at his laptop, hand on his chest, monitoring a steady heart-rate.

Depression. Insomnia. Anxiety.

It's been less than sixteen hours.

Dizziness. Nausea. Paranoia.

He knows all this, looking it up was pointless. This isn't just withdrawal. He's nearly died before, been to the other side and only half returned. But nothing like this.

His phone rings. Reuben. He doesn't answer.

Where the fuck is "out of body experience"? Hallucinations?

He gets up, knocks the bag on the floor, stomps on the pills over and over, and throws the remaining powder in the trash.

Collapsing on the bed and weeping, he throws his ringing phone at the window. It clanks off the bottle of scotch.

He curls onto his side, defeated.

Here he is again. What was it–six months ago?–not long before he found Reuben cheating on his wife.

That's when the ghosts and nightmares and memory loss began.

If it wasn't Alana and Stacey's birthday, Reuben and Fern wouldn't have stopped by.

If he hadn't sounded so stupid on the phone beforehand, they would've stayed in the car waiting; if he hadn't left the door ajar in a hazy stupor, they wouldn't have seen him sprawled out half-dead like a blue-lipped rag.

Unlucky luck.

A few hours after an injection of nalaxone at the emergency room, he wished Alana and Stacey a happy fourth birthday from a hospital bed.

Poor little girls and their ruined plans and abruptly limited trust.

His phone rings again, vibrating angrily on the wooden floor.

You bastard.

That's it, isn't it?–It's the adultery. The guilt.

Reuben stopped giving Jericho drugs when he was fired from Paseka's, when the dope was harder to come by. Jericho's tolerance lowered, he overdosed, and was he a worthless piece of shit or *what*.

But then Reuben's infidelity came and their friendship rekindled as if Jericho was never discarded. Reuben tried his damnedest to get drugs.

Reuben *needed* Jericho in his life, *needed* to compare himself to scum, to a drug fiend.

Jericho grips the blanket until his hands hurt.

He also needed Jericho to be untrustworthy, or Jericho could ruin him.

Reuben has been *keeping* him this way. Why else would Reuben still give him drugs?

Jericho shoots up in a newfound rage, stumbles over and tears through his desk.

Yes, this!–the crinkled photograph shakes in his hands. The ghosts are the unholy product of a damaged brain, drugs, and guilt. This is their runic object.

He stares at their faces. Reuben with his huge smile and eyes glowing red from the flash, the student's arm around his neck, her mouth on his jaw. She's wearing a low-cut dress and a bright yellow lei.

Reckless. Indifferent.

But it's not enough proof. He needs more.

He splashes cold water on his face in the bathroom, takes a deep breath, and checks his reflection. Only half an hour ago, he was questioning his grip on sanity. Now he thinks maybe he doesn't have any at all.

***

The walk back to Blue Coral is a long one. Had anyone seen his panicked escape from Paseka's? His vomiting in the alley?

He passes one of the accidents. It's on a different street, but there's still flashing lights and commotion leaking from between buildings. The racket helps him feel less visible, but now unease is no longer locked inside of him. It's everywhere.

Once at the inn, he pores through months of printed reports until he finds the paper with Reuben's name right at the top, the last check-in. Time stamped: *3:07 AM*. He even ran a credit card, too drunk to realize he could encode the card key without payment. Or perhaps he didn't know. Jericho's righteous indignation is fading.

He pauses and wonders for a moment what happened in the month he and Reuben didn't speak. Could Reuben have confessed to Fern? Maybe he had tried to change–hell, maybe he *did*. Maybe Jericho was just a fuck up after all, and Reuben had given up on him. Maybe he'd empathized but knew Jericho had nothing to lose so he kept giving him what he wanted.

He places the report and photograph in an envelope, writes Fern's name and their address on it, and walks it to his office. Unsure, he hides it in his desk drawer.

It's Saturday afternoon, and the mail is already gone. He can't cross the Rubicon until Monday.

He rests his head for a moment on the desk, wanting to cry, but can't.

The rest of the day is spent checking in Blue Coral's few guests and, for a while, staving off his encroaching anxiety until his nerves settle from exhaustion. The night receptionist, Ian, arrives at five. He expects a comment on his appearance or demeanor, but Ian says nothing, just nods and hangs his coat.

Jericho wonders if it means he's always this nervous and disheveled. He wants to shake him, demand to know whether he looks insane, but he's too tired.

As he goes to leave, Ian stops him. Ian is normally stiff as a cadaver, but in that moment Jericho notices an odd weariness in his eyes.

"I almost didn't come in today."

"Why?" Jericho asks, his throat dry. He's not sure how much longer he can stand, be awake, just *exist* today.

"Something strange happened. I felt really faint around lunch."

Jericho bunches his fingers up. "Getting sick?"

"I don't think so. I feel fine now. But it wasn't just that, I felt faint and I could swear there was–well." He sees Jericho's horrified, puzzled face and stops.

"What? What was it?"

"Oh, just, nothing. It felt like there was a little…tremor. I've been through one of those before. The ones you barely feel, that…just disorient you for a moment. Jostle a couple loose things off shelves. I…was with my fiance, but she didn't feel a thing."

"Oh." Jericho stares at his eyes in silence, then says goodbye. He can't take anymore weirdness for the night.

Once home, he tries to make sense of the day while sitting on the edge of his bed, but he's too fatigued and doesn't know where to begin.

The frustration and guilt surrounding Reuben and Fern and the little girls and Maggie, his waning memory, the violent ghosts, the car accidents, Ian's words, the nagging want for pills.

On his back, he thinks too about the strange girl he saw this morning. She roused an ancient instinct, stirring and soothing like the scent of rain before a storm.

The last thought in his mind before fitful sleep overtakes him is the phrase *vestigial memory*, but he can't remember what it means.

7

Living Fossils

Warm from her bath, Lydia lays above her sheets, listening to the soft ticking of her father's clock in the next room. It isn't the least bit comforting to know it will continue while she sleeps, still keeping track of time.

It must be almost three now—two hours after she locked the front door, many hours since her father fell asleep, and nearly a full day since her morning started, but still it ticks relentlessly.

Until now, Lydia never noticed how the clock repeats itself—tick, tick, tick. There are no tocks, just ticks. She listens until her inability to hear the resting *tock* drives her mad.

She tightens her bathrobe's sash and makes a silent molasses slide down the creaky stairs.

Tapping a pencil tip on her notebook, she waits for ideas. During the afternoon tasting, she considered calling the local paper; maybe they would agree to run a feature on Eden's Vineyard. They could have a little write-up announcing their next tasting, and she could offer tidbits about seasonal wines or pairings.

She writes *call newspaper* beside a bullet. On the next line, *give up and sell gallons of grain alcohol* to amuse herself, then erases it in case her father goes snooping. He doesn't always get her sense of humor.

Looking at the list of missing wine bottles she's stuck in the notebook, she wonders if Reuben bothered looking for them. She asked before he left, and he told her he had—why, he'd searched the entire morning to no avail.

She replaces a fluorescent light in the kitchen that's been flickering, and makes sure there's still plenty of her father's tonic waters in the fridge.

She yawns, rubbing the sore muscles in her neck, and puts the notebook away. Her body is tired but her mind is as steady as the clock.

Deciding a quick walk around the block might help take her mind off things, she changes into a green sundress and sandals, and sits on the front steps lighting a cigarette. There's a chill, but the soft, clean breeze is relaxing.

She locks the door and decides to beeline the few blocks out to the water, maybe take a look at the rolling obsidian from the sand's edge and return by the time her cigarette is done.

Sometimes at night or in the early morning, if she was sure her father was in a truly deep sleep, she slips out to wander the streets, her time and thoughts decompressed. Restaurants would be closed and the bars spilling out drunks. She wonders what it would be like to step inside an ill-lit tavern, into the world of riotous laughter and disappeared inhibition. Other times, like now, it would be too late for that, and the entire world felt evacuated. It all seemed so compartmentalized. A time for sobriety, a time for debauchery. A time for loudness, a time for sleeping. No matter how much she tries to plan her days on paper, it never works out that way.

Half a block from the shore now, she sees a dark figure in the distance, a lone man with his eyes on the cobblestone, and wonders if she should stop. She's usually more mindful that groups of jackasses or strange loners would straggle behind after the bars close. But she had been too tired to think of the time as more than a number, too desirous of a moment on only her terms to wear more than the sundress and sandals.

Then she recognizes him as he draws from his own cigarette, the glow lighting up the shape of his face. It's the man from The Sandy Sparrow. The little shadow.

She steals a glance back at the dark storefront and faded mural, now the size of her thumbnail in the distance. It offers no advice.

The man looks up, but doesn't stare.

"Hello again," she says, deciding on a nervous whim that silence, no acknowledgment, would be more awkward.

"Hi." He stops, and she wonders if she's made the wrong decision. Then he says, "I'm sorry."

"What?"

He takes a drag from his cigarette, looks her in the eyes. "You *do* look familiar."

"Oh."

He exchanges glances with the ground and her a few times. "I don't know."

"I didn't mean to bother you this morning," she says, considering walking again. They were headed in opposite directions, and he doesn't appear threatening, but he is odd.

"No," he says. "You didn't."

"Good. Well, you looked busy."

He looks up again, and after a second lets out a faint but genuine little laugh. "No."

She hadn't meant to be sarcastic.

"I just…" He breathes deeply. "Sleep," he says, ending his fragmented thought with a shrug.

"Oh. Me too. Where are you going?"

"Around."

"Oh. Okay." She prepares to walk again, to tell him to have a good night.

As though sensing her thoughts, he proclaims, "There's a lot of wrecks around here," his voice and face seeking approval.

"I heard."

Crestfallen by her response, he says, "Well…" and somehow—why is it that she cares?—she doesn't like his despondency.

"Did you hear they couldn't find one of the drivers?" she offers, though she doesn't really know if that's true, it's just hearsay from customers.

"Weird."

"How do they look?"

"The accidents?"

"If they couldn't find a body," she says, "I demand an explosive fireball."

He grins slightly, fidgets a bit. "Well." He points in the direction he came. "The only one I saw is that way. I was at work, but… They had to board up the windows of the French cafe."

"Oh. Where do you work?"

"Just a hotel. Blue Coral. It's…" He shrugs and trails off as though he doesn't want to admit it.

Why does that name sound familiar? Someone must've mentioned it recently. But that couldn't be where they met before.

"Oh," she says, self-conscious of how she's punctuating everything he tells her with a simple 'oh.' "I work at a liquor store." It's a lie to make her sound tougher, and she wants to reclaim the silly exaggeration as soon as she says it.

She crushes her cigarette underfoot, looks to the sea. Ten steps from the sand, she starts toward its edge.

"What do you do at Blue Coral?"

He hesitates but follows, looking at his feet. "Not enough."

"I know the feeling. I manage the store. It's hard this time of year."

"Everyone leaves," he says without pause.

"Thank you," she tells him.

"What?"

"For not being surprised. Most people are…kind of taken aback." She sits on the uneven line between sidewalk and sand, kicks off her sandals.

He turns to her, thinking, and she realizes how self-conscious she sounds. "You're older than you look."

"Not really."

"No," he says. "I can tell."

She studies him for a moment. He isn't talking about her age, but she says, "I'm twenty-one. Not very old."

"Anyone awake and not drunk, this time of night…"

"Why can't you sleep?"

He shrugs. "Haunted."

"Did you murder someone?"

He smiles. "Not exactly."

"Look!" She points to the shore. A pearlescent oval of moonglow creeps along the sand. "Horseshoe crab in autumn."

"Weird."

"You know, they call them living fossils," she says.

"Why is that?"

"They're not crustaceans, I don't think. Survived one of those huge extinctions long ago that wiped everything out. They don't have any close relatives."

The pair watch it inch away from the tide, pausing whenever the water washes over the bottom of its shell. So slow, steady, like the ticking clock at home.

"Sorry," she tells him. "I kind of read a lot to pass the time."

She realizes, watching the lonely crab, that she hasn't had a real conversation in a long time. Not someone that isn't her father or Reuben or someone she's buying something from, like Florence who is nice but they talk because they're both *there*. She hasn't talked just to *talk* in years. It's liberating.

"It's okay," she says of his reluctance to speak about whatever haunts him, digging her toes into the sand. "I know what you mean. I'm losing someone dear to me…and can't sleep, because…it's less time, I guess."

He goes to say something, stops himself, then, "I'd think…" He sighs. "I'd think after all these years, knowing what I didn't like hearing, I'd have something to say. Something insightful. But it's just hard."

"So you've lost a loved one. Who did you lose?"

He's quiet for a moment. "We were engaged."

"Oh. How awful."

"It was a long, long time ago." He shakes his head. "But after the pain goes away, you're…used to this, what it's done to you. The sleeplessness."

They watch the crab return to the water under a giant moon.

"This is crazy," she says. "I'm Lydia. Lydia Sortanova."

"Jericho Amara."

"Ok, now we can share our dark secrets." She extends her hand, and he shakes it softly. It feels cold, but nice in her own.

A moment passes. There's a chill, and she remembers she's only wearing a thin sundress.

"Well, I guess I'll run into you again at The Sandy Sparrow sometime."

"Going there later?"

"Maybe in the afternoon," she says, though she didn't have a plan. She stands and something cuts into her heel.

"It is late." He watches the water. "Well, see you around."

She lifts her leg. A fragment of a whelk's shell falls off her foot and into the sand.

"Bye," she says, slipping her sandal back on. "It was nice."

She walks across the cobblestone, slow, heel pulsing from the little laceration. She stops to readjust and glances back.

He seems so lonely, unmoving.

"Jericho."

He turns.

"I don't want to go to The Sandy Sparrow tomorrow."

He doesn't say anything, doesn't look away from the water.

This really is crazy, she thinks, but wonders if he has that modest smile on his face.

"Let's try to find the missing body at that French place," she calls out. "Around eight?"

He only turns a little bit, says "Okay."

"Good night."

She walks home, a strange excitement brewing, wondering what she's getting herself into.

So distracted, she'd forgotten about the shell and the pain until she pulled the sandal off at home and saw her blood smeared over the brown heel.

***

In the morning, Lydia checks on her father, makes both of them toast and brings it to his room.

"I asked Reuben to cover us next Saturday," she tells him. "We can see your play."

He chews for a long time, then nods. Before he's finished, he sets his plate aside.

"I'll finish this later."

"Come on, you can't have pills on an empty stomach."

He reclines and stares through the ceiling. "Your mother always believed names had special meaning."

Lydia gets up, looks out the window. "You have to eat, whether I'm a good cook or not."

It's bustling outside. She wishes he wouldn't insist on being closed on Sundays.

"Do you know what your name means?"

"Oh, lord." She walks back, nudges his plate. "One who is a pain in the ass?"

She can't stand this end-of-life sudden-meaning crap. It's always about her. Why can't he just enjoy the time he has left without worrying about her?

He reaches up and touches her face with the back of his hand. "Light."

"Whose idea was that?"

"I wanted to name you Lucretia, but your mother wouldn't have it."

"Yuck." She sticks her tongue out. "Sounds like a disease."

He cough-laughs. "She always had a way of being right."

"Let's go for a walk. You're turning into a sappy lunatic."

He sits upright, sips his tonic water. "Sit down."

She settles in his wheelchair, shuffling over with her feet.

"I never told you," and he coughs a few times, sips again, "when you were a young girl, I was working the docks"–he erupts in a coughing fit– "I'm fine. A boy had fallen in, not a worker–he must have been about your age at the time, thirteen or so." He stops, drinks. "There are so many electrical faults everywhere."

"He was being electrocuted?"

"Face up, unconscious when we found him. Without thinking, I jumped in to pull him to safety. But once I was in, the entire time I thought"–he coughs and wheezes.

"Dad, why are–"

"Just a tingling sensation in the water. That was all. But a stray current, and that could have been it. The whole time I thought about you."

"You're crazy. Why are you telling me this now?"

"You're more than a bright light, Lydia. You've been a strong woman for a long time. Even then you could have cared for yourself."

"Well, I've gotta haul your butt around." She doesn't understand his point–doesn't want to hear another variation of the greatness-from-tragedy speech if that's what it is.

"I don't need to act strong for you anymore. Let me rest," he says, and settles back down.

"You never did," she says, but he's quiet. She rubs her eyes; they ache, but don't tear.

He breathes deeply. "That's my point, darling."

"So I'll just keep this here for the flies," she says, tapping his plate. "Let them have a fighting chance in autumn." But he's already closed his eyes.

"Lydia?" he says when she's at the door. "Leave the store alone today. Go do something for yourself."

She shuts the door, imagining him reaching for more pills. A warm drop falls on her hand, still gripping the doorknob.

Downstairs, she dusts the immaculate bottles and mops, wondering what to do. She could try to sleep in, but it wouldn't be any use.

Even down here, she can hear the restless clock, *tick, tick, tick*.

***

After spending the day moving from room to room, pacing about on her pained foot, Lydia roots through old mementos and contemplates her decision for the night.

She stands in front of her full-length mirror.

Bowing her head, she places one of her mother's found belongings around her neck, a beautiful celestial sun pendant, its sleeping face behind a cabochon of honey amber. She touches the tiny baby-blue larimar stones encircling the face. Twelve, like a clock.

She still can't shake the idea that meeting with Jericho is crazy. Neither of them know anything about each other; except, strangely enough, why they have problems sleeping at night. But he seems harmless, and it's very much in public this time. Besides, it was her idea.

What does she know, anyway? Only hours ago, she was frustrated by her father's death-scented nostalgia, and here she is rooting through her mother's things.

She sits on her bed and wonders if she's become too untrusting of anyone but herself. Herself at best.

It's been a long time. She'd had a boyfriend in school for a couple years, but she was a girl then. It was all about holding hands and then kissing and then discovering what sex felt like, hiding from each other's parents, writing silly notes. There were real feelings there, too, she'd cared a good bit, but she hadn't heard from him after he left Caligatha with all the other boys and girls her age. She doesn't remember too much heartbreak.

Regardless of what her father says about her womanhood, Lydia could look like an adult, act like an adult, but *be* an adult—was she a woman yet? She knew better than to believe she'd missed that validation through men, but it seemed she'd missed the necessary context required to answer the question.

Staring at the assortment of dresses and pants and shirts she's sprawled across her bed, she wonders if she's over-thinking things.

I don't have to be in control of everything. The clock still ticks. The crab still crawls.

But she wants to be pretty. Standing again, she examines her face, her body, wondering what she should show off, if anything, staring in dismay at her arms. Just a little too much muscle from those trips up and down the stairs.

"Shut up," she says aloud, and changes into her usual jeans and shirt. "The future of humanity doesn't depend on you."

She's getting carried away, pent up. It's stupid. *That* isn't womanhood.

Just as she's content with her reflection, giving herself a smile, it happens again. As she stares into the glass, she can't focus, only sees the flat plane, diluting.

Everything feels like it's sliding away, brightens. She grabs the side of the mirror. Her reflection cascades, leaves trails. Her temples pound, and the whiteness overtakes everything. She leans into her bed, clutching her face. Slow, painful throbbing.

Then it's gone. As quickly as it came, it's gone.

She lies on her back for a moment, listening to faint chatter outside, laughter, the tick of the clock, her calming heart.

Half-expecting it to glow like a protective amulet, she lifts the pendant. Its serene face stares back with closed eyes. She takes it off and tosses it on the bed, it now seeming ridiculously fancy.

This is the second weird spell since yesterday, when Reuben left for lunch and the faintness almost sent her tumbling into a rack of bottles. Then, she'd been glad no one was around to watch her near-collapse, and moved on–too much to do. But today, two days in a row, it's scary.

She's got to get a little more rest, stop depriving herself of sleep, but now the clock chimes.

Seven.

8
Remains

Mae starts up the stairs as Eric closes the footlocker.
"Find anything?" she asks.
"Do you remember?"
She doesn't respond.
He opens the book back to where he left off.

My understanding of Realm is quite unsophisticated, but a key aspect of its operation finds inspiration in the field of quantum physics—something to do with light particles being arranged in every possible combination until they're observed. When these particles are observed, only then do they appear to "choose" their location and activity. According to Jericho, Realm operates on similar principles. Every possibility is considered, and the most logical one is chosen when necessary. But sometimes Realm can't decide, and time distorts. Two things seem to happen simultaneously. Needless to say, this "ghosting" was very dangerous, and how Realm resolved these inconsistencies was unpredictable.

Emma could explain the "ghosts" in less coarse terms, but I'm afraid she has already left with Jericho, and her field-notes are long destroyed.

Anyhow, I digress. I recall that the phenomenon, by the time Leviathan took Realm global, was determined to be early interfacing issues. Nonetheless, I have always found it fascinating how the most advanced and unnatural phenomena find inspiration in the spiritual beliefs they replace. I have begun to find it disconcerting as well.

He closes it again.

"I can't read this shit," he says. "Even drifters like our dead friend in the tub used to have a life worth something. I don't know what pisses me off more, reading technical bullshit or philosophizing about everything."

"If this place belonged to anyone associated with Jericho, it doesn't look like he did any work here," Mae says. "It's too small."

"You don't want to remember either," he says, regretting it.

"Why would we?" Quick, the question already poised in defense. "We didn't all start out soldiers like you."

"We all lost things," he tells her, trying to empathize, but it's useless. Sofia is his guarded secret, the only human part of him left, and she's hidden away.

"Yeah," she mock-laughs.

"I'm sorry. I know your husband–"

"Was dragged out of our store? By crazed lunatics in broad daylight, tied up in a circle with the other men working? Doused in gasoline and set on fire? Is that what you were gonna say? A pharmacist. A harmless man. And after they were satisfied with their show of power, they stole everything. While your old buddies from The Guard stood watch, waiting for their cut."

It wasn't the first time he'd heard this story. It *was* the first she told it.

"You're right," she continues. "Memories lead to softness, and softness to death. Nobody wants to remember."

He starts to tell her there's many reasons he left The Guard, but every fractal of his own story connects one massacre to another.

"I saw something about the building in a letter," he says, returning to the bed.

This time, he dumps the entire contents of the footlocker onto the mattress.

"Here. This one."

"What language is this?" Mae asks.

"It's been translated into English on the back."

Professor Sull,

Sorry I haven't written in so long since leaving. Between all the working, drinking, and that publicized suicide attempt, there hasn't been time for much else. Also, sorry you had to pick this up at the post office and I put a fake bookstore down as the sender. Extra precautions.

Speaking of bookstores, I've been watching. Glad to see you found work. I guess some people still like to scribble in the margins. That's good.

You've seen the news. The immune system has been sold. Soon, millionaires everywhere will never be healthier. And I can't sleep. Somehow, they get ahold of me. One reporter wants to know if I think I'm God, and another wants to know how many more I've secretly killed. One found me entering my apartment and asked if I thought I'd "made up" for what I did to her by trying to cure all these rich people, and ~~I fucking~~ I hit him in the face with my bottle of scotch. It was still in the bag so he wasn't hurt too badly but then I gave him a thousand dollars to not say anything. Don't know how I feel about that. Assaulting a reporter isn't the best publicity. I guess that will be in the news soon.

Don't get me wrong, I prefer things how they are. It's easier. By this time next year everyone will have a daughter or nephew or grandfather still around because of me and if the press loves you, they're less like flies on shit and ~~more like leeches on~~ something, whatever.

Also, that wasn't a suicide attempt, it was just an overdose. ~~I think it~~ Really.

Also, I'm clean now. It's hard to look out for laser sights when you're high.

Anyway, GenAssist thought they got a great deal on the immune system. I settled for a flat upfront fifty million. They said within fifteen years it would be affordable for the middle class, that's when sales would really take off, plus it would have to go through a lot more testing—especially considering the source. And they were setting a precedent with such an unusual deal. So it was really smart for me to take the money now. I would love to see how hard they laughed behind closed doors at my fiscal stupidity.

Fifty million is a drop in the bucket for them. Very easy to make that go missing, compared to what they will pay their lawyers and "independent researchers" to falsify years of study.

Now that I've leaked some tidbits to the press, I wonder how many whole buckets of cash they're paying the FDA to keep quiet. I'm enjoying their story that we're merely in "talks."

It's been six months, so I'm going to anonymously post blueprints online tomorrow so any five year old can cook it up. They and their millionaire friends can fuck off, and have just a merry time figuring out how to sue me when any evidence simply indicts them.

I guess I killed disease or whatever I said.

So now that I have fifty million dollars, I was hoping I could hire you. I need help with something. Don't write back to this address, it doesn't exist. I'll meet you on June 1 at your apartment at 2pm.

Feel free to stroll by 422 Lucretia Avenue at your leisure. Soon you'll be spending a lot of time there. I had a new loft built where I'll be continuing my work, and, incidentally, it's in your name. I'll explain more in person, but consider it your new home.

Please accept this letter as a testament of my sincerity and trust. The paper you hold in your hands is a consciously-designed, unnecessary vulnerability. That, and I know how you are about letters.

Also, sorry about the Esperanto. Extra precautions.

Jericho

"Wait a minute," Mae says. "Where's the chimney for the fireplace?"
Eric looks at the floor.
"You were standing where it should be," she says.
"Maybe they renovated at some point."
"According to the letter, the whole building is too new. That doesn't make sense. Even so, why wouldn't they seal it off?"

9

Aurore

It should be two full days since Jericho has taken any morphine, but he'd found two pills in a pocket this afternoon and talked himself into easing off, downing fragments every few hours.

His pulse and temperature rise and fall, there's occasional nausea, and he's still itchy.

But he's staved off the worst of his withdrawals. He's standing outside Aurore, not sweating and vomiting in bed with intestines knotted into a giant leach.

Alternating between tinges of panic and incredulity, he watches Lydia approach, wondering who she is and why they've become entangled.

But also admiring her aesthetic beauty. Her straight dark hair, thin but shapely lips, mahogany eyes. Her movement is modest yet powerful, deliberate, radiating a hushed and sensuous frenetic power, a person within a person.

"Bonjour," she says, smiling coyly and looking up at the door. "So that's the name."

"Aurore," he reads aloud. He itches and shifts his weight around, worried the prickling sensation makes him appear too uneasy.

"I guess it's more than just croissants."

The windows are already replaced, but the outdoor seating which obscured the interior view is still gone, revealing a dining room of mirrored tables and merlot-colored walls.

"Looks like we imagined the cafe part," he says.

"I guess we're destined for the bar. Shall we?"

The dining room is filled with couples, many of them vacationers appearing to dress the best they could with what they had. The bar is mostly empty.

They sit at the far end, and a young man promptly introduces himself as Farron and takes their order. Lydia requests a pinot meunier, Jericho asks to hold off.

"What?" she asks.

"I've never heard of that," he says, wondering if he looked puzzled, or if she's asking why he didn't order.

"Oh. It's a black wine grape. It's mostly used for champagne. But their house meunier, see"–she grabs the placard off the bar–"I'm curious...lavender, plum, white pepper."

"You know your stuff."

She raises a brow and smirks. "Oh, right. I work in a liquor store. I *meant* to ask for a flaming shot of vodka. Or body shot. Maybe a flaming body shot?"

Jericho laughs. No one has made him laugh so much in a while–not Reuben, not Maggie. But it's easy for Lydia with her sardonic wit and intermittent, warm smiles.

"Well, ya got me," she says. "Confession: I don't really work at some seedy liquor store. I don't know why I said that."

"Where do you work?"

"We just sell wine. But I'm good at it." She waves to the bartender Farron. "Make that two?" Smiling at Jericho, she says, "See? I just sold you one."

"Thanks."

"I guess I wanted to sound...dark. Mysterious."

"Why would you want to do that?"

She gives him a playfully severe look. "Probably because...I was talking to someone dark and mysterious at the time."

The bartender returns with an unopened bottle and displays the label to Lydia.

"Oh, goodness. I thought we were getting glasses."

"The meunier is only available in bottle, madame," he says, reaching for a wine list.

"Well damn. And I've already sold this man on it."

Jericho starts to protest, but she interrupts. "So it is!"

Farron forces a polite smile, placing two stemmed glasses on the table. Jericho stares at the wide bowl and flowering rim, wondering what display of poor etiquette she'll notice. Is he supposed to smell it? Swish it around? It makes him remember his uneasiness, his raised temperature. Somehow, he'd forgotten, but he itches now.

There's a moment of silence, Lydia wanting to say something but waiting for Farron to leave.

"Strange night, last night," she says as Farron pours.

"Yeah. I have a hard time sleeping sometimes."

She smiles. "I was talking about the crab. But sure, be all egotistical."

He wonders if she's serious, but only looks at her after Farron's left. She's staring intently.

"Okay," she says, "You can just chug this like it's mother's milk. I don't care, if you're wondering."

"I *was* wondering…if I was supposed to drink it, or–"

"Toss it over your shoulder? Well…" She picks up her glass, looks him in the eyes. "We have a strange situation here, sir."

"I know." He watches the wine wobble in her glass, then looks back at her, her eyes not having left his. "I've been trying to remember where I've seen you."

She shrugs with one shoulder. "I'm here now. And so are you. But it's bad luck to not toast to anything, so we have to figure something out."

"Bad luck? Is that what they say?"

"Nope. They don't live to tell about it." She sets her glass down, then after a second picks it up again. "Well, then, to–figuring out what the hell we're doing."

She clinks her glass against his and sips, and he resists the instinct to take a large gulp.

"This is nice," he says. And it is, though he has no taste for wine.

"Sorry, I'm just doing reconnaissance."

"Aren't we supposed to be looking for a crash victim?" he says, wishing he had more of value to say. So devoid of conversation, his socializing is always so vapid and flimsy.

"Oh! We'll toast to their memory with the next glass."

There's a moment of quiet, then he says, "I wonder what you think of me. We've passed before…that must be it. Always at a strange time."

"I *think*...I *think* you're right." She stares into her drink, then it's another one of those playfully severe looks. "But so what? You're very self-conscious. Don't be. I asked you here."

That's true. But he's yet to validate her decision.

"Have you always lived in Caligatha?"

"More or less. We used to live a bit outside, but we moved to downtown Caligatha a few years ago. How about you?"

"Ah." He finds himself lost in thought. "Oh, well, I studied."

"How old are you?" she asks.

"Twenty-nine, but–"

"That wasn't a loaded question. What did you study?"

"I was an engineer."

"An engineer!" She raises her brows. "What kind?"

"I made little machines," he tells her, hoping not to get into it, but she only looks more perplexed and amused.

"Little machines?"

He's quiet, and after a moment she laughs. "Like..?" She runs her hands along the bar as though she were guiding a little toy car, makes a *vroom* sound.

"Little machines the size of cells. It was all...immune system stuff. But it didn't work out."

"You mean–" she starts, but clearly can't grasp his evasive explanation.

"It worked eventually," he recants. "I made a bunch of money, saved lives. But..."

"Well, what are you doing at Blue Coral?"

He takes a moment to answer her, still piecing the narrative together. The death is the truest thing. Everything else has sounds like fiction.

"I...I couldn't do it anymore." He stares at the mirror behind the bar, at his own furrowing brow. "It took too much out of me."

"Oh, well," she looks into her drink. "I wouldn't know the first thing about engineering, but I think I understand."

"I still have enough to live off for a long time," he says, hoping he doesn't appear to be gloating.

"How wonderful that you still want to be around people. You could be such a jerk," she snickers. "Still...I wonder why I haven't heard of any of this before. It all sounds like a big deal."

But he can't talk about that anymore. It might be too personal, but he asks anyway. "Who are you losing?"

She gives him a forced smile for the first time. "Did we exchange a hundred words before I told you that?"

"You don't have to—"

"No. It's okay." She pauses, her voice solid. "My father has cancer. The doctors gave him three years, three years ago. It's why we moved into the shop. It's not ideal, but..."

For some reason, Jericho feels weakened by this. Maybe it's his ability to relate, but there's something else. There's no trace of sadness on her face or in her voice. Just resolve.

"My fiancé and I... she was sick too. But it was quick."

"How long ago?"

"Years ago. Many years ago."

"Hmm," she says, probably wondering if it had anything to do with his work. She almost goes to say it, *Did you quit because you couldn't save her?*, but minds herself.

He's about to apologize for asking, but she sits up and says, "Can I be blunt?"

"Of course."

She smiles, more genuinely this time. "I can tell it's left you damaged."

"I wound up with some bad habits, but I'm better now," he rushes to assert, defensive. He can't tell her about the drugs, his forty-eight hour *sort-of* sobriety.

"I'm sure. But...I think I can *see* all that in you. Maybe that's—that's part of why I'm *drawn* to you. I can feel it, fear it. I don't want...I mean, what you've been through, I need to know it's possible to come out of that. On the other side...come out *okay*."

"You're not me," he says. "You're very different." The idea of her coping with pills is almost laughable.

"Maybe." She looks into her glass again, sips. Her smile comes a little slower, more faint, but it's also warm. "This is crazy."

"You want someone to talk to. That's okay."

"Maybe," she repeats. "But that's just part of it. I've spent the last few years being very busy. I don't *just* want to vent at you."

"You can," he tells her. "It's...kind of bittersweet. But even this, it's–far more rewarding than any conversation I've had in a long time."

"No. I mean, I'm not trying to...pry into the grieving process, and I don't want to vent." She clears space with her hands, shaking her head. "I'd like a friend."

He looks down, embarrassed by his abrupt smile. "Sure."

"What's more, I think I found someone more awkward at this than *me*, and that's great."

"Let's have a cigarette." He's not sure if she's flirting, but it makes him pleased and awkward all at once.

Lydia sizes up her half-empty glass and downs it. "See? I'm not really a snob," she says, and laughs.

Walking to the door, Jericho remembers Reuben's words about the girl and old man living at Eden's Vineyard.

"Hey," he says as they walk away from the entrance. "Do you manage Eden's Vineyard?"

"I do." Her face lights up. "Are we solving the mystery?"

Jericho wonders if it was wise to say anything. "I'm...I know Reuben."

She cocks her head. "Are you friends?"

"No. Not really."

"Hmm. I don't know how you could be."

"I see him sometimes. He has a nice family."

"Well, he never talks about them."

"What do you want to do?" he asks, lighting his cigarette. "You seem good at what you do now."

"That's a good question." She's quiet for a minute. "Okay, so that...bottle in *there* aside—I don't really care much about wine. I could make a living, on my own I mean, if...I'd be just fine that way. But—well, I feel like I've been trapped here. For a million years."

"Me too."

"Don't get me wrong," she rushes to add. "I don't resent anything. What about you?"

"I'd like to start over," he says, though it feels hollow. He doesn't know what he wants to start, exactly.

She gives him another one of those severe looks. "What happened to you?"

"What do you mean?"

"After. I mean...you were an engineer? Did working at the inn help you cope right away?"

There's no point in hiding things. She's too intuitive.

Still, he chooses his words carefully, and they're not all true. "Years ago, after...I used drugs to cope for a while."

"Oh."

"It got bad, but I... I stopped. I stopped and started up again and I had an incident. Or to be honest, an overdose. Asphyxiated."

"Oh."

He studies her face, can't tell if she's judging him or just waiting.

"I've had some memory loss."

"You're not *really* telling me—you're an amnesiac or something?"

"No, no. Just things around that time. I can remember things. It's just...fuzzy."

"I see." She seems to reflect, then, "Well, I don't really smoke. Just when I'm stressed." She smiles. "See, we all have vices, don't we?"

He laughs, his body and voice listless.

"Come on." She leans in, pokes him on the shoulder, and he's overcome with the desire to kiss her. "The thing about being human is you can change. *You've done that*, so don't be too hard on yourself."

He wishes it were entirely true.

***

Over the rest of the bottle, Jericho and Lydia discuss the funny things they see tourists do, how awkward they were until emptying their second glasses, Lydia's childhood growing up in Caligatha. Discontent the somber bartender Farron won't confirm anything about the accident or supposed missing driver, and seeming a little looser, Lydia tries to goad him with increasingly absurd hypotheses: a rift in the space-time continuum; or the vehicle piloting itself as an agent of artificial intelligence.

The alcohol slowly begins to soothe his anxiety and itchiness, and he finds himself laughing more and more.

"What else?" She asks Jericho, and Farron leaves after he offers that maybe the car was thrown into the window by a rogue tornado.

Giggling, she covers her mouth. "Sorry," she says. "So, second confession: I don't drink very often."

Whether she's unguarded more from the drink or their conversation, it's beautiful. He envisions her in the green sundress, moonlit, his hand the cool air on her skin.

"You don't drink?"

"Oh, I do, sometimes. But this is long overdue."

"I thought you were good at your job?"

"Hey! I don't have to be a wino!" she says, pouring the rest of the bottle in her glass, then realizes Jericho's is empty. She bursts into laughter. "Oops."

"Never too late to start," he says, and she nudges her glass towards him.

"Share." She places her hand on his leg. "I'm glad you decided to be fun."

They finish, and Lydia insists on paying. Jericho argues with her, reminds her he doesn't know what to do with all the money he has. But she seems to take it personally, so he backs down.

Around ten o'clock they walk together towards Eden's Vineyard. His apartment is only a few blocks away, and she agrees to come up for a little while.

As soon as he opens the door, he regrets the decision.

"Cozy," she says. The bare walls, the dead moth in scotch, even the morphine–*is it still at the top of the trash?*–it all fills him with dreadful shame. The tiny efficiency and its lack of ornaments bares everything, his nothingness.

She sits on the edge of the bed, looks at Alana's drawing. "Why didn't you tell me you were an artist?"

The alcohol's sedation is dissipating, and the comment feels personal. He knows it isn't, forces himself to smile.

"Reuben's daughter made that for me."

"Cute." She lies back and stretches out, baring the light olive skin of her flat stomach.

He looks to the window. "She is."

She rolls onto her side, plays with a strand of hair. "You look out that window a lot?" she asks, noticing the chair, the ashtray on the sill.

He wishes he hadn't suggested she come inside, maybe tried to kiss her by her door instead, and invite her another time after he'd found a way to make his apartment less pathetic.

She pulls him against her body, leans in. "I should go soon," she whispers in his ear. "But I've had fun."

With the pressure of her waist and the weight of her breast on him, he says "me too," and her lips graze his.

He squeezes her side, wonders what she would do without the alcohol. Would she be touching him? Would her fingers still be digging into his pockets, eager to be intimate, probably for the first time?

"We should meet again," he says, avoiding her parting lips.

She buries her face into his neck, mutters something warm, then pulls off. "Okay."

They exchange numbers at the door, and she kisses his cheek, says she should go home and check on her father anyway.

"You're a good person," he says. "He's lucky."

"I don't know about that."

"He is, to spend this time with you."

Her smile this time is crooked, undecipherable. "Whatever he can enjoy, I guess." She straightens her shirt. "Whatever he isn't sleeping away with all the morphine."

Morphine.

It's a stab, a paralysis. Reuben *couldn't* have been selling the same morphine.

The same morphine from the same dying man, with the same daughter reduced to air in Reuben's cupped hands at the bar.

Lydia walks away, flashes of all those tablets staring up at him, Reuben's lecherous voice lingering in his mind, a disgusting orgy of tits, ass, death.

He doesn't know how much time passes between her walking away, him closing the door, and laying on the bed.

He wishes she'd never touched him, his filthy face.

If he'd taken her virginity, he just might disintegrate now into a braindead puddle.

His body begins to boil, molten waves of nausea rolling inside. The ghosts return, too, the walls wavering in sync with his stomach.

For once, he doesn't care, just stares vacantly.

10

Exhumation

Eric kneels at the hearth on the first floor, clearing the ashes and possum bones with the straight edge of his folding knife.

There's only a slab of dirty cement underneath. Crane and Mae are silent beside him, but the disappointment is palpable as Crane leans into Mae's light, trying to grip the cement edges. He wonders if Crane half-expected an inscribed tablet to appear, some holy relic from the old world.

"God damn it," Crane says, still feeling the concrete. "This is it. We *know* this is it."

Eric begins to protest the secrecy, but Crane stands and kicks the surrounding floorboard with his heel.

"Come on," he says, "The cement is loose."

Sure enough, the slab jostles with Crane's kicks.

Mae unsheathes her knife, and they begin working at the rotted, black wood around the hearth. It crumbles easily after years of decay and the drifter's failed attempt to cook the possum.

As Crane sifts through the loft's rubble behind them, Mae stops and shines her light close to the concrete. They've made the sliver of an opening under the slab.

"Hollow," she says.

Crane returns from the kitchen with a gardening trowel, fixing it into the opening. Mae and Eric work their knives under the slab, and it lifts with their leverage.

Eric expects a foul, tomblike smell to emerge as Crane pulls the concrete from the hearth, but the air remains unchanged.

Mae shines her light into the hollow tunnel. The concrete runs easily ten feet to flat ground, with slats carved into the far surface for climbing.

Eric grabs Crane's shoulder before he can peer further down the hole.

"What are we going to find?"

Crane's eyes meet his, wide and wondrous, and Eric realizes Crane has no idea.

But Mae's already started down the tunnel, the light on her rifle bobbing down ahead of her.

Crane follows without a word, contorting himself into the hole, then stops to look at Eric with only his neck above ground. "Stay here," he says gravely, less like a command and more like a warning. He writhes his arm free, and tosses Eric his light.

Eric looks around the desolate loft. Crane's taken the only radio, the only contact with their spotters, with him below.

If Eric were calling the shots, they would all have radios, all be wearing thermogenic sights, and there would be a fourth unit still in the truck.

But he can't do anything about that. Now's his opportunity to search for anything of value to steal. Anything to keep paying the jackals.

"What are we doing?" he asks himself, surveying the rotten trash in the panorama of his light. He could steal the whole room, all of its shattered glass and brittle paper and animal bones, and not fetch a single penny.

He presses his back to the wall, turning his light to the footlocker at his feet.

Carefully surveying the entrance, he steals glances at the book.

***

What does a man do after he's eradicated disease? Cancer, HIV, Ebola, Malaria. Every strain of the flu.

There's no suppressing information. Once his blueprints for the artificial immune system were online, hundreds of millions worldwide, anyone daring enough with access to a printer, swallowed his pill within 24 hours.

Half of America had Jericho's invention in their blood by the time he returned to California that June, and GenAssist had cleared house in an attempt to uncover the engineer or board member that had leaked their prize of the century. Desperate, the new board turned to Jericho for an edge, any edge, over the now publicly-available immune system. He told them in two months' time, he could have an upgrade that scrubbed the arteries of plaque, regulated blood sugar, enhanced the filtration efficiency of the kidneys, lungs, and liver, and eliminated hangovers. But he would need an additional fifty million, and a small percent of sales. Of course, he'd already developed all that in the first go-round. He knew how to play the idiot savant, though he told me he had no intention of using GenAssist again. It was merely poetic humor to him that they'd even asked. This time around, with industry lawyers and legislators and even the FDA in paralysis, he demanded everything be on the books. "Squeaky clean," he insisted.

In another eight months, Jericho released the upgrade along with an open-source online hub under the pseudonym Verminus. The writing was now metaphorically on the wall for the entire industry. GenAssist's chief executive promptly covered the sunlit windows of his forty-third floor office with residue from an antique flintlock blunderbuss and brain matter. Rumor is, he'd been so savage at the end that after the blast shattered a hole in the wall-length panes, no one dared disturb him. For three days vultures freely consumed what was left of his face.

Maybe Jericho wanted everyone to have access to his life-saving technology. Or maybe he'd been so vilified, he wanted everyone to know who the real monsters were.

He then hired a lawyer and, despite a most negligible case, successfully sued for lost sales. He was right—everyone had a father or daughter or niece whose life had been saved. It didn't matter whether tabloids linked him to Verminus. Impartiality was impossible. Despite being the plaintiff and the perpetrator, he was awarded another hundred million, beating a paradox as difficult as he'd left GenAssist's lawyers on the first go-round. GenAssist, as a pharmaceutical giant, collapsed in an embarrassing buy-out that saw it re-envisioned as a producer of novelty genetics tests and other retail goods.

So, when Jericho pulled into my back alley in a decrepit 2015 Volt with rusted sides he'd bought at the last minute for a hundred dollars, I could not fathom what the future held.

There he sat, alternating between staring into the tea I'd served, erratically flipping through an increasing pile of books retrieved from my shelves, and muttering conversational false starts. "You know what's funny about curing multiple sclerosis," and then silence. "It's amazing, what retraining afferent nerves for pulmonary," and then he'd read the dust-jacket of Wuthering Heights, toss it on the pile, and slyly stick another pill in his mouth and force a dry swallow.

He was not, despite his adamant claims, clean.

He finally told me I had "all the wrong books," frowning. "La puta, la puta." Which is Spanish for "the whore, the whore." At this level of absurdity, I couldn't help but laugh.

But he was lost in his serious world. "I can't explain anything on your terms," he said, trying to cut off my laughter. "Everyone has a right to life. Don't you think?"

"Of course."

"And the pursuit of happiness."

I didn't know if he was implying that he'd lost both of these things, and I said nothing.

"I can," he said, lost in thought again. "Everyone has a right to choose how to throw their life away."

Before I could tell him to hold onto his, he muttered a most unusually poetic and chilling line: "What happens to castles built on the clouds when it rains forever?"

I could only think of Oscar Wilde: "Illusion is the first of all pleasures."

Jericho smiled, premature creases showing around his eyes. "Indeed, professor."

Our first, our last.

11

Vestigial Memory

Lydia ascends to the second floor. Her father is sleeping, so she changes into her robe and draws bathwater.

She stares at her phone, wondering if she'll hear from Jericho again.

Why did she always need to be so controlling, so dominant–she shouldn't have thrown herself at him.

He was so reserved, he must have assumed she didn't value their time, the fun at Aurore, that she just wanted an excursion from her mundane life.

And in a way, *was* she guilty of that? There was no particularly good reason to choose this moment, this person, after three years, other than the fact that she was simply drawn to him whereas others slipped by, white noise amidst more important things.

How ironic, if he thought he was just being used for sexual pleasure–she hadn't even felt a void until they touched. And a release would have been nice, but under that opaque shyness, his company was just as rewarding. More so than anything physical, she'd missed that weightlessness. For a night, nothing mattered.

Oh well.

She reclines into the water, and thinks about the approaching week. She'll have to finish calling restaurants tomorrow–it was stupid to have tried calling them on Saturday; she knows better than that. Maybe she'll try to snag Aurore if she hadn't made too big a fool of herself.

Watching the steam rise, her head heavies. She closes her eyes, focuses on her lungs expanding.

Then it happens again—the water becomes hotter, or maybe colder, but it's *different*. She feels every molecule of its pressure on her skin, while the overhead light grows brighter and brighter. Grasping the edge of the porcelain, she struggles against the collapse of her body, pulling herself up and away, terrified of slipping into the water and drowning.

And just as quickly, the faint feeling plateaus and it ends.

She collects her senses, then drains the tub, puts on her robe and hurries into bed.

A bottle of wine on such sleep deprivation was a bad idea.

No matter how long she lies awake, she'll toss and turn all it takes until sleep welcomes her.

***

She stands on the shore, shivering, then realizes it isn't cold.

It's so quiet, there doesn't even seem to be air.

The sky and water are inverted, atmosphere hanging heavy and blood-red, streaming into the steamy horizon.

She reaches to her bare feet and collects a handful of sand. Gray, delicate, light as ash, it floats away like feathery down.

There's a terrible stillness. No ticking clocks here, no life in the water.

She feels her naked body, but the skin of her fingertips or arms or chest don't respond.

This isn't Caligatha.

This is outside of everything, a dream of the unborn.

She walks into the water, and when it's up to her waist it begins to pull her down.

Then the dream is an unseen color, not darkness or lightness.

Everything is blindness in this primordial corridor, a place of forgotten feeling. Lydia can't move, can't sense direction.

Everything is weightless.

She reaches out for loneliness, but even that eludes her in this place of *unbeing*.

Trying to envision the face of her father, of Jericho, of *anyone*, only vague face-shapes flash, blending together, and then nothing comes, and then even names and words are gone, just panic, blaring panic, echoing and speeding up and choking.

She awakens in a ball, slippery, iced. Dazed, thrown overboard and into her bed.

There's the faint ticking of the clock the next room over, the whispering drizzle of rain on the rooftop.

She throws off the covers, drinks from cupped hands in the bathroom and splashes the cold water on her face.

Not one for having nightmares, shaken, she pushes against the darkness of the hallway, telling herself to relax, and settles into bed again.

But it didn't feel like a nightmare–not the scary mishmash of strange, threatening shadows that lurk in the day.

It felt like being born in reverse, a fear beyond fear.

***

Her father is asleep in his wheelchair in the morning. Bewildered, Lydia wakes him and helps hoist his body back into bed.

"What were you doing?" she asks, all too aware of the frailty in her voice.

He seems confused and half-asleep, so she tells him she'll bring breakfast a little later.

She checks his pills–nothing out of the ordinary.

Taking note of the steady mist, she brings her umbrella to The Sandy Sparrow.

"That's better, dear–good to see you dry," Florence says, but then changes her tone when Lydia approaches the counter.

"Hun, you look exhausted!"

She *is* exhausted. How long did the dream keep her awake?

"But I'm not an otter today."

She sits with her usual banana-nut muffin and chai, becoming more aware of how tired she is, picking it apart and chewing without interest.

"No book today?" Florence asks.

No, no book. Nothing to hone her business acumen, no notebook for ideas or planning her day. She should be kicking herself, but there's no energy for that.

Florence grins wide, says one of the staff saw her at Aurore last night with some cute guy. "About time you had a little fun."

Lydia smiles. "I did."

They look to the street. "It's awfully dark out," Florence says.

It is. Dark. Rainy.

She shivers, remembering the ashen sand and dripping-blood sky.

After eating half her breakfast, she buys a few of her father's favorite brioche to bring home, knowing he'll probably only nibble at one of them. Florence tells her they'll have the pumpkin muffins she likes soon.

For some reason, this levity makes her want to break into tears. She grits her teeth, wishes she could wear sunglasses in the dark rain, tries to think of something stupid to say.

"Can I carve the leftover pumpkins?" she asks, forcing a caricature of herself, and Florence laughs.

"You're the light of my life, dear."

Lydia. Good job, mom.

Outside, she tells herself to stop acting like a moody little girl, then walks out of her way just far enough to see the water rolling in the distance, as drab as her dream.

There's beauty in everything.

The beach is mostly empty this rainy day in early October.

Whatever.

Back at home, her father stirs, acknowledges the brioches and settles back into sleep.

Reuben has Mondays off, so she gets the store ready and opens the door.

Antsy, she takes her father's stroll through the aisles, not really looking at anything, then tries reading his paper.

The hours pass slowly; a couple, bored from the rain, take a look around but quickly leave.

By noon, Jericho sends a message: *I miss you.*

She stares at it for a long time, types *Can I see you?*, but doesn't want to sound needy and erases it. Then she decides he sounds more needy anyway, and retypes and sends the message.

He responds right away: *Yes, when? Today?*

She looks at the unceasing rain. *If you can. Do you have a break?*

Here til 5 but you can come.

She checks on her father, still asleep, and turns off the open sign.

***

She almost doesn't recognize Jericho at the front desk in his white shirt and black tie, but he still has the same sad blue eyes, unshaven face. He looks just as tired.

"Hi," she says, feeling the skin on her arms with her fingertips, the thought of her numbness in the dream giving her a chill.

"Thanks for coming."

She's taken aback by this, not sure what he means. "I couldn't sleep much last night," she tells him.

"I'm sorry."

"What? It had nothing to do with you."

Maybe it wasn't the best idea to come here. She doesn't want to tell him about her father, or her dreams, or how tired she is. These are her problems–no, not even problems, they're things she just has to suck up. So why did she come?

He nods and encircles the desk.

They stand in silence for a moment, then he says, "You can stay here as long as you want. There's one reservation for today. I don't think I'll be busy."

She tries to smile, says, "Me either."

"I was thinking." He leans against the desk. "I don't know the things you do. Would you like to redesign the wine list at Tombolo's with–I mean, as in, we get our wine from you?"

"I don't need help," she says. "I can handle myself."

"I know."

She steps to the large window, stares at the rain falling in waves off the roof and onto the porch. "I'm sorry. That's very nice of you." Looking back at him, those sorrowful eyes, she says, "Sorry, I don't know why I'm here. I enjoyed last night, but today isn't going so well for me, and I don't–"

"Don't apologize." He steps toward her, touches her shoulder.

"I'm doing fine," she insists, *I don't need to be here and I don't need help*. But then a growl of thunder shakes everything around them, and as if it were a cue she grabs his face and kisses him, pushing their bodies onto the desk.

"Wait," he says, squirming loose, locking the door. "Come on."

She follows him down a hall behind the desk, unable to comprehend her actions, and he opens one of the first rooms.

They collapse on the bed, and all she can think as she stares at his face is *why can't you be like last night?–relaxed, laughing, making jokes*.

He starts to talk but she pushes her mouth over his, grabbing at his hair, pulling harder than she should.

Whatever it is, that faint familiarity from the moment she saw him—something makes her care, and she can't stand this complacency, pulls his hands onto her breasts. She feels his mouth move into her's, the pressure in his fingers. But it's not enough, she leans into him with all her weight, crushing him with her hips, needing more.

She tries to focus on the sensations, but can't, even when his hand is between her legs, even when he rolls her over and moves his mouth on her bare chest.

Her mind bounces faster than her heart beats—why is she so overcome by a need for this? Is it guilt? Some irrational betrayal of her father? Is she doing this because she feels sorry for Jericho? She tries to look into his eyes, sits up as he removes the last of her clothes, pulls his face to her's.

Those eyes, they hid a landscape as barren as her dream. But there's no sadness behind them anymore. The black ocean within him no longer still, she resists closing her eyes. She won't walk into it and drown.

She digs her fingers into him, forces him onto his back, and loses herself.

Before long, they're breathing into each other's necks, listening to the rain in silence.

Then they repeat everything, less hungry.

It feels better than her boyfriend years ago, but there's something else she can't place. She tries to express this phantom sensation, and only says his name.

"It's like we've always done this," he says between gasps, and it sends a shiver of pleasure throughout every nerve.

Whatever it means, she feels it too.

They take their time returning to the world outside their bodies, redressing in a haze and ignoring the inevitable departure. A heavy, sad happiness smothers the room. She forces herself to say something, but only says "crazy."

Returning to the front of the hotel, Jericho stops at one of the rooms and stares at the door, entranced.

"What's wrong?" she asks, hesitating before putting her arms around his waist, still reluctant to seem too attached.

"Nothing," he dismisses, staring at the numbers. 114. "I keep meaning to…" but he trails off.

She wonders why the room broke his spell.
Then he kisses her again, sadness back in his eyes.
Something in her heart is sent adrift, like ashen sand from her palm.

***

Lydia sits in her father's wheelchair, picking apart one of the brioches.

"I thought those were for me," he says, stirring.

"*I thought* you were trying to starve yourself."

He moves his eyes under half-raised lids, smiles. "You should be so lucky."

"Shut up," she whispers.

He tries to laugh, but erupts in coughing.

Beads of sweat form on his brow, and she brings him a tonic water only to find him asleep again.

A surge of guilt at the sound of his struggling breath almost erupts into panic, but she comforts herself with the idea that happiness and misery are not mutually exclusive. She's tried to control life for so long, she might have forgotten what end of the leash she's on.

She remembers her words to Jericho: "Being human is being able to change."

Or something like that.

12

Sepulcher

And so work began on Realm.

He told me to take whatever I needed from my old apartment. That I should keep the key, and he would give me money to continue paying rent as usual.

Then we spent a couple hours with a cheap 3-D scanner, making sure we'd recorded every nook and cranny.

I asked what we were doing.

"Don't worry," was his only explanation. "They won't be able to eat anything."

Such non-sequiturs were his natural language anymore.

He'd purchased a flat, the very flat where I sit and write now. It was in my name and would later become his wedding gift, after Realm was complete and he'd introduced me to my future-wife Emma.

But then it was his laboratory. He didn't bother furnishing it, and when I rarely caught him asleep it was in his chair, awash in the glow of his endless wall-mounted monitors. Filled with rows of numbers or inkblot-like shapes. Virtual mouse brains, he explained.

I had no idea what Realm was to be. Indeed, he hadn't even given his project a name. For weeks, I was relegated to the mere task of answering calls on his growing collection of cell phones, shunning reporters, and eventually caring for the actual mice that moved into the flat.

One of the mice he named Methuselah and kept sequestered from the others, which he said were "learning to navigate mazes." Except there were no mazes in the loft. Just walls of numbers, inkblots, and lots of mice.

Impossibly, Jericho managed to stay awake nearly every hour of the day, catching drifts of sleep between his poorly hidden drinking and pills. I'd mildly suggested he might be killing himself slowly with the combination of chemicals and labor, but he scoffed and questioned my faith in his immune system. After all, it negated the negative effects of all harmful chemicals ingested. "The chemicals go in, the cirrhosis and pain go out," he'd say.

Soon, I needed time from the persistent odor of rodents to consider the loneliness and lack of meaning that now defined my life. One does not expect to transition from lecturing on Dostoevsky to scrubbing urine from cages. A particular night, about six months in, I'd requested to return to my old apartment, and he vehemently opposed. "It'll ruin everything."

I suppose just to give me something to do, Jericho was insistent I spend much of my days searching the news reports for any new plagues. Sure enough, new diseases emerged. "Superbugs," they were usually called. "Evolution's response." This is exactly what Jericho was looking for in the news, but when I reported to him he would just snicker.

By then, Jericho's immune system had become a rich open-source platform, and the "superbugs" never even spread to the few impoverished fissures of the world without it. By the time I reported to him, such diseases usually had their own module on the hub. Nothing stuck.

At that time, the only story that roused him was quite unrelated, a malicious attack on the new Xumu dolls that had become a holiday craze.

"Those biotoys?" he asked. "The 'expectant mother units' everyone's giving kids like candy?"

"Well, you know they have downloadable faces?"

Jericho nodded. "Yes, there's an avatar marketplace. They're being marketed like fucking pets."

"This morning en masse they downloaded macabre faces with fanged mouths and began attacking their owners."

He considered this. "They couldn't hurt anyone. Their brains and bodies are bio, but their faces are just displays embedded into their skulls." He sat back, a wild grin growing. "Still, I love it. More news like that, please."

Eric looks up from the book, listening intently.

Below, from the tunnel, he can hear Crane and Mae digging through the basement, their voices solemn.

Outside, the sky is turning orange. They must've been here for hours already.

He flips ahead several pages.

It was just before Methuselah's first birthday.

I was reporting on the newest strain of superbotulism when Jericho told me to follow him outside. We took one of the unnamed mice, cage and all, and drove the rusted old Chevy to my apartment. Neither of us had set foot inside for over a year.

Jericho set the cage down in the doorway and opened the cage's latch.

"Okay," he said, "What's a real shitty book?"

I thought he was talking to me, but he started following the mouse. Into the foyer, down the hallway past the kitchen and bathroom. Onto the living room. There, the mouse sat up, whiskers twisting back and forth. Confused.

It stumbled up the nearest chair, then struggled to jump onto the coffee table. Jericho's pile of books was still sitting there.

Whiskers still running back and forth in the air, the mouse stopped at a book, stared at it, pawed it, and circled around.

Jericho picked up the mouse with one hand and fed it a raisin from the other.

"Everyone's got an opinion," Jericho said.

The book was John Steinbeck's Of Mice and Men.

"I don't understand," I told him.

"A mouse dies in it. Number 15 is a mouse."

"I understand the joke."

"Oh," Jericho said, setting the mouse back down on the carpet. It ran obediently back to its cage. "It's used to the raisin being on top of the book."

* * *

Crane works with incredible economy, ripping open flatscreens and metal boxes, removing hard drives and placing them in his bag.

Mae continues further down the tunnel, expecting an order from Crane, but he's singularly absorbed by the massive wall of computers.

She shines her light back at him one last time. In this tight corridor, it refracts brilliantly off every surface. There must be about twenty flatscreens.

Maybe thirty computer boxes. Behind him, already gorged of their organs, are giant computers larger than vertical filing cabinets, taller even than Crane.

The room is pristine, its symmetry and repeated geometry almost holy, their intrusion sacrilege.

Further down the hall, there's a simple metal desk with a glass top. No drawers, no clutter. Only an empty bottle of scotch and a few bottles of prescription drugs. She reads the labels: haloperidol, methylphenidate, diazepam, and the only empty bottle is oxycodone.

Beside the desk are two flat shipping containers.

She kneels, expecting them to be locked but they aren't even latched.

The lid groans open on the first container and she stifles a scream.

Eyes glimmer back from half a dozen decapitated, skinless heads.

She grips her rifle hard, pointing it straight into the container with wobbly arms.

There's something strange about them. They're not merely skulls, but there's no visible muscle. They're bone-white, but not brittle or delicate. They're smooth, as though a veneer of skin could drape across them to complete a natural face.

She expects them to blink in her rifle's light, but the eyes rest still like painted pearls.

With reluctance she reaches her gloved hand to the nearest cheek, tilting it gingerly. Underneath is the base of a spine, also indelicate and smooth, more like a tentacle.

"Don't touch that," Crane says. He'd crept up behind her, his bag full, finger on the radio in his ear. "This is the holy grail."

13

1 Week

The days pass as slow as months, and Jericho's shrinking fragments of morphine are now depleted.

He tells Molly they shouldn't have an *unprofessional* relationship, locking himself in his office and feeling like a child.

That same night, he lies in bed with Lydia, listening to her describe her father's declining health. How she's certain it will be soon, how he doesn't eat anymore, how he's taking so many pills to dull the pain; until Jericho can't take it and kisses her to stop the words and the guilt. Moving over her, Alana's drawing stares at him.

He wonders if he and Lydia are the only two in the world making love in a pit of sorrow.

Could he even call it that? He wanted to embrace whatever new feelings were there, feelings he *knew* he had. But she simply reminded him of what he didn't deserve. There were so many silences, unspoken thoughts. Their time became an effort to develop fire from friction alone, a primitive magic act producing only a warm smoke when they finished.

And she never spent the night, always left *just in case* something happened, leaving him to dwell on how he'd doomed himself to loneliness from the very start.

But most of all–the lingering guilt. It was a death sentence. He'd held onto the envelope addressed to Fern, uncertain. Nothing can undo the travesty of the stolen morphine. The more he lays with Lydia, her breathing growing shallow as she talks about her father, the more he hates himself. And the more he hates Reuben for all of it.

Finally, he stares at the envelope for a long time and places it in the mail.

That night, he tells himself his conscience is cleared, insists on taking Lydia to Milano's.

"Want to do reconnaissance?" he asks, nudging her the wine list.

She stares into space at the leather book, says, "We sell to them." A moment later she smiles. "Thanks."

Her wit lags behind, and she spends more time moving her food than eating it.

Once they're outside and away from any crowds, he stops her.

"Are you okay?" he asks.

So hollow.

She shakes her head no, looks around and sits on the curb.

"I'm going crazy," she says. "I'm not strong enough."

"Yes, you are," he insists. "You're stronger than I am, what you're–"

"You don't understand." She buries her face in her hands. "I'm really breaking down." She watches him, hesitating.

Nothing.

"You can rely on me," he says. But what does he mean by that? He's already let her down.

"What?" She gives him a mixed look of confusion, desperation, even insult. "You don't know what I'm talking about."

His skin starts to itch and burn.

"You're pushing yourself too hard," he tells her.

"No, I'm not. No, no–and these..." She stops, stares at the curb. "These *nightmares*."

He can't thank of anything to say, puts his arm around her. Her eyes turning red, she sniffs. "I'm fine. Let's go."

"What nightmares?" he insists, holding onto her as she tries to stand.

Dissolving dolls.

"Nothing, Jericho. It's stupid. Everyone has nightmares."

"What?" he demands, almost expecting her to have the same nightmares he does, even though it's irrational. "What are they?"

"Just...empty space. That's what's so scary. I try to think of people I know, but there's nothing there. It's like I don't exist."

"Oh." It makes sense, in its sad way. Caring for her father is the anchor of her existence, and his passing consigns her to oblivion.

"I told you it was stupid. Let's go."

"No, it's not. I have nightmares a lot too." He wants to tell her about the ghosts, about his strange episodes, uncontrollable visions, the horrifying experience at Paseka's–but that wouldn't be any good. They're not the same thing. She needs to sleep more, she's judging herself too much. No, it's nothing like the dark edges of his asphyxiation-damaged brain pulling at the strings of his guilt. Her nightmares arise from fear of inadequacy, of aloneness; his from disgrace, from penitence.

Necessary fear.

Self-flagellation.

He realizes he's sweating, longing desperately for another tiny fragment of morphine, not listening while she talks.

She asks to walk along the beach, and they do. It's far from crowded, but with arms across her chest Lydia still looks around, afraid of appearing vulnerable to the invisible hordes.

"He's getting confused," she says.

They walk many steps, the sun melting in lavender water beside them before he speaks.

"There's nothing more you can do."

She nods and whispers, "*I'm going to be alone.*"

The vision of his past love laying feverish assaults him. The emptiness of his apartment.

He stops, and she continues walking a few steps, freezes but doesn't turn.

"Lydia."

She looks on at the sand, and he gently turns her around. Every muscle around her eyes and throat are straining to hold back tears. At the sight of her pained face, he realizes how deeply he cares for her, more than he's cared for anyone in years, and it rouses pangs of bitter nostalgia.

"Lydia."

She grits her teeth, bites her lip. "What?"

"You've never lived for yourself, and it takes a strong person to do that."

She shakes her head and looks away. "No, no."

"Listen to me," he says, shaking her gently, not thinking before speaking. "You are. That strength will get your through. And that whole world you've denied yourself, it's all out there, and you'll thrive in it."

He lets her go, mulling over his words. He meant it all, but it sounded so useless.

Tips for Successful Living from a Damaged Dopehead.

She's quiet for a moment, watching the water creep nearer to her feet.

His entire body begins to ache, each fiber reawakening from its morphine-laced slumber.

"I need to go home," she says under her breath, and seizing on his silence, "I have television to catch up on," smiles.

"You can be vulnerable," he tells her, hoping she doesn't notice his trembling muscles.

After a pause, she whispers something to herself that looks like "I will be."

"I know you don't want to hear me say it, but I'll be there."

She kisses his cheek with the faint scent of invisible tears.

"Good," she says, clutching his shoulder. "Don't go. Don't go."

Then she's gone.

***

In the morning, after a sleepless night, Jericho apologizes to Maggie when he arrives, but she cuts him off, echoing his sloppy words.

"We have a professional relationship, Jericho."

He'd hoped to make her feel better, but forgets about it as he walks to his office, disoriented, sweat beading on his forehead, shirt matted to his chest. Panicked, he reaches his hand into the empty space in his drawer where the envelope to Fern had sat.

After his night with Lydia, he's no longer certain about his decision, or much of anything. Why can he be so contemplative–scrutinize *everything*– but disregard the consequences of his actions? If Reuben leaves his family, are Stacey and Alana better off? What solace does truth bring?

If Lydia knew everything about him, she would be repulsed.

If Lydia's father passed unexpectedly rather than spending an eternity sick, years of acidic tears wouldn't be curdling in her heart.

Truth is the root of all suffering.

He can't think of anything to do, wandering Tombolo's. The chairs rest on the tables, and no smells drift from the kitchen. Within weeks, there will be no bartender until evenings.

He gasps for air.

Lydia fears being alone, but Jericho truly has nothing. What can he really offer her?

Mayor of a fucking ghost town.

But what should he do? He doesn't care about Blue Coral. Lydia tries so hard and cares so much about Eden's Vineyard. Even if it is out of necessity, her stability, her industriousness, comes so easily to her.

Engineering. No, he can't. Even when trying to imagine his past, before Caligatha, some invisible guardian stands before his memories and fills him with dread.

Morphine.

He continues pacing, his fists growing numb, clutching them ever harder as his body cries out for the drug.

Lydia calls. Her voice hasn't changed since he last saw her.

She only says his name, and he knows why she's called.

"Where are you?"

"The hospital," she says, followed by only her breath rising and falling heavier than her words.

"I'll be right there." He repeats himself several times and hangs up before she can tell him not to come.

And in twenty minutes' time he's at the front desk, surprised he remembers her last name. *Sortanova.* One of those details that used to slip by so easily.

Fidgeting with his pass, he wanders the halls of Intensive Care. Everywhere, frozen tension, heavy silence and sighing machinery, like car crashes stuck in time at the symphonic moment of impact.

He's compelled to seek her out, embrace her, and stifle the misery waiting to explode in her heart. But also to run back to the elevator, away from the fake limestone exterior of the hospital, the sterile overexposure inside.

This is a place where everything is laid bare.

When he finds the room, Lydia is sitting in a chair by the bed being spoken to in a hushed voice by a doctor. She's staring into space, expressionless, her ankle shaking mechanically.

He stands by the door, waiting, straightening and curling his fingers across sweaty palms over and over until the doctor leaves. Jericho inches into the doorway.

Her father lays unmoving, lost in a monolithic clump of bedding and tubes, metal and bags and lights and screens. In the middle of it all, a prematurely aged face, thin and unwrinkled.

Jericho never thought about it until now, but despite the ravages of sickness, he's clearly still so young–probably only in his forties.

Lydia's head is between her legs, hair a mess, last night's clothes wrinkled around her fidgeting limbs.

She looks up, expressionless, drifts out of the chair and to the doorway like an apparition of herself. He reaches to hold her but she pulls a pair of sunglasses off her collar.

"Stop," he says, and her body shakes.

"Pneumonia," she says, almost one syllable.

He takes the sunglasses.

"I'm sorry," she tells him. "I shouldn't have called you."

"What did the doctor say?"

"They're doing a blood test to be sure."

"Have you eaten?"

"I'm sorry," she repeats. "This is something I need to do on my own."

"I love you," he says, but she pushes him away.

Stupid.

Her body jerks again, releasing a gasp of incredulity. "I don't know." She steps back, sticks her fingers in her hair, looks around the hallway. "I don't know, I don't know."

They stand in silence. The unbearable fever within him breaks into a terrible cold so strong he clutches at the doorframe.

"I can only handle so much right now," she says. "I need to do this on my own."

The idea of breaking into the hospital's medicine facility flashes through his mind. He studies her face, wondering if she sees how wretched he's become.

"Please keep in touch," he tells her, and she lets him kiss her forehead, her tormented eyes unclosed, both pushing him away and pleading him not to leave.

She swallows, nods.

"Jericho," she says, taking her sunglasses back. "You never did anything wrong."

He walks down the antiseptic linoleum.

At first, he thinks her parting words were about the drugs, but then he realizes that even now, left with her desolate whirlpool of thoughts, she broods over his past miseries, his undisclosed shame. Telling him things she should be telling herself.

What will she do with all that emptiness? Is she to become the caretaker of his tomb too?

His phone rings. It's Fern.

***

Jericho takes Stacey and Alana into Tombolo's and asks the cook to make them something to be sent to Fern's room—the girls settle without enthusiasm on grilled cheese—then brings them back to their mother. Maggie gives him a ferocious squint as they pass but says nothing.

He's made sure to give Fern the largest room, and when he returns she's sifting through her suitcase, lost in thought. She's wearing big, dark sunglasses, just like Lydia's.

Jericho turns on the television, finds a channel with cartoons and tells the girls to sit, handing them the remote. Fern closes the suitcase, wipes her eyes from under the sunglasses and looks at Stacey and Alana. They stare back, confused, quiet.

"You can stay here as long as you need," he tells her.

She slams the suitcase, clenches her fists. "Can I talk to you outside?" she says quietly.

His stomach turns, but Jericho nods, and they step into the hall.

He shuts the door and she smacks him hard on the side of the face.

He's stunned by the force, the rage behind it. He doesn't know how he stays upright.

"You bastard!" she nearly screams, then collapses into his chest, pushing him against the wall. "*Why?*"

"I'm sorry," is all he can manage, arms limp at his side, not knowing whether to comfort her.

"I tried so hard! So many years—*so many years*. Do you know what I've done?"

"I'm sorry," he repeats. Maggie's face appears around the corner then disappears.

"*No!*" She grabs at him, pushes away. "Do you think I didn't know? Do you think I'm a fucking idiot, Jericho? Do you—do you—*they* are all I care about. Do you think I have options? How long do I *need?* How long?"

"You can stay—"

"No, you stupid fuck, *Jericho fucking Amara*—living in your *piece of shit desolate hole in the wall!*" Grabbing and spitting each word. "With all that money leftover! Working at a place like this just for the fuck of it! You don't understand! You don't have consequences! Where am I supposed to go?"

He isn't sure. He struggles to remember if her parents are living, but he feels required to say something.

"What about your family?"

She smacks him again. They must be dead.

"I'm sorry." She falls back against the door, head hanging, takes off her sunglasses and puts her hands over her face. "I'm sorry."

She uncovers one eye with splayed fingers, looks at him through a well of tears. "You don't deserve that. Just—please. Stop. Go away." She opens the door.

He can see Stacey and Alana sitting on the bed, ignoring the television and staring in their direction. They seem to be looking at him for an answer, but then he's gone as the door shuts and they're hidden away in Blue Coral.

He rushes to the hallway bathroom to vomit.

***

Jericho sits in his office at Blue Coral, ignoring calls from Reuben.

His withdrawal is in full-swing. Every surface he touches has a disgusting residue of sweat.

He needs to fix everything.

If he stays he'll just be a cancer growing around Maggie and Fern; if he leaves, it's a concession to his worthlessness.

But what difference does it make? With his arms cradling a trash can in his lap, chin on its lid, ready to vomit, *what difference does anything make?*

He walks away.

To where? The hospital? To further enflame Lydia's agony?

He starts towards his apartment, stopping at Eden's Vineyard. A terrible, dreadful presence emanates from the tall windows.

Is Reuben inside? He must know by now, with all those phone calls. He must be sulking somewhere, quiet, steeling his shameless heart just like when Jericho found him with the student.

Then he notices an overturned rack of bottles inside, grabs the door and rushes in.

An overpowering smell knocks him back, alcohol, a hundred fruits and berries, soaked wood. The floor is glistening with blood-red pools and gnarled glass.

He holds back his curdling stomach, squeezing his jaw so hard he begins to taste blood.

Kicking the larger pieces of glass aside, he steps through the puddles, peering into the aisles. Only dully luminescent bottles stare back, a grim silence hanging in the air.

"Reuben?" he calls out, muscles tensed in pain.

Silence.

"Shit," he says, surprised by his rough, dry voice. "Shit, shit."

Twenty or thirty bottles have fallen from the overturned rack, half of them broken. He kneels to one of the severed necks, lifts the attached string and tag. A hundred dollars. Their stock is far more extravagant than he realized.

"Shit," he says again, looking around.

He opens a door by the stairs, some combination of an office and a kitchen. It's empty, with overhead fluorescent lights humming steadily.

Unsure what he expects to find, he starts up the stairs, calling Reuben's name again. Only now, with the wood creaking beneath his feet, does the violence of the overturned rack sink in.

The first room is empty, a wheelchair beside the bed. This must be her father's room. The only other room on the second floor is also empty, and clearly Lydia's with pale green curtains and bedding.

While reclosing the door, something hanging on the post of a full-length mirror catches his eye, some sort of large necklace. Stepping into the room, he sees it clearly: the sleeping face of a celestial sun behind a translucent and tan stone. He runs a finger across the smooth surface, cool to the touch.

He's seen it before. Somewhere. Just like Lydia.

Thunder grumbles outside, and her curtains sway.

A faintly ticking clock somewhere makes him feel watched.

Here he is, a withdrawing, vomiting mess. A drug addict, intruding on the private home of a woman he loves, wrecked by a friend incensed over his actions, while she's at the bedside of her dying father.

"Shit," he says again out loud, then hurries downstairs.

He locks the door, and finding trash bags in the kitchen, picks up the bottles. Three times, he lacerates his hands, clutching at the glass shards.

There's a mop, but no bucket in sight, so he does his best with paper towels, hands stinging.

His phone vibrates, Reuben again. Unsure of whether he should be enraged or afraid, he ignores it.

How will Reuben explain this to Lydia? How will *he,* for that matter?

Panicking, he closes the door to Eden's Vineyard behind him and hurries to his apartment.

14

Codec

"My old apartment was the maze they'd been running," I realized aloud.

"Not entirely. Two fifths of it. You can only see and touch. I had to rig a dopamine release into eating the raisin, since it's tasteless, or the mouse wouldn't keep going back. That was the hardest part. The rest, it's just cutting off the afferent nerves and feeding in a different signal. It's easy to entertain a lie. That's the mind's greatest gift. It's so eager to turn shadows into anything. But once we find the dopamine release amidst the darkness, our little guiding light, we'll truly believe whatever it takes. Tunnel vision. All that matters is getting back. Again and again."

I still could not tell where all of this was going to lead.

"Anyway. It's all pretty low-resolution. At least, to human senses. And the environment is almost entirely non-responsive. We have a lot of work to do."

As I tried to grasp the implications, Jericho stared at me in dismay. "You didn't really think it took me all these years just to build the immune system?"

"I don't know," I said honestly.

"I'm not particularly brilliant. The difference is..." Jericho almost whispered as he returned to the cage, "nightmares about your mistakes really invigorate the scientific method."

There's a clamor as Crane emerges from the tunnel, and Eric looks up. At first he thinks Crane is pulling someone up on his back, a second head resting on his shoulder, but then he sees the severed spine.

"Jesus Christ."

"Get the truck started," Crane directs. "Take the footlocker full of correspondence. We're leaving."

"What *is* that, Crane?"

"Data. Let's go."

Eric obeys, emerging from the loft with the box of letters and placing it in the backseat as Crane and Mae make several trips carrying the strange severed heads, their gear, and looted electronics.

He starts the truck but stands at its door, nervously watching details of the world around him.

The sky has turned into a pool of blood, with thick purple clouds blooming like orchids in every direction. The peaceful rustle of debris and leaves in the street is unsettling.

Eric has shadowed danger his entire life, infiltrated ranks of murderous tribes across the West, and braced for death countless times.

But now, the fear knotting inside him is of something stranger and bigger.

He slips the book he'd been reading against his back, under his belt, and tightens his jacket until the hard cover fits snug and unmoving against his spine.

A terrible thing is about to happen.

***

Back at their base, Crane stays awake all night in his laboratory with the severed heads.

He restricts entry of no one, but the officers rarely visit anyway. Their barracks and even armory are adjoined to the other, larger building, the upper floor of an old-world slaughterhouse converted into an orphanage. They have no reason to come here unless Crane or Eva requests them.

Here, in the smaller building, Crane has stored a treasure trove of technology culled from a decade of looting and bartering.

Unlike most of them, whom had abandoned the Western Republic's Guard, Crane had no military training. When the last remnants of the world around them came crashing down, he was singularly focused on the more invisible world of medical genetics. Crane was a teenager at the time, gifted with parents who lived and breathed science at Blackthorne's then-safe community compounds and enrolled him in prestigious study programs.

It has taken Eric years to realize Crane has no delusions of finding a cure. From time to time, Crane is excited about a potential breakthrough that inevitably leads to disappointment, but Crane is only doing what he knows how to do: study.

Even the orphanage, despite Crane's conviction of maintaining it against all odds, grew by happenstance, much like the entire hideout.

Eric's parents, too, had worked for Blackthorne, though he did not inherit their scientific talent. He'd enrolled with the California State Military Reserve, and when things fell apart, found himself a part of its devolving remnants. Soon all that remained was The Guard, a messy conglomeration of soldiers and police and vigilantes. Eric and a few of his fellow soldiers left and turned to mercenary work, joining the disillusioned outcasts of the region's other powerful forces—La Bruja, The Cazadores. It was among them he'd met Sofia, and in their roving she'd fallen ill.

He'd hidden her away secretly in the mausoleum, mere days from death, promising the jackals exorbitant funds every month to keep her suspended in the obelisk.

He began directing his fellow mercenaries towards infiltrating shipments of medicine, capturing and questioning anyone who passed for a doctor or scientist. Of course no one had a cure. The best medicines traded merely staved off the disease's progression. It was the same everywhere.

Once Eric and his fellow soldiers reunited with Crane, banding around Crane's warmly calculating intelligence occurred unseemingly, a choice made gradually and without conscious consideration. Crane provided medical knowledge and a chessmaster's long-view of diplomacy with grifters and gangs in the region. Their numbers grew, and eventually they'd established an infirmary and were intercepting shipments of medicine to the region's mutual enemies. As the infirmary grew, Crane surrendered it to Republic control in exchange for their favor and a blind eye towards his future endeavors. As far as the Republic would acknowledge, he'd started the more discreet, more remote orphanage to protect sick children from the general population. The militarization, espionage, and research, they ignored, perhaps unwittingly. Even when they ran operations counter to the Republic's interests, they only witnessed The Guard from afar, never at the edge of their cutlasses.

No matter. It was directionless anyhow. Now that their survival had been secured, and the Republic had annexed such a wide swath of the Southwest, Crane's group did little of importance.

They kept a finger on the pulse of the restless region, but never did anything more daring than intercept medical supplies, Eric stuffing his pockets with whatever currency he looted from drivers to pass on to the jackals.

Crane would work in his lab, running genomic test simulations and synthesizing chemicals for medicines.

There were never true breakthroughs. Survival became the status quo.

Sofia stayed undead, hidden, a secret even from Crane.

Eric learned long ago that to most, the cycle of violence and death could become as routine as anything.

So only he, and Mae, and Crane's girlfriend Eva are sitting in the lab now, aware that anything unusual has happened.

One at a time, unspeaking, Crane has hooked the severed spines to his computer, declining any questions from Eric or Mae.

Separately, he downloads the pilfered hard drives.

Those faces are otherworldly, like human skulls cocooned in a thin white silk. Occasionally Eric thinks he sees one of the heads wince, but it must be his imagination.

With only the muted hum of hard drives around him and the whistling winter wind outside, and satisfied that Crane and Eva are utterly distracted, he slips the book out and continues reading.

From then on, it was really the both of us. No more cleaning cages, though Jericho kept Methuselah, apparently as a pet.

I still reported on the constellation of short-lived diseases. About this time, it became hard to distinguish what was a disease and what was terror. In Europe, artificial immune systems were reprogrammed to consume red blood cells in a seemingly random cross-section of people until a patch went online days later. Then, in North America, synthetic bacteria appeared in pollinating plants, acting as an herbicide and quickly spread by insects. Almost daily, at some point on the world map, a disaster would strike. Very targeted. Nanobots that ate all the asphalt in Tokyo, that sucked all the carbon out of the oil fields in Iran. Immediate damage to human life was limited, but there was a growing dread that an invisible presence had dug fingers deep into the dirt below our cities and had begun to form fists.

My most important reports to Jericho, however, were now far different. Just as his mice had done, I entered into the year-old scan of my apartment. I reported how accurately the color spectrum was represented, or whether fine details, such as interwoven fibers in the sofa, were disorienting while walking. Or how difficult it was to pick up those cups of tea we'd left on the table.

We had to work in maddening haste. "We live in transcendent times," he said.

I suggested, inspired by the continued progress of the immune system unabetted by Jericho, that he collaborate with others, but he refused.

"No. Not until we pass a certain threshold." As usual, he wouldn't divulge any further.

A year passed, and Jericho was right about it being transcendent times. There were reports of others, whole teams of scientists, manipulating the same nerves, afferent nerves. These teams received millions from the military, from DARPA, and from pharmaceutical giants vying to adapt, but I assume nearly all of Jericho's hundred million was invested in the surrounding technology. Eventually those scientists produced mice navigating invisible mazes inside their little heads, but no word of human testing followed.

One day I was poring over reports of a steel-eroding fungus in Seattle, watching the stilted MeDX Medic units scavenge the remains of a collapsed tower, their thin white legs drifting like a swarm of graceful mosquitoes. One by one, the robotic workers fluttered with inhuman grace over dust-painted bodies, separating the living and the dead. It struck me how efficient they were; their thermogenic vision distinguishing warm bodies, their internal organs mixing freshly calibrated cocktails for injection. The scales of creation and destruction grew heavier in perfect balance. But as I pondered this, Jericho appeared behind me, bottle of Famous Grouse in hand, and said, "We're done." Not one for being possessed by the jubilant spirit of progress. No eurekas.

It had been a gradual, painful tick towards his idea of acceptability, and even so his final version of reality was far from perfect. One could not have spontaneously awoken in Jericho's reality and ever mistaken it for the real thing. I felt that I must have seen that living room much as a mouse would have always seen it, for so very long, that if I were to ever see the real thing again in person it would be like setting foot on a foreign planet or walking out of a century-old filmstrip. But he wasn't concerned about perfection. He was concerned about marketability, and that was the last, but most integral, touch.

Once it was bearable to stay in the living room for extended periods of time, he began work on an interface, similar to the visual overlays already common in contact lenses. Thought-command menus, that sort of thing.

I won't bore you with the technical details I hardly understand, but the economic and social foundation behind Realm—that's the "threshold" he'd wanted to cross. He didn't want to just sell a technology, but the seed of what *became a social network so intertwined with all human interaction that, when he sold it, he became a majority shareholder in the human economy itself.*

The lab radiates a brilliant white. Crane has turned on a large wall monitor.

It fills with an ethereal fog, churning into more complex shapes and colors, until watching it is like emerging from the sky onto an alien planet.

He watches in awe as the textures become shapes, shapes become features, and features twist and refine, organically, like geometric bacteria multiplying under a slide. Finally, they stare into a hazy bedroom.

The loft bedroom. Still, quiet, clean. No rotting. No foliage exploding through the window.

Crane focuses on a tablet in his lap, the screen filled with clusters of data, digging through tiny blocks with his fingers.

Eric looks back and forth between the book and the still image of the loft, expecting everything to converge.

So that is the story of how Realm came to be.

He began courting the media giants, and I was there for it all.

I was there when he made his presentation to Leviathan. His technique in marketing the goldmine that Realm would grow into was impeccable. Offer the service for free and in return you sell everything: you sell the environments, you sell the bodies, you sell the experiences. If it has a real-world equivalent, or even better if it doesn't, it can be sold. By the end they were eager to throw any sum of money at him to start development, so convinced at the potential earnings, so starving to be the first de facto platform of the new era in social media. How much did he need, and when would it be done?

Then he told them I'm not his partner. I'm there to perform a demonstration.

Of course, it was unloading a tanker full of blood onto frenzied sharks, only once the pressure peaked, that moment intensified one more unbearable notch. The blood, they remembered, was real.

Because this was Jericho Amano. The man acquitted in the murder of his seven-month pregnant fiancé. The man that tested his immune system on her like a mad scientist, the immune system they all had in their bodies right at that moment, except then, four years ago, it went horribly wrong.

Who was Jericho today? Prometheus or fiend of the fire?

Jericho let the silent moment sink in, perhaps reveling in their terror. For once the blood was on their hands. Their cupped, bloody hands. He'd stopped them just short of lapping it up.

Then he gritted his teeth, hard, and smiled.

"Relax," he said. "Professor, could you formally introduce yourself?"

The screen is no longer filled with the loft. Now it twitches through time and space as Crane's fingers digs into the data. New faces and rooms emerge. A restaurant, a city bus. The way things used to be, crowds of people orderly and healthy. Driving in lanes. Carrying purses.

After I introduced myself, several members of the board were still uneasy. Maybe even more uneasy.

But Jericho had power over them. He made them hungry, terrified them, and even shamed them. He walked with rehearsed grace around the room, speaking with careful enunciation and pacing.

"How many of you here have a daughter, granddaughter maybe, with a Xumu?"

Half of the board nodded. "My grandson, too," one offered.

"The Expectant Mother Unit. The Xumu doll. Lowest-level sentience allowable for retail purchase by our ever-evolving international standards. Tens of millions are sold by GenAssist, hundreds of millions of knock-offs around the world. It cries, it becomes malnourished, you can leave it locked in a hot car on a hundred-thirty degree June day. Of course, no one here's a monster, but haven't we seen our own kids being a little too rough? Maybe... forget to feed it for a few days?"

He completed his lap around the room. "All I'm saying is, don't we accept uncomfortable things day in and day out for less money than this will bring? All I'm saying is, you can't keep the head-start I'm bringing you forever. All I'm saying is...I have a fully-consenting, fully-modeled..." And he paused here, leaning on the table. I don't know whether it was dramatic effect or if he was really considering the value of his words. "Human being. Self-determined. With zero liability."

He gazed at the vice president of sales, who was shifting his weight around, fingering a stack of papers. Hungry. Maybe Jericho was thinking of the last mind he blew, the blood-spattered walls and the vultures.

"Let me do this for you."

When Eric looks up again, Crane is staring him in the face. "It's going to be a long night," he says. "Get some rest."

***

It's been nearly two days since he's rested, but Eric doesn't sleep.

He lays in his bunk for a while, thinking about the old world, about the things he's read, about Realm.

He'd never used it himself, but he was old enough at the time of the plague's origins to remember the world winding slowly to a stop.

The streets became less and less crowded and people seemed to disappear.

Then they exploded back out, frenzied, disoriented, diseased.

Whatever Crane is doing, it's begun to scare him.

Around midnight, he pulls on a jacket and takes the book outside. Sitting by himself in one of their trucks, using the cold to stay awake, he continues reading.

It's funny how time can speed up, slow down. That day seemed to last forever, but the next three years were like a vacuum. Everything happening so fast in an empty space, collapsing at the speed of light.

Realm was sold. And then formally named Realm. It was an acronym. Reality. Enhancement, maybe. Something. Life. Something.

I moved back into my old apartment, a particularly strange experience. It was "high resolution," as Jericho would say, compared to his simulation. The changing sunlight made it feel bigger, the sounds outside made it seem lonelier.

Jericho gave me more money than I could ever spend, but I didn't know what to do with myself. The old bookstore closed. People finally stopped "scribbling in the margins."

For a little while I worked in a grocery, but most people started printing out anything they needed. Everything was changing, shifting economically. Money was still being traded but landfills were sucking up the last name tags and uniforms and packing materials.

Occasionally, I'd meet Jericho in Realm. Each time it was exponentially more convincing, and always in a new, private environment he'd been building. Our conversations felt increasingly hollow, Jericho preoccupied with the restaurants and wine shops and hotels where we met. I asked if he really needed to develop these places to sell on the marketplace–wasn't he rich enough? But he'd just shake his head, say they weren't being made for the public.

"This is my Taj Mahal."

"Befitting, Emperor Amano." Emperor. That was the last thing he seemed to want, whether I was speaking truth or sarcasm.

"Pfft." He rolled his eyes, studied the refraction of buttery window light across rows of wine bottles. "So, read any good books lately?"

Books–as though a publishing industry existed anymore. Everyone started using Realm. Why not? It was free to print out the little tablet. Swallow once. Thirty dollars a month to stay connected. Ten dollars for a new body or a new house, two for an outfit, twenty for a whole city to explore, five for a girlfriend or boyfriend or dog. Who was talking to you from a mind in a real flesh body? Who was just an illusion? It stopped mattering much sooner than anyone would admit. The new economy was here. You could buy or sell any of it, but Leviathan, and Jericho, got their cut.

And here Jericho was, asking about books. The illusion master lost in his own fog.

There's a knock on the driver's side window, and Eric jumps.

It's Crane.

He rolls the window down, and Crane looks weary.

"Trade places," is all he says.

"Where are you going?"

"I'm meeting one of our contacts at the Republic in Big Pine."

"That's four hours." Eric slides out of the truck.

Crane stands beside him for a moment, maybe wondering how much to tell him.

"I'm going alone. I'm borrowing the Owens Valley Radio Observatory."

He enters the truck and looks back. "We'll talk in the morning."

***

Four sleepless hours later, Eric watches Eva encircle the table before him. Her exhausted, expressionless face as pallid as the severed heads laid out in a precise row.

Her gaunt white arm reaches a gloved hand to the nearest skull.

"Are you at all familiar with the old laws of artificial intelligence?"

"Of course not."

"Such fully-replicated human models were rare. They were expensive and pointless in a world full of slaves. But things never change. People prove their power." Her eyelids fall over her purple irises. "And that demands laws. Among them: the physical memory of a human-modeled brain cannot be altered without removing it. And removing a brain must destroy the host."

"These are all–"

"Forgotten things. We've scoured these minds of their secrets. Until now, The Guard has outpaced us. Crane is supplying our contact with a new set of coordinates. We are about to intercept our greatest shipment."

"Eva, what are we bringing in?"

"Jericho Amara."

***

Before approaching the barracks and armory, Eric stands between the two buildings, dawn breaking in the distance.

He takes out the book again, almost to its end, and realizes pages have been ripped out where he left off. The last few pages are all that's left.

The restaurant was bustling, except no one was dressed quite formally enough. A beefy, tanned man was already sitting next to Jericho when I arrived.

"Reuben, this is Keene. Keene, Reuben."

Reuben looked familiar, but I was just as puzzled by the crowd. He never had others in these private Realms of his.

He took in a brief panoramic glance of the dining room, breathing deeply, then cut short a faint glimmer of pride. "Coastal town, quaint, childhood memory stuff," Jericho informed me, dismissive, wanting to move on.

"But I thought this was private."

"It is," he said impatiently. "Reuben, could you grab us a round? On me."

Then he hurriedly told me this wasn't supposed to happen. Not like this, not exactly. All those diseases, I knew what they were, didn't I? Didn't I realize, no matter how ahead of the game Jericho ever was, they were always one step further ahead? Waiting. Waiting for the future. Why else were these diseases always popping up in some of the richest cities in the world?

But this wasn't supposed to happen. He had a plan, too, he always had a plan, but it was going to take eight months. He was coming back to California, and he needed my help. He was working with Blackthorne Aeronautics, and someone named Emma, and he hadn't finished his other project yet, but that was okay because it would all fall into place. Eight months.

It would be okay. It's all part of the master plan.

I wanted to ask so many questions. I didn't know where to begin, because I couldn't bring myself to those gravest of questions. Jericho couldn't have wanted all this, could he? All the death? How did his plan interlock with the invisible master plan?

So I settled on asking who Reuben was.

"Something old, something new," Jericho told me. He stared up at the rafters. "You probably don't remember my old partner. Things went south, but now we'll evolve quite a friendship with all the work out of the way. Please don't break the–what is it? The fourth wall?"

"Wait–Reuben? From University? You've modeled *one* of these things after him?"

I watched the man order drinks from the bartender. Realizing he didn't have a flesh and blood body anywhere at all. Merely an elaborate trick of light and source code.

Jericho only smiled.

"But...you know he's...it's...designed to play off of you. Can you really forget that?"

"I don't know," Jericho told me. "Initially, Reuben was just an experiment to see how complicated it can become, whether reflective intelligence can rival artificial, or even organic, intelligence. I didn't think I could be surprised by someone when I know they're just a reflection of myself. But being human, that's your area of expertise, isn't it?"

I knew scarcely anything about this "reflective intelligence" in Realm. It was all quantum logic, endless possibilities, choosing the most sensible reactions. It was supposed to be smoother, more stable, than other forms of artificial intelligence. And more vain. Increasingly, my "area of expertise" was being defined by its absence.

"At its most basic," Jericho continued, "I'd like to know if using only his DNA and my best attempt to model his memories–or my best guess at them–can produce someone uncannily like him."

"You don't still harbor resentment that he never came to your defense at trial?"

Jericho bristled. "What difference does it make anymore?"

"Jericho," I said slowly, "Reuben committed suicide after years of depression and guilt for contributing to your research. How can you objectively—"

"That didn't happen," he insisted. "Not in this timeline. In fact, in this timeline I'm keeping him far away from my research. I've dumbed him down. He's closer to his family. He doesn't even know the first thing about science. We'll all be much happier this way."

"We?" I began to ask why he was running this experiment, but as Reuben returned, Jericho changed the conversation. "Anyway, there are more pressing matters."

"My area of expertise is extinct," I told him, not without an accidental edge of bitterness. I didn't particularly care that Reuben had returned, that Jericho thought his artificial feelings could be hurt. Feelings that evolved as a response to Jericho's feelings, whether complimentary or otherwise.

"Really? Extinct?" Jericho asked. "Then that should leave you as the most qualified person to finally answer this: What does it mean to be human? Have you found an answer yet?" Perhaps it was Jericho trying a logical checkmate.

I couldn't pin down what I found so appalling. One could easily argue all human relationships could be distilled to this same dynamic. As Jericho himself often said, "We're just our relationships with other people."

Reuben laughed at our conversation. "This shit again," he said. "One day I'm gonna show my friend here how to live."

By now I was too overwhelmed. "I regretfully conclude I might not be the person to ask."

Jericho ignored me. "I'm retiring soon," he told Reuben while pulling two tablets from under the table. "There will be plenty of time for relaxing then."

"You can get high in here?" I asked, surprised.

Jericho waited patiently, staring me in the face until Reuben looked away. "Fourth wall," Jericho muttered under his breath, and I wondered why he and I were the actors in this artificial world, everyone else the audience. "You can get high, you can feel pain, you can do anything but die. I didn't design that. Everyone else did." Reuben leans back in, and Jericho raises his voice again. "Supply and demand. What's being human without misery? Unending misery."

"I don't think that's your answer."

Reuben laughed again. "This guy," he said. "Keene gets it."

I realized then how strange Jericho looked. Unshaven, his hair matted, rings of wrinkles spiraling up his sleeves, weary creases accentuating his young blue eyes. As though entropy had at some point been scripted into Realm.

Reuben downed his beer, said he had to be going home. "Can't neglect the wife and kids too much." He stood, shaking my hand, winked. "Just in moderation."

Jericho's opposite, a freewheeling family man. He was living vicariously.

"It already seems rather complex," I told Jericho, but he wasn't paying attention. Then I had a thought that chilled me, though I couldn't explain why.

"You gave him his wife and twins?"

"Beyond these walls is a whole world. There's a beach…with waters that never stop flowing." His voice tremored. "Enough play. We have a lot of work to do."

He pulled out two more tablets and grew pensive. Pushed them across the tablecloth, back and forth, into each other, away from each other. His lips moved slowly.

It was in that moment I made my decision. In the months that followed, I watched the number of infected rise. I watched their slow, agonizing deaths. I watched captains of industry and government overlords vanish. I watched the very fabric of time and space dissolve.

But I made the decision then, that moment, watching a wounded man under the influence of opiates mouth the only thing that mattered to him.

His lips formed her name over and over. A prayer. A mantra.

Just as mouse 15 couldn't discern the nuances and inconsistencies between two versions of my living room, so too, for Jericho the whole world was low-resolution. A search for his little bit of happiness amidst a sea of duplicitous, irrelevant, and indifferent details.

Why did we leave? I can't answer. I'm still searching.

15

Awakening

The television is dead black, thick curtains pulled shut over the windows. Nothing measures time. Even the machines are arrhythmic, a private conversation.

At some point, a different doctor returned and told Lydia her father did indeed have pneumonia, and had a whole new list of words and terms to make her feel like a powerless child again.

He gave the pneumonia a "score of five," and what's more there was severe *sepsis,* so they were going to administer a *vasopressor,* and also a *corticosteroid.*

"Ok," she kept saying, but there were no assurances, no *"he'll be just fine."*

"Are you going to do an x-ray?" she demanded. "Has the cancer spread?"

The doctor seemed surprised. "We're going to get Claudio stabilized first. One thing at a time." No supportive smiles.

All sorts of people have rushed in and out since then, sometimes asking her to leave, sometimes telling her she can return, but she hasn't checked her phone for the time. Whether five dreadfully slow minutes pass between moments or five precious hours, it's terrifying and uncontrollable.

No one asks if she needs anything, or how she's doing, or tells her those simple things like where vending machines are if she's hungry or how to operate the television, not this time.

They know.

Eventually Jericho returns with a paper bag.

He looks awful, pale and shaking as he sets it next to her. "I think that's what I saw you with," he says.

She looks in the bag. Two of her silly banana-nut muffins.

"Thank you," she says, though she has no appetite.

He pulls a second chair over and sits in silence, his arm around her. She wants to ask if he's alright, but something about his quiet is comforting.

The room grows dark, and Lydia awakens to Jericho telling her she fell asleep.

She stares at the hushed chaos of her father's life support, mad at herself for dozing off.

"It's ok," he says. "You didn't miss anything."

She adjusts, her body stiff. She'd been up all night keeping an eye on her father, and every muscle has hardened to aching stone.

It makes them ache more, but she leans her head on his shoulder anyway.

"I love you, too," she says. She wonders at this, but her heavy eyelids close themselves.

Just as she begins to drift off again, one of the men she's seen before returns, tells her he's broken the rules for her a few times, but she'll have to retire to the waiting area for a while, and he's afraid only one person can stay overnight.

Jericho follows her outside. They light cigarettes, watching cars pull up with headlights flaring like wildfires in the heavy rain.

"I'm going to get cancer myself," she says to her cigarette, then feels stupid and insensitive. What killed his fiancé? He'd never said.

He holds her, and she relaxes, unaware of how tense she had been.

"I'm sorry," she says. "I'm always so—"

He hushes her, and they continue standing in silence until she can feel his phone vibrate.

"Go ahead."

He reluctantly checks, his face growing pained.

"What is it?"

"A friend," he says. "Fern."

"You look worried."

He looks more than worried. He looks physically sick, but she knows he'll deflect any concern.

He says nothing.

"What's wrong?"

"She's in some trouble. I've been helping her out."

That agonized face, those pangs of helplessness. It's the same face whenever he evades talking about his past.

"I appreciate you being here, Jericho. You can go if you have to."

"You said don't go. I'm not going anywhere." His voice is dry, and he coughs.

"That's not what I meant," she tells him. "I'll be fine."

His phone rings again.

"Take it," she insists. "I'll be inside. I'll look for you. But you don't have to come back tonight."

"I will," he says and kisses her. "I will."

She crushes her cigarette and faces the sliding doors alone.

***

He can't control his panic any longer. As soon as Lydia turns away, he retches into a bush.

God damn it.

He's missed both of Fern's calls, and she hasn't left voicemails. She doesn't answer when he calls back.

Returning to Blue Coral, he's certain of the inevitable. Reuben must have eventually come to his apartment, then to the hotel.

Stupid, stupid. Why did he hide her there?

He calls the front desk, but there's no answer. He calls Maggie and demands to know if anything is happening at Blue Coral.

"Have you lost your fucking mind? Have you been high all day?"

He realizes he hadn't checked the time. It's already past nine.

"I'm sorry," he tells her. "I know. I'm sorry."

He hangs up and calls Ian, the night receptionist.

"Ian!" he yells as soon as he picks up. "Where are you?"

But Jericho cuts him off, tells him to check on Fern's room.

A minute later, switching between images in his mind of the blood-red pools of wine and glass and Lydia lying in the waiting room alone, he bursts open the front door.

Empty.

He rushes down the hall towards Fern's room.

Ian is twisting himself into sitting up, his sweater half off, the framed painting on the wall above him crooked.

Jericho steps over him, yanks the door. Locked. He fumbles for his card key.

"They're okay," Ian says. Jericho turns, realizes a stream of blood is running from Ian's nostril to his chin.

"What happened?" Jericho yells, turning back to swipe his card key. He pushes the door, but it's obstructed.

"He's gone."

"Fern!" He pounds the door, then puts his weight on it, pushing it open enough to reveal and jostle out of place an oak armoire.

Shoving the armoire over, he steps into the room, catching his balance. Lightheaded, his entire body uncooperating, like a flesh dandelion about to split into a thousand pieces.

The muted television flickers, the suitcase is open and its contents scattered across one of the beds.

Cold air flows through the sliding glass door to the porch.

"Who the hell was that?" Ian demands.

Jericho ignores him. "Where did he go?" he manages, nearly retching again.

Wiping the blood from his nose, Ian points further down the hallway, to an employee entrance into Tombolo's.

Reuben knows the hotel; he knows the outdoor seating at Tombolo's is in the inner courtyard, giving access to the porches of the first floor's rooms.

"The desk is trashed," Ian says. "He probably has the cleaner's key."

"Disable it," Jericho tells him, "and call the police."

Ian breathes sharply, swallowing his questions, and begins to the front desk. Jericho feels a lump in his throat so hard he can't swallow.

His face is wet–what is it, rain? Sweat? Drool?

Morphine.

Everything is out of control.

Stepping down the hall, he tries calling Fern. He swipes his card at the door to Tombalo's kitchen, Fern's phone ringing on the other end.

The kitchen is empty, all clean and shimmering metal. He peers through the prep stations. No one scrubbing the lines. The mopped floor is dry.

He runs into the empty dining area. Even the bartender's called it a night.

"Fuck!" he screams, knocking over a barstool.

The windows flash with lightning.

Out into the outdoor seating area, he hops the short fence, knees wobbling in pain, and stands in the rain.

Quiet. The first floor porches stare back from across the common area.

Only the sound of rain hitting water in the fountain, insects hiding under the benches.

His blaring heartbeat, a drum of death.

He calls Fern again, pacing in a circle.

A hard blow explodes near his temple, and the phone breaks across his face, sends him tumbling into the grass.

***

"Miss Sortanova?" A hand touches her shoulder, and Lydia jumps.

She hadn't been sleeping, had only just sat down, but the buzzing lights and distant voices and stale air all blended into a nauseous half-consciousness.

"Yes?"

One of those big white coats sits in the chair next to her, a broad and rosy face. He shakes her hand.

"My name is David," he tells her, but the identification hanging from his coat pocket says D. Aitken. She stares at it as he begins talking.

"I'm very sorry, but," and all that unnatural light and ugly air swarm around her, "cardiac arrest," laughter from the television tumbling out like rending metal in a car wreck, and "defibrillator." All eyes in the room fall on her, not *her* eyes but her shoes and knees, sheets of numbing-cold rain, "trauma team. I'm sorry."

He's watching her face, his frozen stare saying *time can start again whenever you want it to.*

She hears herself make a sound, an "uh."

"I'm sorry, Miss Sortanova."

Then he asks if she has anyone, and she wonders what that means.

***

"Where the fuck is Fern, you asshole?" Reuben is yelling. "What do you think you're doing?"

"I don't know," Jericho tries to say, but his dry throat gives out. He rubs embedded gravel off his face, sits.

Reuben grabs his collar, pulling him all the way up, face-to-face. "You listen. You say one word to anyone, that's it."

Jericho remembers Fern's covered eye, the sunglasses–he thought she was wearing them to hide her emotions from the little girls. Was she developing a bruise?

"What did you do?" Jericho demands, twisting free.

"Whatever she told you, she's full of shit. You say anything to anyone, I'll kill you. How many months before a fucking soul even notices you're gone?"

He shoves Jericho back into the ground and steps away.

He sits there, overcome with rage, wanting to leap up, topple Reuben and tear him to pieces, to reveal all the demonic black bile inside. Always preying on the weak–himself, Fern, the student–how long had Jericho been naive?

"You broke her arm, didn't you?" Jericho yells, but his body lies unmoving.

"Fucking dopehead," Reuben says, and already Jericho can hear his self-assurance returning. That burning, cocky sneer.

He watches Reuben walk back into Tombolo's, and lays on his spine staring at the starless open void above.

Damn it.

He needs to find Fern, needs to find a way for her to be safe, needs to get back to the hospital.

Damn it.

He searches for his phone, finding only scattered pieces of plastic, glass, silicone.

Red and blue lights flash from behind the building, and soon several porch lights turn on.

He gets up, scraping off the larger pebbles and clumps of mud, and heads inside. Reuben is gone, probably through the restaurant exit.

At the front desk, Ian is explaining his confrontation to an officer, flakes of blood still above his lip.

"Christ," he says at the sight of Jericho.

The officer asks for Jericho's story, and he doesn't know where to begin. Between gasps for air he starts with Reuben's affair and then the broken arm and then the smashed bottles at Eden's Vineyard. The officer keeps interrupting until Jericho stops, unable to breathe.

He leans on the desk, encased in pain.

"Please," he manages.

The officer's two-way radio crackles and someone's voice says something about the third floor.

"Sir, I'm going to ask you to stay here," the officer says to Jericho, interrupting him again, then says "copy" into his radio, heading for the stairs.

Ian and Jericho stare at each other for a moment, then Jericho runs up the stairs, falling twice.

Fern is standing at the far end of the third floor near a fire escape, calm and composed with Stacey and Alana.

He yells her name, and the same officer sternly tells him to go back downstairs.

Fern doesn't look at him, covers her face, but he glimpses it. There it is, that dark red circle around her left eye.

His hate for Reuben turns into a cold clutch into his chest. Lightheaded, he descends the stairs as the walls begin to slant again.

"Fuck," he pleads. "Not now."

He clenches his fists until they hurt beyond any feeling.

"I can't do this," Ian is saying. "I'm going home for the night." But everything sounds like it's underwater.

Jericho collapses behind him in the chair, lays his face on the desk, envisioning the ceiling slowly pushing down on his back. For a moment he can feel his body being crushed as he retches over and over.

The taste of vomit in his mouth grows sharper until it's a spiny ball of death, shredding his tongue with every inhalation.

Fucking dopehead.

"*Go away!*" he screams and pounds a fist into the wood, a high-pitched squeal ringing through his ears, the white wallpaper glowing brighter and brighter.

The terrible noise, the nausea goes on for minutes, tens of minutes, burning and burning.

Echoes descend the stairs with bulky black bodies, radios crackling like a live wire. His face drips with sweat and pulses with pain. Blood drips from his mouth as he lifts his head.

Fern descends next, and the girls follow, sniffling. Fern's red-eyed stare sucks him in, flays him.

Then there's only one officer in the room, talking in snippets barely audible under the relentless squeal.

"Not pressing charges," and "own business," and "nothing we can do."

Jericho tries to focus on the officer's face.

"–damage to the hotel?" the man asks.

"Where?–where is she going?" Jericho manages.

In his blurry vision he sees a gargantuan frown, hears something about Ian, and then the officer's gone.

Burying his head in his arms, Jericho embraces the invisible flames around him, the spinning inferno of noise, wishing it would consume him.

Fern. Alana. Stacey.

He stands, stumbles over the desk, throws open the door. In the wavering black there's nothing, no cars, no people.

Lydia.

He runs to the pier, collapsing on his knees.

The water seems to rise up, twenty, fifty, a hundred feet tall. He lays prostrate, waiting for the crash, the destruction of everything he's ruined: Lydia's father, Fern's broken face.

"*Kill me,*" he whispers to the ghosts.

Then silence. The air grows cool.

He looks up, lets his fists fall limp. The tide rolls, mid-dream.

Never has he longed so desperately to be carried into oblivion, staring into the pathetically low sparkling crest beyond.

***

It's all an endless sequence of visits, words, directions.

Would she like to spend time with *the body*, here is a counselor, please sign this, here is a list of funeral homes.

All the words are no longer threatening. Now they're maddeningly banal, meaningless: *arrangements, executor. The body.*

She finds herself standing, walking through a doorway. Someone is gently calling her, "*Miss Sortanova!*" but she keeps walking.

Out into the cool air, the sideways rain, steps turning into blocks. She lights a cigarette, noticing it tremble, but it's soaked before she can take a drag. She crushes it in her wet hand.

Past endless facades of candlelit tables and banks and novelty shops with their stupid trinkets in the windows.

Now what? Now where? Now who?

She tries to light another cigarette, but the whole pack is soaked now.

That faint feeling returns, and she leans against the brick storefront of a bicycle shop. Her palm slides on the slick windowpane and she almost falls.

***

Jericho runs up to the double doors, but they don't open. The vestibule is empty, nobody in the general area.

He bangs on the glass, frantic. He's failing everyone.

Finally a security guard lumbers over, opens the doors, and he rushes past him to the elevator.

He has to see Lydia, has to be there, has to do something right. He'll stay there with her at the bedside, or sleep by her in the waiting area. As long as it takes.

She's gone.

***

Heavy with rain, Lydia stares ahead at a giant building, disoriented. Without thinking, she starts up the stairs, streams of rain running down her temples and off her nose.

Her body almost seems to move itself, the cold holding on and hoisting her away.

She walks through the arched doors, past idle bodies, past a concession stand. The smells and lights and chatter blend, a wash of mocking sensations.

Someone in a suit approaches her, but she can't look above his shoulders.

A loud voice bounces off all the walls, "If you can look into the seeds of time–" and she shivers, frightened.

All eyes are on her again, but again not her face. This time in disdain, at her dripping body plastered with waterlogged clothes.

She realizes she hasn't changed in days, hasn't bathed, and is standing in the lobby of Caligatha Ensemble.

This, the theater, today. This is where they were supposed to be.

"–And say which grain will grow, and which will not, speak."

The invisible speakers are projecting the only sound in the room now.

She runs back out, and for blocks and blocks, until her chest burns and she can't breathe, stopping beside an empty laundromat.

The faintness returns, stronger now. She tries sitting, leaning against the brick, stumbling into the wall. It responds to her touch, lets her sink into it like a pillow.

Somewhere below her inflamed lungs something stirs, and she twists around, everything becoming white, still hearing the echoing voice from the theater. She has the strange sensation that she doesn't stop twisting around, that her body is falling apart.

The revving and splashing of a passing car is the last sound she can clearly hear before she's enveloped, opening her eyes wide but unable to see.

She's sucked into that terrible place of nothing, tries to remember Jericho but his name won't come, his face won't come.

16

A Long Rest

Lydia comes to on her back, staring at the ceiling's dim light. It's just a tiny line, a little sliver, but it glows so bright.

She tries to turn, but her head doesn't agree, either weightless or extremely heavy, but she finds herself looking at a wall of switches and lights.

The hospital.

Everything seems so close, like the inside of a coffin.

Her eyelids slowly fall again. She almost feels at peace, almost riding a wave far out in the ocean, far beyond Caligatha, just drifting away and away.

***

Keene stretches, removes the tubes from his arm, the straps around his waist and ankles.

He slides the monitor away from Emma's still-sleeping face. It's passed like mere seconds of sleep, but their bodies need more time before looking at all that crap. For now, he understands enough to know that both of their vitals are in the green.

Emma stirs with a hum.

"Good morning," he says, grinning. "Any good dreams?"

Her eyes still closed, she moves her mouth, squirms. "A or B?" she asks. "What'll it be?"

"You know I like my coffee before the morning news."

"Always with the hedonism. Gravity?"

Keene pushes off the table, headed out of the control room.

"I like falling on my ass," he says, reaching for his clothes, but can already feel himself drifting downward.

He dresses in no hurry, and by the time he's descended the stairway to the main hall, pressure has returned under his feet. There's that strange realization of having a body, the clothes hanging like a second skin.

He makes two cups of coffee in the dining room, and picks the little bits out of Emma's cup while the eggs and fruit are being prepared.

She ambles into the room a few minutes later, still pulling on her shirt.

"Thanks." She says it with a flat voice, but smiles.

"When was the last time I told you how beautiful you are?" he says, setting her up.

"Eight months ago."

Keene laughs, pulls the fruit out of the thawer.

It's all jokes, of course, but watching her sit at the table, he studies the refined features of her face. Even if all their time here has felt like only three consecutive days, they still need the humor. It's too unsettling to talk about all that passing of *real* time not spent together.

"If it's not..." She stops, chews a strawberry. She fakes a smirk. "Thanks for breakfast."

"Happy anniversary." Keene gets up for the eggs. "It's the least I could do."

"You're a few weeks late," she says.

"We don't know that yet."

She smiles a little more. "Isn't the first-year anniversary gift traditionally paper? I guess soy egg protein is a real treat."

They finish their food and return to the main deck.

"If it's not, we should consider waking Jericho," Emma says, finally finishing her thought while double-checking their awakening vitals. "Well, we've been running smoothly."

Keene watches her switch through the rest of the passengers, one at a time, muttering "A or B, A or B?" That's the ultimate question. He knows she wants to skip right to it.

"Just a minute. We've got something interesting. These oscillations–she's awake."

"Who's awake?" he asks.

"Jericho's...Lydia."

"What? Why?"

"I don't know. I don't have anything out of the ordinary until the last hour."

They stare at each other, unprepared for this moment.

"We have to put her back in." Emma readjusts and folds her arms. "It's inhumane."

"That would be worse," Keene says. "I'll check on her. Go ahead and find us some good news."

***

Keene hesitates over the girl's body. Sure enough, her eyes are darting back and forth under her eyelids.

She's dreaming. A real dream. But of what?

Will she even answer to the name Lydia?

"Hello," he whispers. There's no right word for something like this.

The eyes open, and she mutters, "Where?"

With this one word, he knows he's made the right decision. That one word–and she's *real*.

Her eyes try to open wider, adjusting to the dim light. Keene steps back, but the girl surprises him by sitting all the way up, examining her IV.

"What happened?" she asks. "What'd I do?"

There's no method for this. Nothing.

"Take it easy," he tells her. "What's the last thing you remember?" But she's looking at the straps around her waist and ankles, furrowing her brow.

The girl looks at her IV again. "I feel so sick," she says.

"Lay back. You'll get used to it."

She doesn't, examines his face instead. It's such a confusing, haunting sensation.

"I left the hospital...in the rain. I fell at the theater." She's thinking hard. "Who found me? What's in this IV?"

Damn you, Jericho. This is impossible. Horrible.

"You're okay now," he says. "But you should get some rest."

"Where am I?" she repeats, starting to undo the straps.

He watches her, wondering what to say. Somehow, he refused to believe this moment would come, no matter how serious Jericho was. He could wake him now, but it's too late. She's on her own.

"You were in a hospital?" he asks. Maybe he can keep the illusion going until her body's ready.

"I need to..." She looks around, puzzled. "This room is so small. I need to finish...I need to–"

Her face is wrinkled in effort, working through waves of disorientation and nausea.

"Rest," he says. "I can give you a sedative, if you'd like. If you don't feel well."

"Wait." She reexamines her thin white shirt, then stares at him. "Who are you?"

"My name is Keene." He tries to keep his smile warm and real. "Keene Sull, and Emma Sull is also here."

At this, she tears off the IV, all but falling off the edge of the bed. Catching herself, she must realize she's not in a hospital bed, backs into the corner with her legs against her chest.

Keene motions under the bed. "There's more clothes under there. I'll give you a moment." He pauses for a deep breath as though to emphasize his patience. This won't be easy. "I recommend rest, but I understand."

Moving back with slow steps, hoping to appear as nonthreatening as possible under the circumstances, he closes her door behind him. Emma is already heading down the hall.

"This is going to be hard," he tells her. "I can't imagine how it must feel."

"She's not the only one in for a surprise," Emma says. "You're not going to believe this."

***

Jericho bangs on the door of Eden's Vineyard a fifth time, presses his face to the opaque windows.

Nothing.

It must be past midnight by now.

He sits on the steps, indifferent to the onslaught of rain.

He shouldn't have left the hospital, shouldn't have sent the photograph–but why end there?

What was the last thing he did right?

***

"I don't understand," Keene says.

Emma shakes her head. "I don't either. But we got a reply pulse about two hours ago. The exact same signal we've been broadcasting."

Keene nods. "Which is why it woke us up? This is what we've been waiting for–it wasn't the usual eight month waking period. Right? *Scenario B.*"

"Okay. That's what you'd think." Emma pulls up the log of their vitals, enters an historical view. "But look here. This is the beginning. A whole eight months. And then we awoke, *Scenario A*, everything onboard was running smoothly, we began our second period. And then–" She continues swiping the screen, revealing month after month, turning into years.

"We were out more than eight months?"

"It can't be–but…it keeps going."

"How far back does it go?"

"Just shy of…forty years, but that's impossible, so…" She trails off.

"*Years?* So–" Keene says, but doesn't know where to begin. "We *couldn't* be out that long."

"Something went wrong, but I don't know what. *Everything* is off like that. Every log either reads forty years or is maxed out, looped back around."

"What does that mean?"

"And our energy capacity is *higher* than it was, which probably means the gauge is malfunctioning."

There's a moment of silence.

"Should we wake Jericho?" He doesn't understand how any of this could be, but it doesn't sound good.

"Soon. It's not as bad as it sounds. We're just floating in space with a broken wristwatch."

Somehow, that's not very comforting. He almost says *that's a pretty big bug*, but doesn't want her to take it personally.

"First," she says, "I want to look at the pulse again, make sure it wasn't just an echo. It's possible it was just an acoustic reflection from a leftover satellite. And see if there's anything else it didn't pick up. We're broadcasting much more than an SOS, you know."

A loud thump sounds out from the main hall, and Keene runs down the stairs. Lydia staggers forward, disoriented, then hugs a support column, sliding to her knees.

17

Shock

He doesn't tell her more than she needs to know right now–he's never seen anything like her, doesn't know how she'll react.

Staring into her glass of water, she doesn't speak.

"So what you were living in," he coaxes, "is what we call a *Realm*. Every bit as real as everything around you."

Her eyes don't blink.

"Everything you felt–everything you thought–it all has meaning. You are still–still *you*."

What a hollow reassurance. It all sounds like bullshit. It all *is* bullshit. She looks through him, that look of someone facing death. He resists a shiver.

"It's life, but–like stepping into another room, or another continent, another world. Life from another angle."

He lets that sink in, playing uncomfortably with his hands. He sounds like a Leviathan ad campaign.

"Some of the people that you probably know–not all, and I wouldn't know who, but some–are with us."

"*Why?*" she asks. Sharp.

"Why were you–"

"Where is this? Why was I put in–in, in *there*? Why don't I remember anything before?"

He hesitates. "This is very hard," he says slowly.

She jerks up, smacks the glass of water with the back of her hand, sending a liquid trail flying across the room, jumps from the table and covers her face. She cries in jagged heaves.

He looks at his lap. They need to wake Jericho soon.

"Where am I?" she sobs, backing into a wall.

She's going to lose it. But what choice does he have? If he denies her the truth, she'll fly around like a moth in a lampshade until she's completely lost whatever sanity she has.

He retrieves the glass, fills it with water again.

"Where am I, where am I?" she repeats through gasps for breath. His back turned, in his mind he can still see her chest pumping air like an injured bird flown into glass, a million beats per minute.

"Okay," he says, sitting. "There was a little accident a while ago down home." He thinks. "Do you know Jericho?"

"*Do I?*" she tries to scream, but it turns into a drawn out sob.

"Jericho...Well, all of this is to keep us safe. The Realm, this place. We're biding time. This is his, or at least mostly his investment."

"What kind of accident? Where *is* everyone?"

He can't overwhelm her. Just a little bit at a time. Not too much.

"Everyone else is still in Realm, or chose to just sleep. Truth is, we don't know why you woke up."

"*What kind of accident?*" she insists, still pressed against the wall. Her eyes are dark red.

"A...big one. We left to–to be honest, to spare our lives. Now, we're waiting. Hoping. Hoping someone down there survived, put the pieces back together. We send a signal from out here. We–Emma and I–we've been waiting for someone to hear it and respond. We sleep, too, eight months at a time, just not in a Realm. We wake up automatically every eight months to make sure everything is running smoothly, but there's also a mechanism in place to wake us if there's a response to our signal."

She's staring into space again. Too much information. He's overdoing it.

"I don't know why *you* woke up, but today–today might be the day we've been waiting for."

"Caligatha," she says, staring through him again. "Everyone's dead."

"No," he tells her. "No, Caligatha is fine, because it's not on Earth. Caligatha is just a Realm that Jericho...Well. Many of those people are right here with us."

"There's no Caligatha?"

Keene sighs. "Just a template. California beaches, early European...gothic architecture. *Caligatha.* Two things you liked."

"I..." She wraps her arms around herself. "Why don't I remember?"

He thinks of how to calm her. He considers the metaphor of her life as a puzzle, a big jig saw, that's been cast into a thousand pieces, but can be put together again. In a new way.

But that's just more bullshit.

"Jericho...can explain all of this better than me."

"This is crazy. I can't, I don't believe this. He wouldn't. He *didn't*."

"He–he loves you a lot."

***

"I never want to do that again," he says.

"You shouldn't have to." As always, he can't tell if she's making a moral judgment or a statement of fact.

"She's going to need a while. She's...intelligent. I feel bad for her."

Emma looks up at this. "I told Jericho. A scientist that plays God dabbles with his own irrelevance."

He's not sure what she means, decides to ignore it.

"I guess he wasn't even playing by the time we met." That might have been sarcasm.

"Well, let's get him. I think he's running a little late to the scene."

She slides the monitor away. "Oh. Bad news. Are you ready for this?"

Keene sits. "The signal was just an echo?" He'd wanted to be optimistic.

"No, it's real. It didn't come from us based on acoustic models. So that's the good news. There's almost no doubt. I was preparing to wake everyone with the news, and–we can't interface with the construct. It won't respond to any requests."

"We can't pull him out?"

"He should have woken up instead of…her, and now…no, we can't." Emma takes off her glasses. "I have literally no incoming connection. Zero. We have physiological data from the immune systems, of course, but no construct. No Realm."

"That's impossible. She was just telling me about it. Something about a hospital, a theater."

"It *is* still be running. Everyone's log is consistent with being in Realm, brainwave patterns as you'd expect. Even if the log does go on forever. Remember, we interface with the hardware, with Realm, when pulling someone out. That's what's not responding. But that makes it all the more inconceivable. Only Jericho has override capabilities."

"It couldn't have been forty years. That's insane."

"I agree. For the time being, only one person can clue us in."

"We can't pry her for information," Keene says. "Not yet. She's going to be a mess for a while."

"We're not out of options. They're just not very attractive yet."

He leans back, looks at the ceiling. "So we've lost track of time, maybe lost everyone on board for now–but we might have a signal from Earth."

"Don't forget our energy supply is replenished, or, more likely, the gauge is faulty. It's a mixed bag."

"Happy anniversary."

"Strange day." She smiles halfheartedly. "We still have a few options. For one thing, we *can* return on our own. And as for the construct, there's two things we can do. We could always shut it off manually."

"No, doesn't that cause brain damage? It's not worth it."

"It's possible. It would all be reversible, but we don't have the immediate means. Or–when she's better, she can go back, figure out what's going on."

He thinks of her fragile scream, her body curled in her bunk. Alone.

"Maybe," he says.

"I am curious. When I said brainwave patterns as you'd expect–well, one thing is odd. Mind you, our timeline is already suspect, but given the forty years–the whole damn thing is scrambled every six months. Regularly, every hundred and eighty-some days. But then again"–she puts her glasses back on–"the log is fucked up, so who knows what a few months means."

***

Lydia lays on her side.

Beyond, there is nothing. A black colder than Caligatha's ocean at night. No serene waves, no whispering wind.

Questions come and go, followed by panicked pacing and an implosion of screaming and crying. Then she collapses, defeated, having barely made a sound. She goes through this cycle for what feels like days, but there's nothing to keep track of time.

In one of her calmer moments, she'd accidentally discovered that the wall above her head was actually something of a screen. Awakened by her touch, it offered temperature and lighting controls, and to dissolve the wall nearest the bed. It was horrifying at first, until she realized it was still there, invisibly separating her from the vacuum outside. She'd opened a window.

She expects to see something that will make everything she's been told undeniable, but nothing ever passes the huge window—no flaming comets, no floating pieces of rock, no suspended clouds of a rainbow nebula in the distance. Even the ancient maps etched in the stars have been stolen, all dimensions skewed beyond sight—where is north?—when is now? Reality has become a freefall.

There's a small mirror by the door. She'd studied her face for a long time. Everything was how she remembered it—the couple of small freckles under her left eye, the imperfections in her teeth, the dense fractals in her brown irises. It hadn't seemed possible: no lie—*whatever* version of herself was a lie—could be so complete, so perfect.

Then, feeling modest and vulnerable, she'd undressed, examined her body. Her complexion was, maybe, ever so slightly lighter, and she couldn't recount every stray freckle. But the feel of the finest invisible hairs, the elliptical shape of her navel—everything was *the same*. Then she caught herself in the mirror, noticed her arms, the lack of muscle tone from lifting her father's wheelchair up and down the stairs. Holding back tears, she examined the underside of her foot, where she'd stepped on the whelk's shell on the beach. The skin there was smooth.

It was one of the few times she could really cry the way she wanted to. The kind of crying that feels like being wrung out.

Outside, the blackness persists. She wishes she could roll right off the bed, into the emptiness, let all the air in her lungs get sucked out like so many stolen memories.

So there was no Caligatha. Even the name was nothing but cheap wordplay, *California gothic*.

Why couldn't she remember? The word *California* rolls around in her mind, but gathers nothing. She can't remember loving the beaches, loving the architecture—not *outside* of herself. Of course she did—she loved it as Caligatha. It was home.

Every moment in Caligatha remains so vivid. Every scent, every taste, big and small—the vast and eternal ocean's salty air, the complex flavor of the simple meunier at Aurore. Her father's pained laugh. The cold iron ache in her stomach as she sat by the hospital bed. The stabbing, pulsing pain of the damned shell that's left no scar.

The warmth of Jericho's embrace.

And who was he? So all of this—Caligatha, this big floating coffin in space—*all of this* was his? How could it be? Jericho, the pained little shadow. He seemed no less entwined with the fabric of the town than her. Unarticulated worry and angst bubbling inside him—the flashes of sadness in his eyes when she talked about her father, the half-healed wounds of his past losses still too sore for him to share.

One of the last things she said to him was that she loved him.

No, it's impossible. Jericho didn't know. Her father didn't know. So many people—Florence, Reuben, all those crowds on the beach and in restaurants and at the hospital, from as far back as she can remember up until her collapse at the theater.

There's a pain in her eyes and throat, but no more tears.

Now everyone's all gone. Only her own face stares back at her in the window.

✻✻✻

Closing the door behind her, Lydia looks up and down the hall. So many doors just like hers, all the little windows pitch black.

Her body still trembles. One uneasy step at a time, she makes her way out of the hall, more careful than before, rebalancing herself with the support columns until she's found the bright open room she sat in with Keene.

Standing in the doorway, she watches him stir what looks like a cup of coffee, stopping to pick out something with a spoon, stirring again.

He shudders and looks up.

"Hello," he says uneasily.

Lightheaded from her walk, she stares at the cup.

"How are you feeling?"

This almost makes her burst into tears again, and she wants to run back to the bed in her tiny hole, where she's less naked and vulnerable. But she crosses her arms, bites her lip, focuses on all the bad feelings in her body.

"Tired. Hungry."

He draws a chair for her, and she sits, looking around to keep her bearings.

"It's been a while. And you're used to food."

She watches him, unsure, but he seems to be watching her too, as though she were a wild animal and he were afraid she might do anything.

"What kind of food do you like?" he asks, opening a compartment in the wall to remove a cup.

She watches him fill it with water from another compartment and place it beside her, then realizes her face is hot and wet.

"I'm sorry," she says, choking and looking away. When she looks back, there's nothing but hurt on his face. Is he genuinely bothered by her sadness?

Neither of them speak. She reaches with a trembling hand for the glass, sips until her throat feels a little less sore.

Breathing deeply, she tries to swallow all her vulnerability with the rest of the water, but can't finish it.

"I promise I won't make a mess this time," she says.

He makes a little choking, laughing sound, seeming to hold back his own well of sadness, surprised by her words. He stands and walks away from the table.

"Really," he says, "there's anything you could want here. Provided you don't want anything *too fancy*."

Staring at the soft white finish of the table, she swallows the rest of the water. She wants to force herself to say something, think of some food, but she can't.

He turns, the smile gone, and it only makes her want to shrink away again. More than anything else she just wants the terrible loneliness to go away.

"Here," he says, resting another glass and spoon on the table. "Your stomach needs to work its way up to solid food."

There's a thick, shimmering puree of minerals in the glass.

"It's mostly just sugar," he assures her.

She nods.

"Other than tired and hungry," he asks, "how are you holding up?"

"So what are you?" she says, ignoring him. "A scientist?"

"No. Not at all. My wife is. Emma. You can meet her whenever you're ready."

She doesn't say anything. There is no *ready*.

"I was a professor of literature, but now I guess you could just say I'm the luckiest man alive."

"I'm sorry I don't remember."

He sits next to her. "Don't be silly." He takes his time, still careful with his words. "I know anything I say will sound demeaning or cruel, given the situation. But I mean it when I say...If there's anything I can do to make this more bearable, I will."

She considers this. "You said the people I know–lots of them are here."

"Yes," he says. "Many of them."

"I want to see them."

"You will. We're working on that."

"Something is wrong," she says, thinking aloud. "I don't remember anything before...Caligatha. I don't remember you. You said–you said you don't know why I woke up?"

He explains everything to her again, how there was a *big accident* a while ago, how they fled, how they don't know how many survived, how they send out an SOS signal for everyone below, how he and Emma sleep for eight month periods, how the system wakes them every eight months or if it thinks the SOS got a response, how they seem to have gotten a response now.

But this time he tells her new things. How only he and Emma and Jericho are supposed to wake up, how they're supposed to wake everyone else if they can confirm the response. How something happened and they're not sure how much time has passed. How they've lost their control over *Realm*, can't wake everyone else up. But they're working on it.

"You're taking this very well," he says, almost sounding proud.

"What choice is there?"

"Can I call you Lydia?" he asks gently.

She's confused by this, almost expects another wild story and to get another name, but realizes she has a last name too. He's just being polite.

"Of course."

"Lydia, I'm...I'm astonished. Your intellect, your strength. We'll get through this."

Intellect? She feels so worthless and overwhelmed. She studies his face, still too tired for any of this.

Picking up the spoon, she digs up a pea-sized bit of the paste, puts it in her mouth.

Blueberry. Like every other artificial blueberry flavor she's tasted for twenty-one years. Her stomach aches at the taste of sugar.

"Go slow," he cautions her.

"My father," she says, afraid she'll start tearing up again. "Is he here?"

Keene places his hands on the table. "No, Lydia. I'm sorry."

She waits for the tears, but they don't come. "I was supposed to take him to the theater," she says, listening to her flat voice and strange words. "But he died."

"My God," he says. "He passed a long time ago. Long before the accident."

She listens to his words repeat in her mind, watching the paste melt on the spoon.

A long time ago. A long time ago.

"Jericho." The name has become a mystery. "He made Caligatha of things..." She trails off.

"He wanted you to have what you enjoyed," Keene tells her, looking away. "What made you *you*."

"I need to see him. We need to fix this."

"We're trying," he says, still not looking at her.

"I need to. That's what I want. I have questions."

He looks at her again, but not in the face. Just like the people at the hospital, or when she walked delirious into the theater.

"That's what will make this more bearable."

"Lydia, in Realm...What's your...relationship with Jericho?"

She wishes he would really look at her. "You're afraid, too," she says. "Afraid we *all* forgot the world outside Caligatha."

"Truth is, Lydia, we don't know what to think yet."

"He was an engineer," she says. "He wouldn't talk about it, *ever*. It made him sad. He said he neglected her when she needed him, when she was sick. He was mad at his work. He–"

"Slow down," he coaxes, but it makes her angry.

"No, he remembers," she insists. "Maybe not all of it, maybe not all of–*this*, the accident, but–but–"

"We're hoping," he tells her.

She stares into space again, catching up to her words. Jericho not remembering parts of his past didn't sound too different from her own apparently damaged memory. Had it all just become a big jumble of things that had really happened to them, set in a place that didn't exist?

"I'm so confused," she says.

"I know," he tells her. "I know."

She forces herself to continue eating, and for a while he seems lost in thought.

"Yes, Jericho is an engineer," he finally says. "A very brilliant one. His breakthroughs in nanotechnology changed a lot of things. First, health. He was a big contributor to the artificial immune systems we have today, though they've evolved a lot since then. Now you don't even need that food you're eating, really, and aging is mostly optional."

Lydia stares at the spoon.

"But he stopped working in the middle of all that. His—well, the short story is…he'd fallen in love with an undergraduate at the University, deeply so. They were expecting a child. But she became sick, and he lost both of them."

Keene stands, retrieves himself a glass of water. She can tell he's scripting his speech.

"He blamed himself for not being able to save them. That is true. He wasn't the same after."

Lydia stops eating.

"But eventually he rose from that depression. Finished his work on the immune system. Developed Realm. He became one of the most successful pioneers alive."

"That's not the Jericho I know," she says. "None of this makes sense."

"No," Keene tells her. "None of that ever mattered to him. The money, or being the Edison, Ford, Gates of his day; whatever the fame—he avoided all of it. He was determined, but not prideful. All that mattered to him was you."

She focuses absently on the taste in her mouth. It's impossible to believe any of this.

"I can't say I ever agreed with Realm, or like the idea of biding time in a fantasy, but he has saved all of us. And—at the end of it all, you may well be the only reason he had to keep going."

She doesn't understand where she fits into anything, but she's beginning to feel exhausted.

"I need to rest," she says. "I can't do this."

"You have all the time in the world."

***

Sitting there on the ledge, the remaining half of her glass has melted into blue water.

Infinite space behind a blueberry slushy. This is what absurdity everything has come down to.

She rolls onto her back again, thinking about Jericho.

Was he looking for her? Had she vanished from Caligatha like a shadow? He must be worried sick.

She wishes she'd forced him to talk more so she'd have more clues. The Jericho she knows–how could he have made all *this*?

Sitting up, she wonders if she'll ever see him again, then she wonders if she'll see *anyone*. What if she's one of only three people left alive?

No, it can't be. She would rather live in Caligatha. Convince herself it's real. She's already forgotten everything once. Surely she can do it again.

Staring at the window, she longs for the ticking clock but hears cavernous silence. So this is the end of time.

She gulps down the melted blueberry stuff, looks in the mirror.

This powerlessness, this frozen time, this non-existence–she won't have any of it.

Leaving her room again, she examines the doors. They're locked. Etched in small print in the corner of each window is a last name.

Sortanova.

And directly across from her's is Jericho's–*Amara.*

None of the others are familiar, but had she known many last names? Her failure to develop closer relations haunts her still.

She imagines each person she knows as she passes, living their separate life, clueless. Florence opening the Sandy Sparrow, Reuben locked out of Eden's Vineyard–what's going on *there*?

It doesn't matter anymore. She needs to get everyone out.

Navigating to the main hall, she looks around, follows voices up a stairwell.

Keene is sitting on a bed coming out of the wall, just like her's, but it's a much larger room encircled by unfamiliar black objects with dull lights and a window almost the whole width of the room. He's leaning forward, listening to a woman speak, her face obscured by several hanging tablets. It must be Emma.

"Lydia," Keene says, startled.

Emma slowly moves the glowing objects away from her face, and Lydia is struck by how young and powerless she abruptly feels.

Keene and Emma must be nearing their fifties, but she hadn't noticed it until now. Keene was so soft-spoken and gentle, it gave his ethnically ambiguous features a sense of youth despite the few lines under his eyes and few gray streaks in his hair. Emma and her square but delicate face, glasses, all drenched in monitor glow, makes Lydia feel like a child again.

"How are you feeling?" he asks her.

"I'm ready," she says.

Emma moves everything entirely from her face at this. "I hope you're not planning on getting fresh air."

"Ready for what?" Keene asks.

***

"Are you sure you understand, Lydia?" Keene asks again. "This–this could be bad."

"Yes." On her back, she looks again out the window into the darkness. "But...what happens when I come back?"

"What do you mean?" Emma asks.

"How do I...disappear–from Caligatha?" She stumbles for the right words. "How–what happens to everyone I leave behind?"

"It's a simulation," Emma tells her.

She wonders at this. "No," she begins, but can't find the rest.

"Inconsistencies are programmed to be ignored. No one–unless they're here on board–will notice that you're missing. In other words, unless, like you, they have a room and bed on board, they do not exist until you interact with them."

"Okay," she says, though she doesn't entirely understand. And it doesn't answer her unasked question. What is it she's really looking for?– still the validation that everything she's cared about, a fake universe, needs her?

"There's no pulling you out of this yet," Emma says. "There should be at least one ejection spot, probably very accessible to Jericho. I have every reason to believe they still work, but we didn't anticipate any of this. It's impossible to know where they are until we reestablish a connection. Do you understand?"

"I'll take him there. I'll come back with him."

"He knows where they are. He designed it that way. There is likely one wherever he's living," Emma tells her.

"Okay."

"If you don't find it," Emma begins, and looks to Keene.

Keene changes tone, slows down. "Lydia...there is a chance–"

"I'm doing this," she insists.

Keene walks to the doorway, looks back at her and Emma. "If you don't come back, we'll get you out."

"I'm going to reiterate one last time," Emma says, looking her square in the face with furrowed brows now, "Caligatha is possibly an unstable Realm. We track vitals, and we've routinely had brainwaves coming in scrambled every six months. We've lost our incoming connection." She turns to Keene. "I don't know what either of these facts mean, or whether they're related, only that they're highly abnormal. We'll do what we *can* to get you out."

"Fine."

"You are entering right at the beginning of another cycle of disruption. That six month period is due. I don't know what to tell you to expect. Possibly nothing."

"Let's just do this."

"In fact, it may be any moment. One last time, I'll urge waiting a day or two until–"

"No. Enough. Just wire me up."

"It doesn't work that way, dear," Emma says, walking to the foot of Lydia's bed. "Everything you need is inside already."

Lydia wants to ask what this means, but says, "Okay."

Emma touches the corner of her window, and little white lines fade into place.

"It's not a window?" she asks, betrayed again by an artificial device posing as the natural world.

Emma fleetingly smirks and says nothing, tapping through menus. Lydia watches, surprised by how accessible, how nontechnical the minimalist screen is.

"Whenever you're ready–your afferent nerve pathways will be blocked. There might be a half second of disorientation, since you're not used to this. But then you'll be in."

Lydia lies back, staring at the ceiling now. "Okay." Somehow, the inability to glimpse dead space, no matter how cold it might be, has begun to chip at her resolve.

The hesitation in the room is claustrophobic. She digs her fingers into the bedsheets.

"Whatever you must do, I implore you to be quick," Emma says.

Keene starts to say something very serious sounding, but she can't turn her head, goes limp.

18

Return

Lydia wakes to a faint ticking sound, dizzy.

Her hands feel around, fingers knotting the familiar sheets of her bed. She's wearing a green sundress.

Sitting up, she takes in the room, the aging wooden floors, every piece of furniture.

She twists up her leg. The scar from the whelk's shell forms a line across the heel of her foot.

She stands and touches the curtains. The mirror. Her mother's pendant stares back.

"Okay," she says aloud. "Okay."

She knew she didn't have a plan. She tried to ignore it and jump in with anxious instinct, but now she's paralyzed.

Find Jericho—then what? She can't even sort out how she feels. Why should she even want to leave Caligatha again? But the illusion is ruined.

She checks her father's empty room, closing her eyes and listening to the silence broken only by the clock.

Tick, tick, tick.

Seven in the evening. Jericho should be home.

Descending the stairs, an overwhelming stench of wines makes her cover her mouth. The floor is sticky under her sandals, and an entire aisle is toppled over.

She runs into the kitchen. Paper towels and shards of glass are stuffed to the brim of the trash.

Confused, she calls out Reuben's name, but then tells herself it doesn't matter. No one answers.

Walking the two blocks to Jericho's house, she avoids eye contact with passersby. Are some of them *fake?*

So many dreaded questions.

Her heart pounds as she knocks on Jericho's door, looking back at the world, but it does nothing to assuage her dread. No, everything–*everything* scares her now. Everything in her own room, the sunshine, the *people–everything* is so real.

She knocks again, and hears something fall inside.

"Jericho?" she calls into the door.

Something unintelligible in Jericho's voice cries out.

She knocks harder, calls his name again, and again a slurred mutter.

"It's Lydia," she yells louder. "Open up."

Something scrapes against the door, and her heart races even faster.

"Jericho," she says, cringing.

The bolt turns, and she grabs the knob, throwing the door open. His body slumps against the wall.

"Jericho!" she screams, grabbing him, but he falls back, head hitting the painted brick.

He looks up, eyes closed, dully pronounces the consonants of her name. She shakes him, saying his name again.

His eyes open, lizard's eyes, all bright blue without pupils and gazing into another dimension.

"Come on," she says, hoisting him up and heading to the bed, his legs moving out of rhythm.

"I'm sorry," he mumbles.

He collapses in a pile of limbs, and she shakes him, rolling him over.

"What happened?" she cries.

"Love," he slurs.

"What?" she screams, looking around the apartment, realizing she didn't think to grab any belongings before leaving the shop–where would they even be?–where the *fuck* is her phone?

"You."

There's no landline anywhere to be seen.

"Where's your phone?" she demands, shaking him again, checking his empty pockets, but he stays limp.

She runs into the kitchen, tripping on garbage strewn across the floor.

"What?" she yells at the floor, looking at the upside down pale, pulling at her hair. The trash has been thrown everywhere, like he was looking for something.

Kicking everything out of her way, she returns to Jericho, yells his name.

He says *Lydia* one syllable at a time, unmoving, eyes closed.

"No, no, no, stay with me," she pleads. "Don't go, don't go."

She shakes him harder, smacks his face.

"Don't go, don't go."

She listens for breathing, hears nothing.

Running out of the apartment, she starts banging on all the other doors, screaming "*Somebody!*" over and over, runs back into Jericho's apartment.

"Don't go, don't go," she sobs, pushing on his chest, then breathing into his mouth.

"*What the fuck!*" Tears fall on her hands as she presses down. "*What is going on?*"

Her arms give out and she collapses over him, wailing so hard her lungs feel like she's drowning, then her whole body feels icy and numb, heavy.

Hearing herself gasp for air, everything goes black.

***

Lydia wakes to a faint ticking sound, dizzy.

Her hands feel around. The familiar sheets of her bed are under her body. She's wearing a green sundress.

She jerks up, frantic, disoriented. Her limbs are leaden, and it takes a moment to remember what happened.

"No, no, no," she hears herself say.

Her room. Everything is the same.

Except her window is open, and her summer floor fan is propped by the door, set on low and blowing warm air.

She stands, her legs shaking, walks a tight circle.

The pendant is gone from the mirror.

"No, no, no," she chants, her whole body quaking now, staring where it was hanging.

She runs into the hall, into the closet, throws everything to the floor, and grabs a dusty shoebox.

The pendant is inside, right where she'd found it.

She crashes into the wall behind her, hands over her face.

Over her rapid breathing, she hears a cough from down the hall.

***

Emma taps the window on Lydia's open door, and Keene looks away.

"Something's wrong," he tells her. "Look."

"Everyone's brainwaves are already scrambled," she says. "Being impatient was not a good idea."

They stare at Lydia's heaving chest, her darting eyes.

"Christ," Emma says. "There's nothing we can do. Except—we can shut it down."

"We shouldn't have done this," he says, standing. "She can't take it."

"That's up to her. She's already demonstrated that she's not anyone's slave, not Jericho's, not our's. Give her time." Emma breathes deep. "There is good news. Before I saw the brainwaves, I was looking over a new signal we've detected. It's not just a duplicate of our own this time."

"People are alive?"

"People are alive." She smiles. *People are alive.*

She lifts her tablet. "Our message is repeated, but it concludes with an original signal using frequency shifts to establish a binary system."

He looks at the screen, seeing only numbers.

"These are coordinates."

***

"What's wrong, dear?" her father is asking.

"Nothing," she says, voice wavering as she walks down the stairs.

Her father is alive. The pendant is unmoved. No sticky floor.

She tosses receipts and the newspaper from the register counter, searching for her notebook. The last entry is dated May 4th.

This can't be happening.

In the kitchen, she leans over the sink, waiting for panic to overcome her, to purge itself from her weak body.

Nothing happens. Her shallow breathing sounds hollow in the metal basin.

Standing upright, she notices it's nighttime.

"Okay," she tells herself.

Figure this out.

She looks up the number for Blue Coral. A woman named Maggie answers, almost doesn't seem to know who Jericho is, then says with a laugh, "Oh, *Jericho*–he's almost never in."

She hangs up, turns off the open sign, and runs to his apartment. She pounds on the door but no one answers.

Back at Eden's Vineyard, she paces around.

Weren't Reuben and Jericho friends?–But if it's May, she wouldn't have his number on file. Reuben didn't start working in the store until, what, June or July?

She tries hard to remember his phone number, but it's impossible.

But she does remember his address. It was simple, the same as her birthday. 323. Perch Street.

She runs all the way to the little townhouse, rings the bell, tells herself to calm down.

A woman with curly brown hair answers, face flush from anger or crying.

"Jericho," she blurts out. "Reuben. Does Reuben know where Jericho is?"

Her face hardens. "Are you his girlfriend?"

Lydia tries to catch her breath, doesn't know what to say.

"As far as this home is concerned, he can piss off for a while."

"Wait," she gasps, catching the door. "Wait."

"Look, hun," the woman says. "He's already ruined my daughters' birthday with his overdose. If that's news, I'm sorry to break it to you. It's late."

She pries the door from Lydia's grip, closing it.

Lydia stares.

This can't be happening. She's trapped.

***

Lydia sits on the beach, contemplating her next move and watching the multitudes shop just past the pier, walking around with their food and trinkets.

It's late now, past ten, but it's May, the height of Caligatha's busy season.

She shouldn't have rushed in. She should have gotten more answers from Keene and Emma.

All these people—what *are* they?

What if she has to break into Jericho's apartment to find her way out? She's known nothing but a world of rules and consequences.

If she resorts to violence, do these people feel pain? Besides, which are just like her?—if anyone is just like her, their real body a secret even from themselves—*they* can still feel pain. Very real pain, even if the scars won't be there when they wake up.

Picking up a handful of sand, she watches the grains fall, drifting in and out of each other. Each is so real, so unique.

Such extravagant effort for a lie.

She throws the rest of the sand, angry, but it catches in the breeze and blows back at her.

Her eyes begin to well up.

So today is May 4th, six months before October. She remembers Emma's warning about everyone's brainwaves being scrambled every six months.

The woman's words at Reuben's house, too, stick in her mind: *"He's already ruined my daughters' birthday with his overdose."*

But it doesn't make sense—he'd told her he'd been clean for a long time; it must have been longer than six months! Was it all a lie? And was that an overdose when she *first* arrived?

Why build a world with such misery? Jericho was not happy—Caligatha itself seemed built to reinforce his unhappiness. Drugs, his miserable friendship with Reuben, his lonely detachment from the transitory crowds.

No, it wasn't hard to picture him using drugs only six months before they met, and it wasn't hard to picture him using again. Jericho always seemed trapped in his own mind.

Unable to escape his mind. What fucking irony.

She brushes the sand off her dress, shivering.

Six months. Bookended by overdoses.

Looped.

If she hadn't somehow left Caligatha and reentered in the middle of the loop, would she even remember leaving?

Until now, had they been doomed to repeat the same six months forever, never realizing it? How many times had she lived the same days? Made the same decisions again and again?

Watching a family leave one of the beachside restaurants, parents walking hand in hand, she wonders what her father is doing.

They pass a sign, a woman in sunglasses holding a margarita. *GET LOST*, it says.

What a cruel, cruel, cruel world.

"We are, Jericho," she says aloud. "We are."

19

Realm

Keene is useless.

Lydia's body has settled, but while Emma pores over endless technical information, he paces the ship.

He really was, as he told Lydia, the luckiest man alive. If it wasn't for Emma, and Jericho's grace, he would not be alive.

Still, stopping outside Jericho's door, he wonders what it's worth.

"The mind is its own place," he tells the door, "and in itself can make a heaven of hell, a hell of heaven."

John Milton. Paradise Lost.

There might be new truth to those words. He wonders how Jericho's heaven has turned out.

Death, so called, is a thing which makes men weep, and yet a third of life is passed in sleep.

Byron.

All these things may well exist only in his own mind now.

These snippets of literature describing ancient ways of life. Trapped in his mind. Fossilized.

A living fossil.

In a world where anything is possible, metaphor and truisms are quaint. The natural order has been turned on its head. Even if there are survivors below, the humanities are to be esteemed only in their context, like the Temple of Artemis or Nazca Lines to modern humans—incredibly complex, breathtaking, but little more than eroding monuments to long-gone, primitive, backbreaking efforts.

Or maybe not.

Jericho never had much of an opinion on the future. Everything was just a means to an end.

"The way people are changing," Keene had asked, "do you think they're in danger of losing their humanity?"

At the time, the three of them would often meet in cafes or quiet bars, often Aurore. Emma and Jericho would discuss their work, while Keene was too entranced by the dizzying distortions in the world around them. Everything he knew and loved seemed to be like a candle burning at both ends, dying at the hands of technological change or dying much, much more literally.

"I don't know," is all Jericho said, pausing before sipping his scotch. "It's the big question." But he had no interest in answering things like that anymore, he hadn't for a long time.

"I guess," Emma offered, "it depends–whether you see humanity's quest as one for survival, or one for perfection."

"Or happiness?" Keene asked, knowing Jericho didn't care about either perfection or survival, but he didn't take the bait.

Survival. What a thought. If anything was immortal it was death itself. It wasn't for nothing they were orbiting Earth in a several-billion dollar time capsule.

Nature abhors a vacuum.

Aristotle.

Keene has become the new Library of Alexandria. He and Jericho had discussed the importance of saving all that information, but it had to be put together so quickly.

900 zettabytes of human history. Aside from Realm, Jericho said it was the largest chunk of the two yobibytes on board. And it had been amassed in two months' time.

Keene still has no idea what that means.

One of those conversations took place in Aurore, as usual, right before leaving. They'd escaped the accident early, once again working at lightning speed on one of the uninhabited Orkney Islands off Scotland.

They sat at the same large rectangular table, its surface a mirror. "Let me know if you notice anything different," Jericho had said of the restaurant, as though it somehow mattered amidst their sleepless nights.

Unable to look away from his reflection on the table, Keene wondered why, more and more, they couldn't just talk in person now that they were finally all in one place. At least before, he'd understood the practical need; it had always only been he and Emma, or Jericho and Emma–there was always someone separated. But it was almost zero hour, and they were all together. And still in Realm.

It was hard to focus on conversation, contemplating the ramifications of Realm. He remembers asking Jericho if those 900 zettabytes was *everything*–from Chaucer to Van Gogh to Miles Davis–but Jericho had dismissively informed him that the human brain itself stored "less than six terrabytes of data," so yes, it was a lot. Seeing Keene still lost, Jericho said with a little more enthusiasm that the 900 zettabytes he'd allocated was equivalent to *300 million human brains* worth of knowledge, so if those people he mentioned were important at all, "then yeah."

While Jericho and Emma talked, Keene had mulled it over. Math was Jericho and Emma's second language, not his. But the idea that *all human history* needed less storage space than Realm required didn't sit right. He knew the worth of human history couldn't be quantified, it wasn't just *information*, but he knew that Jericho would counter that Realm wasn't just information either.

But he couldn't let it go.

"If all human history is 300 million minds' worth of information," he finally asked, "and Realm is a whole...yobibyte...how many minds is that? What is the...worth of Realm, measured in human minds?"

"It's pointless to measure it that way. It's like saying, 'How long is the Prime Meridian measured in snails?'"

"I know," Keene told him.

"I guess I should leave metaphors to you. Just under half a trillion," Jericho said casually, rubbing the lip of his empty tumbler. "That's more human brains worth of information than have ever even existed. But remember, you're talking human history. Realm requires a ton of information just to support a single species of grass effectively."

It was impossible to imagine. Every capable thought, idea, memory of every person that had ever lived–that's how much power Jericho wielded. That was the size of Jericho's world. And then some.

"How much more?"

"Twice, I guess. But I don't like giving numbers to abstract things like that. It's not black and white. Things like that are meant to grow, be organic."

At the time, Keene thought Jericho was speaking about the human mind being something beyond quantification.

But maybe he meant Realm.

Their server, a tall brunette woman, spotted Jericho's empty glass and whisked it off the table, and Jericho smiled at her politely.

Even though she wasn't real.

Even though it was all quantum logic. If none of them were in that restaurant, the server wouldn't exist until they returned.

If Jericho returned tomorrow, and asked her how her evening was after they left, her response would be selected from a vast array of possibilities. Even if those possibilities were meant to "grow, be organic," they only grew based on his interactions with her. Whatever response was the most compatible with Jericho's previous behavior would be chosen. Only by serving him again and again would she take on the illusion of being truly organic, ever more nuanced through their shared history.

Keene stared him dead in the eyes.

If Jericho was rude, she might act accordingly. If he flirted, she might reciprocate, or she might not. The appearance of chance, hinging on ever-finer nuance, was the magic.

She might spontaneously wear her hair differently. She might paint her nails a different shade one day. Yes, she was kaleidoscopic.

But unless it had been specifically scripted, or unless it was the result of a major chain reaction initiated by Jericho, that server would never start tearing up in the middle of taking his order, take a moment in the bathroom to assure herself she would get through the day in spite of an argument with a lover. She would never slip up beyond her usual margin of error, bring him the wrong drink because she was thinking about needing to repair a broken window at home.

She might say these things happened, but only reflexively. Only if Jericho's interactions caused them to happen retroactively. Only if Jericho told her his window was broken, and she began to empathize, would she organically grow backwards, like a root, inventing a history she would have to permanently uphold. Then, her window would have broken last month, unless he'd been around to notice otherwise.

Realm only grew backwards.

Jericho watched her walk all the way to the bar, still smiling politely. Because *she* had been polite, and he wanted her to *know* he appreciated it.

Keene didn't notice what was supposed to be different about Aurore that day.

But something was different about Jericho.

"You look good," Keene told him. "Considering the stress. I've seen you worse. You look healthy."

Jericho finally looked away from the server. "We're almost there."

***

Lydia listens to birds' feet dancing on the rooftop. So many voices outside.

I can't cry anymore, she tells herself.

Laying on her bed, she knows this is it. The point of no return is coming.

She couldn't find Jericho last night. The hospital said he was discharged. There was no response at his apartment. The girl, Maggie, at the front desk of the inn, again needed a moment to remember who he even was.

She returned home. Thankfully, her father was asleep.

But throughout the restless night, she realized what she had to do.

She would try to find Jericho again. Then, failing that, an ejection point must have been at the hotel. Where else could it be? It's just a hunch, but that room he'd stopped to stare at—there was something strange in his eyes.

She had to steel herself for whatever Jericho might do or say. And who knows what would happen at the hotel.

But most of all for right now.

Pulling on her clothes is readying for execution. Her last day alive, at least in the only world she's ever known.

Make it good or make it bad. The choice is her's.

She checks on her father. He's in better health, already awake.

The pneumonia—his death—she can't stop thinking about it. She could stay, prevent it. She knows when it will happen.

But the truth has ruined her: she also knows this is all fake and inconsequential.

He isn't real.

Still, whenever her life in Realm began, whether *any* of her memories happened in or out of Realm, it doesn't matter. For now, outside of the sterile hospital and shuffle of doctors, she has an opportunity to make her strange peace.

Until then, it will stay too real inside of her.

"Come on," she informs him, "We're going out."

Though he's healthier now, he still protests, but she's firm.

They stroll along the beach, stopping for breakfast at one of the crummy diner-themed restaurants he likes, her father grumbling the whole way.

"No," she interrupts as he tries to save money and order scrapple, "he'll have his lobster benedict" she tells the waitress.

"What's gotten into you?" he asks, but she ignores him.

"When I was little, you'd bring me all the way into town on the summer weekends just for cotton candy, do you remember that?"

"Of course," he says, smiling. "You didn't even like it," then he laughs, "It was just the colors you liked, but you'd be so happy to get it each time."

"Then eat your lobster."

"You couldn't pronounce it when you were little. You called it cloud candy."

Nothing makes sense anymore, but this mutual moment of happy nostalgia makes her smile.

Watching a little girl toss bits of her waffle to a seagull, Lydia sees her plan crystallize.

Find Jericho. Get everyone real out. And let the rest have their peace.

It's a chilling resolve–a whole world, in her hands. Oblivious, automated, scripted.

Afterward, she insists on wheeling him throughout the town, recounting more bygone memories, and finally she lets him rest.

What happens when she exits Caligatha? How can he be *unaware* of her disappearance?

But she can't think about that now.

She leaves Eden's Vineyard and, standing outside Jericho's apartment, wonders what to say.

The strange sense that they'd always known each other–won't it still be there?

She knocks and waits for minutes, and finally she hears him leaning against the door, checking the peep hole.

There's a pause, and he opens.

He doesn't look well, only half of himself, like his face is a mask or some parasite is feeding off him.

He stares expectantly.

"Hello," she starts, and he continues to stare, blinking.

When he doesn't respond, she repeats the plan in her head. No backing down.

"I'm Lydia," she tells him. "Do you remember me?"

"No," he says but doesn't move, then, "Maybe."

"We've met before."

"You look familiar," he admits.

It's like we've always done this.

"Good," she says. "Do you know where?"

He studies her.

What to feel? She wants to shake him, scream *why?* a thousand times.

"I don't know," he says, uneasy.

"Yes. You do," she insists.

"What is this?" He slips his hand back onto the doorknob.

"Think, Jericho," and at the mention of his name he starts to close the door.

She throws her palm against it, leans in and waits for his eyes to meet her own.

"Jericho. I'm Lydia. You run Blue Coral and you do drugs because you're miserable and blame yourself for the loss of a woman you loved. She was sick and you thought you could save her."

His face falls, expressionless.

She puts her weight on the door, stepping one foot in, but something in him breaks and he pushes her back, slamming the door in terror.

Lydia leans against the painted brick, that familiar headache returning. Bright, white, and making her body drift.

She focuses on her breathing, trying to stay calm against the fear of disappearing again until it's passed.

***

Emma is quiet.

He can tell she's wavering on the precipice of admitting a rare defeat.

Finally she says, "I'll turn MAIA on. Go down to the greenhouse and grab me a leaf."

He's puzzled about the leaf, but just says in sympathy, "She can't do anything you can't do."

She gives him a vacant smile. "It's no time for pride."

Descending to the lower level, he hears Emma activate MAIA from the bridge. Really, MAIA still makes most decisions while in sleep mode, but doesn't take directions unless awake.

MAIA—acronymically named according to its functions of systems monitoring, autopilot, and information analysis—was not particularly intelligent, at least as far as artificial intelligence goes. But that wasn't the point. Emma had developed MAIA for long flights with crews in stasis to make important flight or ecosystem control decisions. Emma hadn't played God, but as she ascribed to Jericho, she had *dabbled in her own irrelevance*. After everything went to hell down below, it was MAIA and not Emma—much less himself, of course—that was onboard the evacuation ship with the world's dignitaries, headed towards a confidential destiny. Most likely the Gliese System, Emma had said. It'd take a near eternity to reach, so of course they'd probably be using Realm in tandem with MAIA. The two were interdependent anyway—MAIA operated on a small percent of Realm's massive allocated resources.

Keene opens the first pressurized door, air blowing through him, decontaminating him. Then the second door depressurizes.

He pulls the handle and jumps back as overgrown foliage bursts into the vestibule, so dense he can't even see the red LED lights overhead.

It hadn't been this way—the assortment of plants had been tidy and organized in their long bins of strange soil, evenly spaced leaves and stalks, roots in little marble-like orbs. He'd only stepped into the room once before they took off for orbit, but he remembers the labels: wheat, rice, bamboo. Algae in tanks. Now it's a veritable jungle.

What the *hell* happened?

He snaps a leaf, mystified.

As he's about to close the doors, a quiet chittering sounds at his feet.

It's Methuselah. For whatever reason, Jericho insisted he come along. His habitat in the greenhouse must've been destroyed by the overgrown foliage.

Keene picks him up, rubs his tiny scruff.

"You're not *that* old, are you, friend? What's happened here?"

Methuselah sits up and twists his whiskers.

***

It's evening before Lydia decides to get out of Caligatha.

After her confrontation with Jericho she's realized the futility of her situation. No one will listen. No one will remember.

Against all her visceral judgment, she refuses to return home–she *can't*. She can't just accept that life continues, indifferent to her disappearance, that the hole she leaves behind is just a *continuity problem*. But she can't stay, either, plugging that hole and driving herself mad.

There is no unknowing.

A blood-red sun behind her on the beach of Caligatha, Lydia starts up the steps to Blue Coral.

Inside, a young woman sits at the front desk.

"Can I help you?" she asks. Her name tag says Maggie.

"Yes," Lydia says. "I need a room. First floor."

Maggie squints at the monitor in front of her. "I'm afraid I only have second and third available."

Lydia looks down the hallway. She'll have to pass the front desk to reach that strange room. And she'll need a staff member's key. There's no way she can pull it off without a room on the first floor.

"Are you sure?" she asks, thinking as she speaks. "Jericho told me it would be no problem. I have a guest in a wheelchair. The stairs won't work for us."

Maggie bites her lip.

"Could you call him, please?"

She takes the bait, picking up the phone.

"Do you have a restroom?" Lydia interjects.

Maggie points down the hall, and Lydia slips behind her, looking back. Maggie's engrossed on the phone, trying to find Jericho's number.

She runs down the hall, turning left at its end, then retracing her steps and turning right. There's a housekeeping cart, but no key.

This is it.

She returns to the front as Maggie is hanging up the phone, taking note of the room, 114.

"I'm sorry," Maggie tells her before she's returned to the end of the hall, rising again from her chair, "but I'm afraid Jericho can't be reached right now."

There they are. Her keys are on a band on the desk.

"Could you try again?" Lydia asks. "Tell him *Miss Sortanova*."

Maggie hesitates, but picks up the phone again, and Lydia runs back down the hall, tries the door. Locked.

No. There's no way around it.

The muscles in her stomach tighten. She heads back to the desk, grabs the band, and begins to run, but Maggie's grabbed the band behind her, yelling some warble of surprise.

Lydia stumbles, turning around and almost losing her balance.

Maggie's face is incredulous. "Hey!" she yells, and before she realizes what she's doing Lydia's hands are on her collar, pushing her back against the desk, but Maggie rights herself immediately, face still bewildered and half-crazed.

They're both frozen in place, both confused by her actions. Was this really the only way to go about it?

This is it.

Lydia again only sees her fist hitting the side of Maggie's face, spit ejecting from mouth. This time she lets go of the band.

Without looking back, Lydia runs down the hall, sweaty fingers fumbling to face the card's magnetic strip out before she reaches the door.

The word *hopeless* screams through her head as her feet pound on the carpet.

"Please," she begs, swiping the card. The lock grumbles, and she throws it open, stealing a look down the empty hallway as she blindly enters the room.

20

Decision

Emma folds the leaf in her hand, lost in thought, something reverent overcoming her.

"Thank you," she whispers, staring at Methuselah.

He tells her about the overgrown foliage, and she nods.

"What do you need that for?" he asks, but she walks in silence to the lab.

He sits in the bridge, at the nearest printer, as a simple box and dish are assembled for Methuselah, soon overhearing Emma talk to MAIA.

An engineer, a literature professor. No doctors, no pilot.

There's no control, he thinks. We're at the mercy of Realm and MAIA, drifting in infinite space in a very expensive tin can.

Emma returns in a moment with the leaf, her eyes weary. She waits until Methuselah's new home is printed, and the mouse tucked inside.

"It's been a long time," she says.

"What do you mean?" he asks.

She pulls up a chair, sits closer to him than she has since they woke up. Rubbing the leaf between her fingers, she begins to cry.

"There's molecular sensors in the plants," she whispers. "In case we need them to, they can sprout and flower on cue, or we can track a bad generation."

"So?"

"So every other log tracks some sort of system activity, and is maxed out or reporting the fortieth year. This is independent."

"I don't understand."

"Each generation is tracked. This is a," but she begins crying again, stops. "This is a thirty-second generation bamboo leaf."

It can't mean what it sounds like. That's not possible.

"We've been asleep thirty-two years?"

She shakes her head. "Longer. Each generation is a little over a year. The logs are probably accurate."

"That can't be," he insists. "We only planned for five years. How are we still–how is the mouse...?"

"It all works," she sobs. "It all works *perfectly*. Physiologically, no one onboard has aged a day. Even the mouse."

He tries to say something, but can't. *It can't be.* Something is wrong.

"It all works perfectly. Just perfect. *We're gods.*"

***

Lydia grips her sheets, wide eyes taking in the dimly lit metal of her cabin, curling into a tight ball.

She closes her eyes.

What has she done? She's saved no one.

Exhaling, she sits up, tells her heart to settle.

The black screen stares back. No stars.

"God damn it," she tells the wall.

There's no time for that she hears her invisible conscience say, and she wishes it would show itself, tell her exactly what she's supposed to do.

She walks to the bridge.

Keene is holding Emma while she stares into space.

"Hello, Lydia," he says, not at all acknowledging her with his usual gentle severity.

"No luck," she tells him, but they don't respond until she brings up a seat.

"Okay," Emma says, sitting up and wiping her face. "Okay."

Keene is quiet. Something is happening.

"Okay, this is it," Emma tells everyone. "We give ourselves a day. Twenty-four hours. We decide whether to stay here or go home."

Lydia tries to consider this, but it doesn't feel like a choice.

"I don't have a home," she says.

"What happened in Caligatha?" Keene asks, but he doesn't look interested.

"I don't know." That's the truth. "I...went back in time."

"I don't understand," Emma interrupts, and Lydia isn't sure but it sounds more like a protest, almost like she's angry.

"When I arrived...I found Jericho, and he died. I'm guessing an overdose, but..." She wraps her arms around herself, feeling cold. "And then–"

"An overdose?" Emma sneers. "An overdose? In Realm? Jericho had an *overdose* in Realm."

"He'd told me before about his problems. But...then we seemed to go back in time. Everyone, everything. But he seemed to have an overdose that day, too. At least that's what someone told me."

Emma stands, quiet but appearing to withhold an eruption, and begins walking out of the bridge.

Lydia looks to Keene, but he lowers his eyes, and they begin following Emma to the sleeping quarters.

She places her thumb on the corner of Jericho's window, next to the little name *Amara*, and the door makes a quiet huffing sound.

"You bastard," Emma says, opening the door.

And there he is, just as she remembered him, chest rising and falling in deep sleep. She tries to take it in, this new reality of Jericho, but Emma's leaning over him, touches his screen.

She stands cramped in the doorway. The room is so small.

"MAIA," Emma says after the screen over Jericho's body fades in, "Do you have a record of physical activity in this room?"

Lydia wonders who Emma's talking to. Her voice is no longer detached and observational.

A woman's voice, "Security surveillance, Emma. Jericho has set his logs marked private." It seems to come from everywhere at once in the room.

"Give me the last feed."

The entire screen fills, at first an almost black gray, then becomes a mirror image of the room, except their bodies are missing.

In the screen Jericho's body sits up, dazed, and Lydia realizes it's a video. He sits still, broken by random bouts of shaking and rubbing his arms as though cold, and the silence in the room is crushing.

"Speed up," Emma says, and Jericho begins rocking back and forth so fast it makes her feel panicked. He stands and circles the tiny room. He must be walking very slowly because it looks normal now, then he stops.

"Slow back down."

Jericho stares back at them, his eyes dead. Lydia almost can't take it anymore, but he speaks.

"We can't," he says, seeming to study them, then falls silent for a while.

"What did you do, you fuck?" Emma says under her breath, and as though to answer her Jericho speaks again.

"MAIA, create a new partition in Realm."

He sits, looking away from them.

Lydia consults his sleeping body over Emma's shoulder and shivers.

"My last back-up–copy that to a synthetic, but remove every reference to Lydia Sortanova. Don't let him remember anything. Respawn him at day one."

He looks at the screen again. "Yes. Good."

He rubs his temples and forehead in silence as he considers his next action.

"Pull up our passengers. Everyone."

His eyes burn back at them, studying them again carefully, looking through them. Then he begins listing names.

"Gregory Mentz. Rowan Scanlia. Timothy Regis. Wallace Friedman."

His voice is so hard and commanding, in stark contrast to his beaten, almost transparent presence, like a man burned by the same divine fire he's brought down from the mountaintop.

"Samantha and Max Benning. Garret Huck."

He goes on and on for minutes, a deliberate pause between each name, but steady and determined.

Finally he stops, thinking, almost defeated, then says, "Wait. Remove the women," even though he's said only a few women's names as far as Lydia can tell.

He stops longer now, breathing deep and long.

What is he thinking? Lydia wonders. She wants to ask Keene and Emma, but even Emma's stone cold glare has fallen, her mouth agape.

"When the partition is ready, queue them up," he says. He's doing something huge–catastrophic–but what? "Queue them up. Then disconnect all outgoing transmission in two hours. Disconnect all of Realm."

He stands, walks away from them, through the mirrored door, but then the video jumps forward and he's walking back in.

Studying the screen, staring through them again, he says, "Prepare to transfer that new partition to a freeform edit mode. Lock everyone. Queue me—no, queue me and—" He chokes on his words and brings up a glass, taking a long gulp of something amber. He must have left the room for the drink. "Queue me and erase all the physical wetware, do you fucking understand?"

Fiery wrath again.

That everywhere voice that responded to Emma speaks again, but this time, in the video, it's thinner and hard to hear, coming from the screen.

"Start me in administration, then lock me in one hour. I want a blank canvas. No one leaves. No ejection points. No death safety. No matter what I say, lock me in one hour once I'm in. Then transfer all my administration privileges to Lydia Sortanova. Everything, not just Realm."

Watching his chest still rise and fall in peace, Lydia wants to grab him up from the bed, shake him until everything is normal again, until the life she's lost is regained.

What has he done? To himself?—to her?—to everyone?

"Do you understand?" he asks again.

No. No, I don't understand, Jericho.

But the voice speaks for her again.

He stares at the screen for a long time, mulling over what must have been a vast swath of information.

"Bring up my private video archives," he says, setting the glass on the ledge by the screen and reaching under the bed, taking out a thin metal box.

He pulls out a few things she can't see, moving closer to the screen and sitting.

"Play all," he says.

Then he lifts one of the objects. It falls, long, from his collar past his chest.

Her mother's pendant.

Then, muffled, the voice of a ghost, she hears herself speak. Her voice. Some Lydia long-forgotten. Something she doesn't remember.

"Turn that thing off," the voice says. It's her sounding playful. Laughing.

"Oh, come on," Jericho's voice is saying, a hollow echo. But he's staring through them with reddening eyes.

He's watching a video, too, but they can't see it in this mirror image.

"Don't you want to remember?" Jericho's voice asks.

"I can remember just fine," Lydia's ghost says. "But there won't be anything *to* remember if you don't put that down and come here."

"Stop," Emma says louder than she's ever spoken. "MAIA, turn it off. That's enough."

And just like that, Jericho's weary face and red eyes are gone. Just that minimalist screen, white on black.

"That's enough," Emma whispers, backing out of the room.

***

Even with all of Jericho's casual speech, Keene doesn't really understand what Jericho asked MAIA to do, wants Emma to explain. But he understands enough–she doesn't want to be the harbinger of doom.

She sits in the bridge. He pulls up a chair next to her, but Lydia remains standing, looking ready to explode.

"We still have the signal," he says. "We can still go home."

"Yeah," Emma says, unphased. "We can."

"Look," Lydia almost shouts, seeming to jolt even herself with surprise, "I need to know what's going on. I need some answers. How–how can I know what to do when I don't–I don't have a past. I don't know what's going on *now*. How can I–"

"Okay," Emma says. "Here you go. Jericho couldn't bring himself to be with you in Caligatha. At some point he overdoses, because even Jericho's paradise needs drugs. It kicks him out of Realm. He gets up, wishing he was really dead. But the problem is, he has over seventy people on board who've contributed to a several billion dollar orbiter waiting to go back home. He could just blow his brains out, but no–atonement is meaningless unless others suffer too, right Jericho?"

Lydia clutches herself.

"No, he *can't* just sit around waiting and he *can't* go back to Caligatha and he *doesn't* just blow his brains out. He sends an artificial Jericho that doesn't remember you back into Caligatha to, oh, be your *savior*, maybe? The man he wanted to be, the man without guilt? And then he sends himself and everyone else he hates into a new Realm–I don't want to know what that...what his idea of hell is."

"An–an *artificial* Jericho?"

"We've been out for forty years because of that." Emma's voice rises. "You said he overdosed twice. Well, you just watched him get kicked out the first time. You die in Realm, you get kicked out. Death-safety. But it's the copy he sends back. Even without the memories, Jericho is still Jericho. Probably even worse, because I'll be damned if he could just cut out all his memories and emotions so cleanly. The poor bastard sent back in, he does all the same shit."

"Oh no," Lydia chokes. "I understand. Those drugs—my father's missing drugs. We still met, and when my father dies Jericho can't take it and overdoses."

"Whatever the reason, he can't be kicked out now because this copy of himself isn't linked to a physical body. *And* Realm can't force a short backtrack of only a few moments, do a rewrite, because his last backup had administration privileges. The idiot removed privileges from himself *after* he made the copy. Realm can't override administrator actions. You've been living in a feedback loop, Realm trying to make sense of it—when he dies it sends *everything* back to his first overdose. His copy's point of origin. Even *our* time was synced to Realm because it's such a sophisticated fucking clock, which is why we stopped routinely waking up."

"Why?" Lydia demands.

"Why what?"

"Why is all of this because of *me*?"

"Maybe you should watch the old home movies," Emma sneers, and Keene feels it cut through himself.

Poor Lydia.

"But—I didn't do anything," she says, fighting back tears.

"And you're just fine, aren't you? We're all just fine."

"What did he do to all those people?"

Emma almost laughs, so angry she doesn't consider her words. "Who cares? They all deserve it. I guess he was right all along."

"No," Lydia says. "I don't believe any of this."

This seems to remind Emma of Lydia's vulnerability, her innocence. She closes her eyes.

"Twenty-four hours," she says as Lydia starts off.

Keene watches Emma's face, her clenched muscles.

He draws near, kisses her throbbing temple.

"I didn't mean that," she says, watching Lydia disappear. "Look at her. Jericho doesn't know the meaning of misery."

"There's nothing you could do," he tells her.

"I know," she says, eyes still closed. "That's the problem."

It's been so long since they've been able to look at each other the way they used to. The steeled nerves, the resolute determination. All this has replaced the woman he knows.

Jericho, Emma, Lydia–he's become a man surrounded by martyrs.

Well, scratch Jericho. Where the hell did he go?

"If we land, and everything–" He pauses. "I know we don't know, but if everything *is* fixed down there...we can fix all this too, right?"

Emma looks up. "Jericho disconnected Realm and gave her all his administrative privileges She can reconnect and pull everyone out. But you and I have only been asleep. Caligatha on the other hand–Jericho fucked it up, that was a *well*-documented error and *exactly* why Leviathan required Realm's users register by their DNA profile, so that they could minimize liability in the event of someone pulling this kind of half-assed cloning bullshit. If it hadn't been so long, it might be one thing. They've been living the same moment all this time. The level of EDP is probably off the charts. God only knows what it'd be like to pull them out now. And everyone else, everyone Jericho took with him–do you want to see what mental state those people are in after forty years of...wherever he took them...some Realm he created in a rage...after *that?*"

"I guess not," he says. "But those in Caligatha...Lydia is doing as well as we could expect."

Emma rubs her forehead, exasperated. "For now. Realm is the only concept of reality she has."

"We need to go back home," he tells her. "Something's down there. We can go back and fix everything."

"But at the same time, even *if* a few people survived below, Christ. In 8000 BCE, humans were still painting in caves and just learning to plant seeds. I'm not sure anyone that survived would have the necessary skills for *that* level of civilization let alone regenerative neuroscience."

"Something is down there, though." He thinks of Lydia, stands. "What we need, maybe, is a reason to have hope again."

She gives him a look like he's gone insane. "What? That even the humble bamboo plant carries on?"

They stare into each other's eyes for a moment, hoping the other's nerves will relent.

"That's the spirit," he says. "Meet me in the dining room in an hour."

As he steps away, he hears Emma's words again: *the level of EDP is probably off the charts.*

Ghosting? Wasn't that fixed long ago?

***

Lydia sits on the edge of Jericho's bed. It's all too reminiscent of the hospital. But Jericho isn't dying.

Or he's not dead. Or not alive.

She resists the urge to touch him. In spite of all that's happened, she wants to fit her body into the tiny bed, try to find that missing spot in time where she could curl against his form, cradled in his warm breathing.

She stares at the blank screen, reaches forward to tap it. It fades into the familiar menu. She doesn't know what to do, says Jericho's words aloud, looking around to be sure no one overhears.

"Bring up Jericho's video archives."

The screen fills with little thumbnails.

"Play all," she says.

Then she's staring back at herself.

Except this Lydia's in a bed she's never seen before, in a contemporary bedroom with light green drapes. The walls are filled with oil paintings of ocean scenes, a couple of European cathedrals drenched in a buttery warmth rivaling the room's sunlight.

"Turn that thing off," she watches herself say.

The camera pans closer, until her face fills the whole screen.

"Oh, come on," Jericho says behind the camera.

She watches the scene play out, Jericho and this stranger that looks like her. She convinces him to set the camera down, and they kiss, diagonally framed, until he reaches across the bed to turn it off.

Then they're outdoors in sweatshirts. Lydia has the camera.

"So here we are," she says, and pans across a city below. They're on a mountaintop overlooking a valley of verdant pine. The buildings are glowing red before a setting sun, purple and stars weighing down overhead. "I finally got someone out."

"Yeah, yeah," he says, suddenly in the frame, kissing the lens.

This isn't the Jericho she knows. He's so loose, so at ease.

"Stop," she tells the screen. "Turn it all off."

What did Emma want to do? Drive home the fact that she couldn't remember all these things?

"Come on," Keene says from the doorway. "There's nothing for you here."

"These people–they–it's not me," she says.

He looks to the ground in reverence. "Can one remember love? It's like trying to summon up the smell of roses in a cellar. You might see a rose, but never the perfume."

"What? Is *everything* going to be a riddle?"

He smiles, and it's good to see that again–not very reassuring, but at least someone can flash signs of levity.

"Sorry," he tells her. "Words of an old playwright."

"I don't know what to do," she says, and reaches to feel under the bed until her fingers touch the box. She pulls it onto her lap.

"Doubtful you'll find more understanding in a box than you will in tomorrow."

She pulls out the pendant, just as she remembers it.

"This is my mother's," she tells him.

"It's beautiful."

"It's the only thing...Nothing else has come over with me from the other side."

There's scraps of paper in the box, but she doesn't want to read them, leafs with forlorn detachment around until she finds a little velvet box.

She opens it, and inside is a glimmering square-cut diamond on a rose gold band. It isn't new; there's the faintest couple of nicks on the band.

"He was going to give this to me again when we got out of Realm," she realizes aloud. "When everything was okay down below...but why don't I remember? Why was he going to give it to me a second time, and I can't remember the first?"

"Some things have followed you. Come on."

She watches the dull overhead light in the diamond's glow for a moment, then hurriedly places everything but the pendant back under the bed. Somehow the pendant seems assuring, perhaps because her mother was always missing, always a concept, the only person who remains constant and can't betray her. Maybe even that isn't true, but she places it around her neck and tucks it under her shirt.

He leads her back to the bridge and beckons her to the wall-length screen.

"MAIA," he says, "Let Lydia see what's outside."

Just like that, the black becomes a sky of deep blue and white, moving slow and graceful like a distant storm over the sea of Caligatha. She watches, speechless.

"Perfect timing," he says.

"We're so close."

"We have some limited flight ability, but we're really just an orbiter just beyond the atmosphere. Looks like we're facing straight down."

"It's just like laying on the grass and watching the sky."

"Some things," he tells her, "rarely–but some things look the same from wherever you see them."

"Thank you," she says. "I expected it to be so much smaller."

"You took the wrong pill, Alice." He smiles again. "The sort of freedom you've found has made for a much *larger* world."

"I prefer it just how it is. Is this a screen or–"

"No, a special glass. Palladium. The overlay is just more of that embedded nano-crap." He smiles again. "Go ahead."

She steps forward and places her palms and forehead on the cool glass.

"We've really been here all that time?"

"I'm just along for the ride, too, my dear, but it seems that way."

"And now we're going back?"

"If we decide. Emma believes someone sent us coordinates."

"Coordinates. That's a far cry from a word like *home*."

Keene smiles. "I should say."

"No one's ever told me what happened."

"A lot has happened."

"The *reason*."

"Right," he says, beginning to pace.

"I might've been born yesterday, but I don't think all of *this* is over a forest fire."

"Remember what I said about Jericho's little machines?"

"Yes. Artificial immune systems. Nanotechnology."

He breathes long and deep. "Jericho was only one of many pioneers. Pioneers across many fields. We lived in what he called *transcendent times*. Many, many rules had begun to bend at the hand of nanotechnology, gene therapy, robotics, artificial intelligence. This produced a lot of good, and a lot of bad. This trade-off has always plagued us. When you make waves, you produce peaks and troughs."

He pauses with his arms in the air, mid-gesticulation of a trough, lost in the thought of bygone horrors.

"I understand," she says. And so far, she does. "What was the bad?"

"Accidents. Terrorism. But most of this was contained. Just as nuclear technology, miraculously, was scarcely used for ill in the entire century since its inception. So too were nanoswarms, intelligent and destructive machines in the form of dust clouds–or, synthesized microorganisms designed to destroy architecture–or, engineered diseases–*all* these things were crushed by the average goodness and ingenuity of humanity."

"Okay," she says. "But something got through?"

He breathes deeply again, but this time only says, "Yes."

"Who did it?"

"Who did *any* of it? It depends who you ask. Some attacks were claimed by terrorist groups. But many of the attacks appeared indiscriminate. Every organization had a stake in pointing their finger somewhere. Anyway, there was very little death, very little destruction. There had been foresight for many of these things since the 1980's. Until–it hit. Many people called it many different things. Saitei. La Peste. In English it was mostly called *it*. I…suppose my English-speaking brethren are not always equally inspired." He tries to smile, but it's forced.

"It?"

"Just before leaving, it'd been formally dubbed Vesper Syndrome, after, in a reverse from usual nomenclature, the only case of apparent immunity. A woman named Vesper. It was different. Invisible. No one has managed to isolate it. Without isolating it, we couldn't perform animal tests or simulations. We don't even know how it works, but it seems to attack the haptic system and ruin the ability to interact with Realm."

"That's all?"

"No, it acts like a sort of… neurological autoimmune disorder. It convinces the body to attack itself. By hijacking the haptic system it spontaneously deprives specific arterial pathways of oxygen, leading to tissue degeneration and loss of limbs or worse without immediate medical intervention. Its tendency to strike frequently and randomly in sufferers makes it very difficult to manage without constant medical supervision. I don't know if I agree, but some speculate Vesper Syndrome is intelligent, that it spread to…synthetic…people in Realm. It was able to simulate its own potential mutations and evolve at a speed unachievable in nature. And it took those lessons into the real world, changing at will. Camouflaging."

Lydia watches the white and blue twist lazily beyond—is that all that's left now? Water, wind, and dust?

She turns. "So is everyone dead?"

"Shortly before this all began, Emma was contracted to develop MAIA for Blackthorne Aeuronautics, with consultation from Jericho. While a very low-level AI, MAIA has the specific purpose of being an intelligent autopilot for a ship navigating deep space with a crew in stasis for a very long period of time. And interfacing with Realm. This was for scientific purposes, supposedly. There was never more than loose talk, but..."

"Where did they go?" She hadn't thought of the idea of *more* beyond this ship—or orbiter, as Keene called it—and Caligatha, and whatever was left of Earth.

"We're not supposed to think they–anyone—went anywhere. But in the end dignitaries and captains of industry disappeared. There was also talk of underground bunkers amongst the common people, but it's doubtful that would have been feasible long-term. It all depends what you believe."

"And what do you believe?"

"Some believed they were headed for Gliese...a very far away planet. The only inhabitable one we know of. But that would take a very long time. It's twenty light years away."

"Twenty years? But we've been—"

"No, no. That's a measure of distance. Emma says it would take *half a million years*. So it doesn't seem very likely. But then again—our orbiter is based on many of their concepts, and, though I suppose you could call it a devastating success, we're here, and we're the only ones doing this."

"Well, what made everyone here so special?"

"Money," Keene says without hesitation. "That's all."

"But what about you? Didn't you say you were a literature professor?"

"I told you I was lucky. Emma worked on MAIA with Jericho, and after Realm brought Jericho his money he had a lot of *friends* with money. Friends that apparently did not make the cut with everyone else. This is all their funding. Get enough billionaires together, you can do just about anything."

It's taken a moment for it all to sink in, but now the realization hits her: this isn't the remnants of human survival. It's an escape vessel full of cowards.

"I'd worked with Jericho before, and Emma was integral of course. We–Emma and I–happened in that last year. It might seem obvious for us to be here...but Emma belonged on the first ship out. I'll forever be indebted to Jericho for saving the both of us."

She's confused—why would some nanotechnology engineer collaborate with a literature professor? But it doesn't matter; she's too betrayed by this new idea of escape.

"So you copied their plans and ran away?"

"I'm sorry...there wasn't much to run away from. By the end of our time secluded on an island off Scotland, we'd lost all ability to communicate with the outside world. We survived the only way we could. The entire operation is built around the hope that others did as well, in their way—better, hopefully."

She turns back to Earth. "That makes me feel like a coward, but I don't remember."

"You're far from the guiltiest person on board."

At this she turns again. "Why? Why was Jericho so upset at those people? All those names?"

"Like I said, money. There was only room for those with money to help fund this orbiter."

"So?"

"With limited room, and the price of...admission...some on board made...certain choices in regards to their children and families."

"What?" Unbelievable—her skin pricks with rage. "They let them *die?*"

"You can rest assured Jericho felt the same way. Anyway, they are the minority. And many here, like me, are lucky and indebted, one way or another. No matter what you think of the rest, remember that."

"How many?"

"There are seventy-four passengers all together. And Jericho listed, what, twenty?"

"They deserve whatever he—wherever he sent them."

"Maybe. I'd rather not think of it yet. One consequence at a time." Keene looks away. "But I'm glad to see you angry."

"Why? It's a horrible thing."

"We need more than sadness. We need reasons."

She can't think of anything to say, hopes the bastards never wake up. But then she can't help it. "Did you have children?"

Keene looks back, but not at her. At Earth.

"No," he says, unflinching. "We can't."

"Oh." She wants to apologize, but she's still under the adrenaline rush of anger.

"Well, you're not alone," he says. "It struck a very personal chord with him."

"Over his loss? That's not the same. That wasn't a choice, losing his wife and child."

"But you'd never convince him of that."

"I don't understand. How, if he'd been so permanently affected, had he been able to fall so in love with *me?* What happened to her?"

"Just as I'd said. She was sick, and he didn't finish his work in time."

"What was her name?"

He smiles sadly. "If you really must know, it *was* tragic."

"I think I need to."

He sighs, thinking for a moment.

"The only work he'd shared with the University was theoretical. We didn't know his team was performing animal tests on the artificial immune system off-site. But, as it turns out, they had gone smoothly for quite some time. He administered her. It was certainly a risk, but one they were both willing to take. However, the artificial immune system could not discern that there were two unique patient DNA sets—mother and child. I don't quite understand what happened on a technical level, but...it assumed one of them to be a cancer."

"She died."

"Yes, from that. In a more horrifying way than any of us would care to know."

He'd killed her, trying to save her.

"Whatever existential crises he hadn't already faced, he met head on at trial."

"At trial?"

"He hadn't been cleared for human testing. It was an act of desperation. He was found innocent of murder, in part due to technicalities and mishandlings and in part due to a sympathetic jury. It also helped there was a wealth of video documentation of her enthusiasm for the procedure. But..." Keene trails off.

"But what?"

"As I said, it was tragic."

She shivers. "Thank you for explaining," she says, sounding more like she's apologizing.

Turning, she watches his face, his absent eyes, and regrets becoming so angry.

"Whenever he was down on himself, really down, he'd watch it again...as though to reaffirm his guilt. I told him so many times to destroy it, but even that wouldn't have helped. It was all over the Internet, being as ghastly as people–" He stops, looks up at her, seeming to hold back tears. "Lydia..." He pauses, shakes his head. "I apologize."

She's as shapeless as her envisioned Earth below of wind, water, and dust. "No. I need to know. What happened, who I was."

"You are who you are. Don't let that weigh you down."

"But that scares me the most–not knowing if I'll ever remember who I am."

"You'll become what you're meant to become."

"But–these are different rules. You said so yourself. Death is–*dead*. And Jericho..."

"Life and love persist. So does death. Rules don't break, no matter how much humans may bend them."

"I don't feel human anymore."

Keene studies her in remorse, then pulls a little piece of green out of his pocket. A little leaf.

"Here," he says, handing it to her.

"What is this?"

"We have a greenhouse on the lower level. They gave it rules on how to grow, but it's a bit...impatient. It's been waiting for you a long time. To decide whether to bring it back home."

She runs her fingers over the leaf's veins and looks back at the world below. "What happened to the Vesper girl?"

He sighs. "Vesper White was kidnapped by a fundamentalist cult which refused to believe the only glimmer of light left in the world was a…former pornographic actress."

"Oh."

"If her body had been found, perhaps we would know more. In matters of life and death, ideas are more dangerous than disease."

"I see." The world below might really be empty.

"I'll leave you," he says. "You have much to think about."

She listens to his footsteps.

"Keene?" she calls out, and the steps stop. "I didn't realize...I thought you and Emma had been together forever."

"We have now."

She turns, but doesn't know what to say. "I'm sorry," she says, disappointed.

He smiles. "Life and love persist." But at this his smile drops, and he nods in a moment of silence before leaving her alone on the bridge.

Do they persist?

Water, wind, and dust.

The muscles in her stomach and jaw begin to clench in anticipation as she makes her way back to Jericho's cabin.

***

Emma meets him in the bridge after a little while.

"MAIA says if we begin our descent in sixteen hours, we'll have the best chance of settling near our target."

"I don't want to talk about that just yet," he tells her, taking her hand. "I have something to show you."

They retire to their unused sleeping cabin amongst the others. In his room, he instructs her to lay down.

"What are you doing?" she asks.

"MAIA," he tells the screen, settling beside her, "I believe we're ready for Echo Park."

"What?" she says, turning, but there's that cutoff feeling of an involuntary yawn.

Then the sensation of moving air. Crisp, alive.

Elysian Park Drive, that familiar stretch of gravel and dust overlooking the steep Echo Park. Timeless and verdant, not so much sunken as hidden in broad daylight, an ancient sanctuary of foliage whose crater still chokes any encroaching neon.

"You hate Realm," Emma says, her eyes still closed.

Really, just on the other side is Dodger Stadium, and they're only a couple blocks from the bustling traffic of Sunset Boulevard. All meticulously replicated in its peacefully industrious hum.

But this spot is their own. Something about the topsy-turvy Los Angeles topography had formed a barrier, leaving the rows of duplexes in tranquility.

"Everything has its place," Keene says.

Hand-in-hand, they watch the gentle breeze rustle the palms.

It's sundown. In the distance, a pair of joggers unsettle little clouds of dust underfoot, while a terrier sprints in wide circles around a young lady.

"Strange," Emma says. "All this time has felt so brief...a few days. Yet, it does seem like eternity since we've been here."

She means the real Echo Park, of course, where they'd had a little loft on Lucretia Avenue.

An eternity, but it was also such a brief pass through the corridors of time.

"I was hoping to make up for a missed anniversary," he says, and she places her head on his shoulder.

A few days awake in space without the shape of her hand or the scent of her hair.

"I would have been fine with the soy egg protein. Thank you."

He gently turns her face to look at his.

"I'm not scared with you," she whispers, losing her stoicism. "Not of death. Not of our uncertain immortality."

They kiss, embracing against the smells and chill and hush of nightfall.

"To know you is to transform love into eternity's grave, to lose you is to remove its headstone and lay within."

Emma considers this in silence, then smiles. "Who are you quoting?"

"Just some old, retired hack."

"Come on," she says, squeezing his hand. In her eyes twinkle not the solid edges of overhead LED's or the wash of anemic screens, but the diffused glow of the moon. *Everything has it's place.* "Let's do this."

✳✳✳

She watches the details at first, observing the strange motions of her body, every forgotten word from her mouth. Then, unable to accept the mystery of this stranger with her skin and mannerisms, skips from scene to scene, rushing through endless snippets of candlelit dinners, afternoons on the beach, days lounging in the sunbathed flat.

She remembers nothing of this past life.

Then Jericho has the camera, focused straight on her abdomen.

"This is week number eight," he says. "Day fifty-something."

She listens to herself laugh. "Oh no," she says, "Am I going to go through this *every* day?"

"Only a little over two-hundred more times. We'll figure it out, exactly."

It can't be.

The camera pans to her face. That look of playful scorn, unable to hide her smile. She knows it well.

"*I'm sure* Autumn will appreciate the documentary," she says.

At this she skips again. It's not possible. There has to be something, jumping scene to scene, that will explain it all away.

The seasons morph as shirts become sweaters at night, but there's a more subtle change.

Less laughter. Less outdoors.

By the time her belly has grown to what must be the second trimester, half of the videos are in bed.

She still smiles. Sometimes it's genuine.

Most of her smiles now are the sort she's used to giving her father, brandished for courage.

"No," she says aloud, her double on the screen stroking her bloated belly. "It *can't* be. It *can't*."

Her heart pounds until blood rushes through every vein, pushing at the tips of her fingers, roaring like a hot river in her ears.

And there it is. It's a different camera this time–something about the colors and quality is not right. It's a lab camera. And the room–it's empty. No warm, buttery bedroom with green drapes and oil paintings. No encouraging smile.

She's laying on a table. Jericho strokes her hair, tense, trying to soothe.

Her double looks away, and Jericho chokes up, stifling what might be tears with an arm across his face.

"Yes," he tells her. "Just a prick and it'll all be better."

Syringe.

"Nothing to fear."

It enters her arm, slowly and more gently than any shot she can ever remember.

"One night here," he says.

"And home in time for breakfast," she finishes for him.

The Lydia on the screen lies still, but here and now she's itching, waves rolling in her stomach.

Jericho's talking, but she can't pay attention, holds herself and looks away from the screen.

His voice goes on and on, alternating between a drone and reassuring pets of comfort.

In this dark, cramped little room it's just her, Jericho's motionless body, and his disembodied voice.

She sobs, biting her lip until it beats harder than her heart.

Jericho's voice changes. Wavering. Still trying to soothe but louder, alarmed.

She looks up at the screen with eyes behind fanned fingers.

"Stop!" she yells, but she can't enunciate it right, it comes out mangled in her sobs. "Stop!"

It doesn't.

She watches herself writhe, Jericho screaming and knocking the counters clean, falling to his knees as she collapses from the table.

Lydia on the screen seizes, eyes only corneas, all white and open impossibly wide as they roll to the back of her skull. She gurgles up salival foam as blood pours from her nose and ears. Jericho grabs her, her arms flailing and bending at impossible angles. Her skin sticks to his coat, his face, the floor. It pulls off in loose clumps. Her torso falls apart in a shower of pulsing segments into Jericho's arms.

What's left of her settles into collapsing pools.

She dissolves.

***

It was only their bedroom he'd crafted differently from the template, down to the wispy curtains revealing their overgrown flower garden. Matching everything from memory.

But it's not perfect. No replication of the real world in Realm ever is.

Anytime they make love and drift asleep in Realm, Keene dreams.

Elysian Park again, more vivid and imperfect and real in his dream than any Realm template.

He knows this moment as soon as the brisk frost settles on his face. It's an early December day, the first morning they spent walking about the world beyond their flat together.

Emma is in his arms, their hands clasped in her peacoat, watching a Japanese family make their rounds. To the other side, tourists with folded paper directions, two adventurous children running far ahead of the rest.

"Keene," Emma says, watching the children, and her fingers grow clammy. She doesn't say another word.

She was so soft back then, so desperate to believe the things he'd promised, but she had these moments of freezing up and swallowing some invisible, poisonous thought.

Back then, he'd worried Emma doubted their legitimacy, felt forced to share her life with him. Children playing dress up in a world falling apart, with nothing else to do with their shrinking freedom.

He couldn't think of anything to say at the time, had fallen too silent for the rest of the walk, but time skips ahead in his dream.

Now they're in bed an hour later in this dream, slipping into a generic template of a bedroom that isn't their own.

They make love, and Emma begins to cry.

"It isn't the same," he says.

"You don't know what the same is," she tells him.

He wakes up here, as he often does from this dream-within-a-dream, wishing it were really that moment, and he could say something less apologetic, less neutered.

Emma is beside him, but she's not crying. She's asleep.

Gradually, she'd adjusted to the fact that they could only make love in Realm, that they could never have children. What else was there to do?

Always at the end of this dream, lying awake, he hears Jericho's voice from a different time and place. One of their meetings in Aurore.

They were almost finished, and Emma must have been reflecting on being left behind by Blackthorne Aeronautics.

"Why us?" Emma had asked. "I know little, if anything, that you don't know."

"I need more than people with money," he said, and for once he seemed to care about what he was selling. "I need people to provide for the future."

They all wallowed in his ambiguity for a long while. Maybe, with all of these impassioned contradictions, Jericho never had a plan.

"You know," Emma said firmly. "You know we can't have children. There's no reason for us to go."

"Yes, I do. I know," Jericho said, in yet another mystery left unsolved.

***

She's dead. Dead. *Dead.*

The woman in Jericho's home movies, the woman of so many stories, the woman with her face and voice.

She's dead.

The woman with her history, her sick father.

Dead.

Her body shakes so hard she's sure she'll collapse into a pile of broken limbs.

Dead.

Through the hall, to the bridge. No one.

She runs back to the cabins, trying all the doors without thinking.

What does she even want to find? Herself?

As though she'll find the fake Lydia in these movies, still alive. Not dead, not melted into a puddle. No, not dead. No one's dead, not on Earth, not her, not her father. No one.

All one big fucking joke.

She begins touching her quivering thumb to the windows, one by one, swinging the doors open.

So many bodies, sleeping, lost in time, lost in space.

She wants to shake them all, demand everything be given back.

She stops halfway down the hall, looking back at the mess of flung open doors.

Transfer all my administration privileges to Lydia Sortanova.

Jericho.

She has to find Jericho. Not the fake, simulated Jericho. Not the breathing shell in his bed. The real one.

The one quarantined with all the others he'd damned.

The only life she remembers is some falsified feedback loop. In his miserable idea of heaven.

For answers, she has to go to hell.

No ejection points.

She makes her way to her own cabin, sits on the bed, resenting the reflection of her own face in the black screen.

21

The Descent

Emma and Keene emerge from their cabin to discover half of the hallway's doors open and Lydia asleep on her bed.

"She's going to lose it," Emma says. "It's inevitable."

They return to the bridge, and Keene watches her discuss the logistics of a landing with MAIA.

Since the orbital isn't designed for navigation, their best opportunity for landing near their target is only ten hours away.

"Well?" Emma says.

"What about Lydia?"

***

She feels her body, her clothes.

Green sundress. It fills her with rage, this feeling of being dressed by someone else.

A long hallway lies before her.

Cool, milky light glows from gargantuan windows stretching from the marble floor to the ceiling far, far overhead. Elegantly trimmed trees, their trunks and branches wrapped in knotted vines, line the hallway in pots so tall she could barely reach their rim.

She steps to the first window. Everything is the palest blue, clouds drifting lazily below.

Between each of the windows is a door.

According to the diagram MAIA produced, Jericho and everyone he brought with him is at the far end of this hall.

But now the skeleton whale that swallowed her in her sleep is alive, has flesh.

She's here and the tables have turned. The thing that was impossible to fathom is itself asleep with all of its denizens, unaware, just a dream floating in the sky.

Etched in the first door is the word *Panacea*. According to MAIA, there are four people wasting away here, two men and two women.

She pushes the door and it glides wide open, revealing a glowing panel of white. Stepping through, the panel dissipates, and behind her is now a curtain of beads in its place.

There's a spiral staircase surrounded by paper lamps leading down to another curtain of beads, and a dense and sweet fragrance hanging in the air. She pushes through the second curtain, and rather than surprise is overwhelmed by disappointment.

An elaborate opium den opens before her eyes. Ornately-patterned silk hangs from the walls. A hallway to her left is obscured by more beads.

Low-lying beds hug the corners, suspended in midair. On one next to her, two women in loose dyed skins are listlessly pleasuring one another, mouth on mouth and hands in thighs while on another bed a man and woman watch in disinterest.

The second couple immediately pull pipes from their mouths, staring at her. A lazy specter drifts from their lips in place of words.

In a far corner, a naked couple are copulating slowly, but at the sight of her the man takes his hands off her breasts and pushes her back by the stomach until she stops, resting on her arms. Without breaking his stare, he snickers and reaches to a tray, grabbing a square glass.

He sips, then laughs again, motioning her near.

The other man and woman continue to stare at her, their smoke now long floating snakes, while the two women continue, oblivious.

She had no plan, and certainly none for being so underwhelmed. She had expected desperate, trapped people. People who would rush to her rescue, people at the edge of madness with a thirst for freedom. Instead, she's found wallowing slugs in a lethargic sandbox of carnal bliss.

She approaches.

"Drink?" the man with the square glass says, motioning to the tray.

"What is it?" she asks, not knowing where to begin.

"Laudanum. Opium tincture."

Of course.

"Lovely." He sets his down. "Blackberry."

"No," she says, stopping.

His smile grows and grows until he erupts in a screeching cackle that reminds her of a stalling engine. His eyes never leave her face. Then, without any transition, he barks, "*Why* are you here?"

"It's time to go."

"Time to go," the couple beside her echo in unison, but they've taken to watching the two women pleasuring each other again. But now the women's faces are different. They'd both had brown hair, and now one is blonde.

"So," the man says, now fully pushing off the woman like a bedsheet. "Everything is...back to *normal*."

"No." She stares at the woman. She must not be real. "It's time to wake up."

"Ha." He sips the laudanum again.

"Do you know how long it's been?"

"*Hummm*." The woman to Lydia's side lays back, stretching her arms. "A year," she yawns, disinterested.

"No. No, it's been much longer than that."

She doesn't respond, and the man beside her stares through Lydia.

"Much longer," she appeals to the man with the laudanum.

"Things are not back to *normal*. As though *normal*–" He stops, reaches for his own pipe. He draws for a long time, and blows in her direction. "I think we'll ride out *normal*, if we have a choice."

"This isn't *real*," Lydia protests, stepping forward. "This is all the same. You're–you're fucking *cartoons*."

"My dear," he says, now picking at the indolent woman's silk. "I used to have consequences. I used to squander my time on the search for meaning. I spent my days empire-building. Amassing things. People. And happiness is always, *always* fleeting in that world."

He sips the laudanum, staring at Lydia. Then he begins moving his hand over the woman again. "Not because of struggle. Not because of pain. But because there's a difference between the *unreal* and a *lie*. What I realized is the world we'd lived in for so long was never real–everything that held society together, like money, is just another fabrication. But it's worse. It's a lie. You *tell* yourself it's real. You see?"

He leans toward the woman, grasps her face with both hands and runs his fingers across her chin and mouth, parting her lips. He settles his thumbs on her cheek bones.

"But now we don't have to believe anymore. No more anxiety. No more lying to ourselves or each other."

He moves his thumbs to her closed eyes.

"Accept that everything is unreal. The lack of *inherent* truth will set you free."

He looks at Lydia, smiles and reaches a hand to the square glass and sips again.

"Everything going to shit, and nothing being *a lie*, is the best thing that ever happened."

He reaches to the woman's face again and begins pressing his thumbs into her eyes as she lies solidly still.

Lydia surges with anger, grabs the lamp with its dangling pipe and slams it into the wall. She steps back, watching in surprise as a tiny spark begins to glow and burn into a flame.

He grabs the bare shoulder of the woman, picks her up and shoves her to the wall. Still unflinching, she pulls the burning silk into herself, curling into a smoldering ball.

He laughs, standing now, reaching his hand to Lydia's face.

"Look at you," he says. "So unfulfilled. A life of frustration. You still embrace your pain. The fulcrum of your life."

The woman moves, uncurls and rests on her side, but she's not the same. Her broad face has become narrow, her pink lips red, her shoulders more jagged, her brown eyes blue.

"I've had so many like you," he says, fingertips digging into Lydia's neck, turning her face side to side, examining. "But real, feral thoughts in your head. How exciting."

She smacks his arm away, and he rests again, already disinterested.

From the soft ticking and clacking of the bead-obscured hall, another woman arrives carrying a lamp, rests it beside the bed. Lydia watches her prepare the opium.

Was there something wrong with her to be so distraught by this rupture in reality?

The second woman finishes and reclines on the bed. In her eyes is nothing. There's no careful design in these people, these things. They're not at all like everyone from Caligatha. They're sloppy, designed for sensation in a haze.

"You're all *dead* inside," Lydia tells them. "Dead, *dead!*"

The word rings out in her head again. Dead, dead. Just like her, dead. Who is she to call anyone dead?

"*Dead!*" she screams. No matter what her circumstance, she has her will.

"Then here we are," the man says, and blows smoke in her direction again. He motions to the suspended cloud. "Join the danse macabre or leave. Your penchant for sadness is no good here."

Lydia says nothing, looks to the hallway.

"Be gone," he tells her.

She takes one last look around the room, backing through the beads. After all this time, she's not cause for alarm. She's novelty.

She continues down the dark corridor, discovering another beaded doorway. She parts them and steps through.

At once, with one step, a dense noise washes over her. An orgy of elegant booths of neon, silk, caged birds and macaques. A vibrant chaos of sight, sound, and smell. The sizzle of live shrimp in woks of leaping liquor-fed flames; pale pubescent girls, nude save their checkered boarding school tops; chopped serpent chunks writhing on platters. Those tending the open tables and booths are motionless and sullen, unspeaking. The noise is its own self-sustained black magic, like the ocean roar, everywhere and nowhere at once.

As she passes, each twitches and jerks alive, shouting its thrill, but these too are carnivalistic caricatures of real people: drain and taste the blood of this living man, little lady!–crush these baby chicks with your bare hands!–defile any of these chained women anyhow you please!–and then, after she passes, each again falls quiet.

So this is a Realm dedicated to fulfilling uninhibited desire and bloodlust. Urges pinched off in the ancient brainstem and left to rot. A romanticized, womb-like den of bliss. And steps away, violence, modeled on a shadowy interpretation of a black market's worst in Shanghai or Mumbai; or perhaps, depending on the participant, of New York or Los Angeles.

Hyperrealist decadence.

Therapy. *Panacea.*

More than disgust, she's struck by the lack of surprise, the lack of creativity, the insincere sameness. The wrathful parts of the mind care only about liberation from shame. All reviled passions look the same in sunlight.

She passes children in bamboo cages, tanks offering the temporary sensations of near-suicide by tigerfish, the leashed men and women implanted with absurd sexual devices full of prongs and teeth and blades for pleasure or torture. Finally, there is an open area with benches and a veranda serving as an infinite wall.

Invisible birds chirp cluelessly.

A woman sits at one of the benches, back turned, head up to the sky. Matted black hair falls in dirty tangles to her waist.

"Hello," Lydia calls out, but she doesn't move.

She's compelled to run back to the beginning, out of this awful place, but she steps forward.

The woman is still as stone. Lydia circles around to discover one of the slaves with his face between her legs, engaged in cunnilingus.

Her eyes are glossed, her mouth agape, neck crooked. She's been drooling for so long, her clothes are plastered against her skin from chest to waist.

Dead. Dead. Dead.

The word swirls in her mind again, whipping into a tempest.

Feeling her heart pound in her fists, she forces them flat, slaps the woman's face hard.

"Wake up!" she screams.

But they won't wake up. As her hand begins to sting, she realizes there's nothing she can inflict in her wrath that they haven't already experienced.

She steps back, cradling her hand, thinking of how surprised she was to strike Maggie. But now she was seeking catharsis, enraged to feel. Now there was no surprise. She strikes out like a mad storm unable to contain her thunderous friction.

The woman reels back, settles her eyes on Lydia. Her lips mouth something silent, one or two syllables of air.

More in puzzlement than anger, the woman grabs the slave by his hair, throws him off in a string of saliva without breaking her stare into Lydia's eyes.

Lydia steps further back, stares into the slaves expressionless face, and races toward and through the market and all the reanimating vendors. Through the black rainbow whirlwind of neon and blood.

"It's not real," she says aloud, gasping, looking back for any sign of being followed. "It's not real."

She crashes into a large body hard. Steps from the beaded curtain, a man stares at her, unphased. He's fully nude, and in his right hand he holds a long knife. "I told them," he mutters, plunging the twelve-inch blade into his side with a giggle.

His entire body is covered in scars and oozing sores.

He lifts the knife and Lydia screams, grabbing his wrist. But there's so little force in his arm, it swings back without tension.

"Time to go," he breathes, hot on her face.

She screams again, grabbing the blade from his hand. She wrangles his fingers loose with too much force. It flies in her hand, slices through his mouth. His jaw dangles and flaps as he giggles again.

He steps towards her, blood gurgling from the open gash. She kicks him in the stomach and swipes the knife across his face as he doubles over, choking and laughing, and she strikes him again with the hilt until he falls to the dirt.

Her chest heaving, she plunges the blade with all her strength into his back, pinning him to the ground.

Overcome, his laughing stops. There's only the liquid sound of blood choking his breathing.

Lydia rocks in place, staring at her bloody hands.

Her scream is not one of terror. It rises from her belly like a world splitting in half until her lungs are empty and she's an empty vessel.

She rushes through the first and then the second set of beads, expecting scornful laughter or an ambush, but the room remains silent, undisturbed from its standstill rhythm.

Onward out of the opium den, up the spiral staircases, and then into the marble hallway.

The gentle breeze from nowhere gently licks her hot skin as she stands, catching her breath.

"It's not real," she says again, trying to clear her mind of all those tortured people. "They're only there when I look at them. They're not real."

The blood on her hands is gone.

Below, through the windows to nowhere, neolithic mists still twirl across a pale blue sky.

She looks at all the remaining doors.

Elysium. Harmony. Rapture.

She thinks of the student she'd judged back in Caligatha, when she was sitting at the bench waiting for her father's medicine. She'd been so quick to project ignorance and selfish indulgence. Why? Because she had no indulgences of her own? Is this what ultimate liberty from responsibility looks like? A mad race beyond temptation, beyond pleasure? A race to the most forbidden, to the most unthinkable?

Is it possible to appreciate pleasure and pain only when the pendulum swings beyond our reach?

No one here wants to be saved. They'd rode that pendulum swing into a directionless circle.

She begins to walk to Jericho's nameless door.

***

"I don't know," Emma says. "It may be wisest to compose a new signal. Try to communicate further."

"Does it matter? Someone wants us to return."

Emma nods, tells MAIA to display the coordinates. The screen splits into a sinusoidal world map and several other blocks of text.

"Assuming these are the international standards we're used to," she says, tapping an area near Arizona, "roughly 34°N and 114°W...we can expect to land somewhere near the California-Arizona-Nevada tristate area. That would specifically be Mojave Valley."

The screen fills with a topographic map of the region.

"But as it doesn't appear anyone will be laying out the red carpet, nothing about this landing would be specific."

"Back to the beginning," Keene says. Less than three hundred miles from where it all began.

***

A ground cold and damp sinks under her feet like moss, the door behind her, her only way out, sucking up dead air until it's disappeared.

Everything is dark. Only the dimmest of eclipsed-moon violet lays a razor's edge of light.

Organic tendrils, not quite trees, form wide swaths of crooked path, hanging loose from invisible walls, brittle and dying on the ground.

She forms her lips to whisper Jericho's name, but holds her breath.

The air is salt, rust, rot. Strange and alive.

Beyond is a dark clearing with scattered boulders.

She makes her way forward, feet sinking, moist soil spilling over and between her sandals and toes, until she realizes they're not boulders and gasps.

No longer moving, no longer struggling, are the torsos of the men Jericho has brought to hell with him. Only their rasping gives it away in the darkness until she squints her burning eyes.

Behind them are children, their bodies decomposing and falling apart. Bones sticking through disintegrating flesh.

Jericho has recreated the left-behind children, gnawing at the shredded legs of their fathers. Feeding.

As she watches, the fathers' limbs slowly regenerate, growing new flesh, repairing the bloody torsos.

And the feral children swoop their necks down, snap new tendon, raising their bloody mouths to the eclipsed moon.

Jericho's mocking them.

All the healing he brought to them now keeps them alive to be tortured forever, tortured by the memory of their own lost children.

***

"If this is our decision," Emma says, "We shouldn't burden Lydia with our landing procedure. She's been through enough."

Emma goes over the process again. When ready, they'll proceed to the detachment pod. The engines will fire until they stop orbiting and reenter the atmosphere. Then it becomes a glider, but there's no runway, so at ninety meters they'll be ejected from the detachment bay which will expend its boosters, settling down lightly, maybe two-hundred meters from wherever the orbiter stops. Additionally, a separate pod of MeDX, those thin-legged medic automatons, will be released. In a next-to-worst case scenario, they should be able to revive anyone who's injured, but there is a slim chance of instant death by landing in the Mojave Valley. After forty years of fuel regeneration, there's enough fuel to return to orbit, but not for a second return to Earth. And they would have to crash land next time anyway, unless they reattach the pod to the detachment bay.

"So we should be sure this is what we want to do."

***

Lydia continues through the clearing.

The tortured faces of children turn to watch her pass with eyes wide and yellow before dipping bleeding jaws back into their meals, bare scapulas glinting in the invisible moon.

None of the men move, save their expanding chests, breathing slow, everything else snuffed out long ago.

The spongy clearing twists, becomes rocky, and her stomach turns as she realizes the soft, sinking soil was immersed in forty years of congealing blood.

Finally, at a precipice overlooking a black void, Jericho.

The little shadow. His back turned.

There's a muted hum, like a million tiny wings.

His body is ragged and torn.

"Lydia," he says.

Everything seems to stay still. This place, this moment, is somewhere far beyond the universe.

"Jericho," she whispers.

He turns, his blue eyes burning bright.

"I tried."

"What happened? What am I?"

He looks to the fissured rock below.

"Love never dies."

"No," she insists. "Shut up. What am I? What did you do?"

"You're perfect," he says. "Every experience you've ever had. Every dream."

Nothing moves. The air carries only their voices and the mysterious hum.

"You've been with me every step of the way. You fell apart. And I've put you back together."

"I watched myself die, Jericho. Someone exactly like me, but it wasn't me."

"It took me so long, but your love stayed with me. Guided me. Through every genetics black market. I've put every piece of you together from memory. With love."

"What did you do?" she asks again. "How many have you..."

"No," he says softly. "It was never meant to be this way. You were supposed to be reborn. A new, clean body. An empty mind. I grew it all myself. I built Caligatha from everything you'd ever loved. I scripted every experience you'd ever revealed to me. Every heartache you'd endured. The day you discovered your mother died in labor. Your old boyfriends. The day you ran away from home because your father boiled the lobster. Cloud candy."

"No," she says.

"You turned out just right. The way you started writing in your notebook. Your father would die and eventually the notebook would turn into memoirs. You would write, and it would be so beautiful."

"No."

"I was so afraid you would become something else, but you became you. You became Lydia. We were supposed to fall in love all over again, and the best part is, it was going to be real. All of it was being written right into a real mind, a *real mind*. Slowly, we would emerge, into the real world, into our old home. We would make Autumn again. She would be born."

"No, Jericho, no."

"But that world isn't real anymore. The *real world* isn't real, Lydia. I only wanted to end the suffering that took you away. But people need their suffering. So they've destroyed everything, just to have their selfish pain. We had to leave. We had to get away. And I really hoped it would still work. When I met you in Caligatha, we fell in love. But when I touch you I don't feel the right feelings. I feel all the pain. The disease. When you lay beside me...the billions dead lay with you. And you melt away, melt away with Autumn inside of you."

"I'm not real," she says. "I'm...I'm fake."

"No," he says gingerly. "You are made of love. You're the only pure thing left."

"I'm not real," she says again.

"I would do anything for you," he says, his voice wavering now. "I've done almost everything."

"I know."

"But I couldn't...Do you know how hard it was to realize–*realize I was the deadest one?* So many years of work, and–I...I couldn't recreate myself. Before. Before the good in me died. I tried to give you myself, without all the...*fucking pain*. But I've had a lot of time to think about things here, and I know it didn't work. I knew you would come here eventually."

"I came for answers."

"I should have sealed this Realm."

"Jericho, you have to make everything stop. All of this. Make it all stop."

"These?–These *murderers?*"

"Look at what you've done, Jericho."

"They'll be here forever. Don't you see? I've made it so they'll never die. What they've always wanted. What we've *all* always wanted. This is my Realm, my rules, and finally, the immortality they deserve."

"Jericho, did you create the disease?"

"I'm the conduit. Vesper Syndrome. It doesn't matter anymore." He steps aside, and the hum grows louder. Behind him, a black figure writhes. "Oh, Verminus. Tell her! Tell how we've conquered death."

The body pulses, waves punctuated by dull shimmers. Flies. A body swarmed by flies.

"*Tell her!*" Jericho screams. "How *everything* is perfect now."

"Jesus, Jericho."

He breathes heavily. "You're here. That can only mean one thing–there's a signal from Earth."

"Yes," she tells him.

"Keene and Emma will guide you. I wouldn't trust anyone else."

She says nothing.

"Now there's only one more thing I can do for you," he says.

He reaches out his arm. A revolver.

"My love is so cold," he says, breathing heavily again.

He turns, fires three shots into the humming mass of flies.

The explosions ring through Lydia's ears.

"You'll never die, Verminus. *None of you* will ever die. I've designed this place to keep you alive forever."

"Jericho–"

"But not me. I've turned off my death-safety," he says. "I'm disconnected from a real body."

He holds out his palms.

"Please," he says.

The metal glimmers, dark purple.

"Make it right. I've waited for this moment. Our old selves may die, but we'll be together forever in my dreams, a new you and a new me. It couldn't be any other way."

She feels the gun. As icy as his hands.

"I am going," she says.

He closes his eyes.

"But not with you."

She presses the barrel to her head and pulls the trigger.

***

"I'd implore us to consider all possibilities, as there are far more negative than positive. It's even possible that we've been mistaken for the craft that may have headed to Gliese. Anyone with the ability to send us that signal might suspect that we have resources and technology to plunder. Or, obviously, they may want to exact revenge. Even if they're not hostile, they might be the last remnants of human life, excepting us, and have no cure."

"What if they don't?" Keene asks. "We stay here? Hoping–actually *hoping*–that they die out down below, and take the disease to the grave with them? *Hoping* we have the opportunity to repopulate the world with a group of so-called humans formerly so affluent they have no concept of reality? Whose idea of drudgery and toil was having to shell their own clams? Men and women so amoral as to abandon their own children?"

"I know," Emma says. "I just don't want anyone's expectations to be too high."

"I don't expect to return to a new Eden, a place of innocence and hope. I don't expect anything. But I've begun to believe that no matter what's below, right here, on this craft, there is nothing human."

"You think landing will change that?"

"Why are we here, Emma?"

"To preserve humanity."

"How human do you feel, then? Because I'm not making the case for anyone else on board, and certainly not myself."

"I don't want that to be true, Keene."

"Before I came to meet you on the island, I tried to write an explanation. A letter. It was more to myself than anyone. I could only conclude that I was part of a futile search for another man's happiness. That I had to see how the story ended. What would happen to Jericho when he discovered that he couldn't just build himself a maze, practice running it, and find his happiness at the end like so many of his test subjects? Isn't that the summation of this entire human experiment? Designing our own maze? Predicting every turn? Because that isn't how it works—we *are* the maze. Forget about Realm. Our social delusions were the first artificial construct we bought into. The idea that we had to navigate through other people. Every time we twist someone's fate with our own conclusions, try to nail their behavior with our own convictions, we turn them into a wall. In this supposed age of boundless horizons, there were so many walls, so much predictability, it's no surprise the whole thing toppled so easily. Everyone's idea of freedom was just another person's intended action. Down to the last minute, Jericho might have been the most clever man of all in navigating his maze, but I just *had* to know what would happen when all the walls, *all the walls*, were down and he realized he was really, truly, alone. That she would not return."

"Keene..."

"But he took the delusion one step further than I could have imagined. Just before we leave, he unveils his hidden passenger. His reconstructed idea of love. He knows she will never, ever be the exact same person. At the end of that maze she was what he was waiting for. But he knew she wouldn't be there. So he finally, after all these years, turned her into his last wall. Out of all the things he knew. All the history. All the predictability. Forgetting that the most precious moments he'd spent with her, she changed him in some way. Accepting that truth was his way out. But he turned her into the last wall of his maze, and now there is *no* way out. We're trapped inside."

Emma says nothing.

"So even if Lydia is the only chance at there ever being an honest life, I say we return. Because, I'll be damned if it makes any sense to me, but I feel more compassion and empathy for this woman, pieced together like a golem, from some perverted black magic biology...than I have for anyone but you. And we've already made our share of choices."

Emma nods. "She decides."

"We go," Lydia's voice says from the doorway. She sips a glass of water, staring through them.

"MAIA," Emma says. "Let's make that landing happen." A silhouette against the screen's morphing boxes and colors, she says, "Let's hope this isn't a mistake."

But Lydia's gone.

"Stay here," Emma says.

22

Downward

Lydia lays on her back, staring at the dull slit of light above her, wondering. All those dreams of nothingness, an in utero landscape.

For a moment, she considers going back into all those other Realms, Caligatha and Panacea, putting a gun to everyone's head and pulling the trigger. Forcing everyone awake.

She hears breathing, but doesn't move. Emma is in her doorway, looking down.

Neither say a word, and Emma approaches the foot of her bed, sits.

The silence continues until Emma bursts into tears.

"It isn't fair," she says. "Those with the gift to create life only create more pain."

Lydia closes her eyes.

"I didn't know, Lydia. We didn't know until the last moment. We didn't know what to do."

Emma wipes her eyes.

"I've seen the worst in humanity. I've seen people hurt each other, throw each other away like trash. Keene and I...I've spent so much time feeling like the bastard child of humanity."

Lydia sits up. "You have no idea what that feels like."

Emma nods. "My entire life, I've only wanted to do something of value, to watch something good come from me. And all I've done is help the worst people turn their money into delusions and more pain."

"That seems to be a thing ever since I've woken up," she says bitterly.

"I don't know what the best thing to do is, I guess I never did, but I want you to know you're the only reason we're still here."

Lydia lays back, closes her eyes.

"Keene doesn't know this, but before we left, after we found out about you...I cornered Jericho in his cabin. I closed the door. We have armaments on board...in the event of a hostile rescue. I put a gun to Jericho's head and told him just how fucking crazy I thought he was. That I've always doubted the reliability of his equations predicting mass human extinction. But I've had my own cross to bear. I've wanted more than anything else to raise a family, maybe...not even to create life, not to be a mother, just to...feel normal. And Keene wants that, too. I'm guilty of wanting that too much, and to make him happy. I love Keene more than anything, and it pains me so much to see him think of himself as a mere practical joke. So I've overlooked these things. Told myself I was protecting something. Giving us purpose. But I couldn't overlook it anymore."

"I don't care about your motherly intuitions," Lydia says, unmoving. "Or your infertility. Or your purpose."

"I know. You shouldn't. But even the purest things can lead to such terrible delusions. I asked if it had already started. You were already alive. I didn't know what to do, Lydia. Which is why I'm trying to act on justice rather than love. I could have ended all of this painlessly. I could have shut all of this down. But you're here, and you're very real, and even now I'm still trying to protect, when what justice means is for the one person who hasn't acted out of love or self-interest to determine their own future."

"All I want," Lydia says, pacing her words with deliberation, "is to feel the ground beneath my feet, and know what real loneliness feels like. Not lonely like a fish in a bowl. Lonely like the last fish in the ocean. I'm owed that. I want to go to the place everyone else calls home, where I've never been, and if nothing is there, I just want to walk the beach alone."

"Okay," Emma says, stifling her cry.

"Every second since I've woken up, I lose more and more. I'm already the living opposite of life. And I'm disappearing. Living backwards, down to the point I'm nothing at all. I've been unborn. I just want to come out and see what's on the other side."

She means it, really means it. Want isn't a feeling she can understand anymore, but to be able to walk the surface of the Earth in true loneliness, finally know she's out of things to lose. It's the only conclusion that makes sense anymore.

"Okay," Emma says again, standing. "We'll begin our descent soon." And after a hesitation, considering word after word but finding nothing to say, she leaves, closing the door behind her.

But Lydia can still hear the sobbing, rolls onto her side.

How is it possible, having not only lost everything, but having discovered she never had anything to begin with, to still feel hurt? She wants nothing more than to stop Emma's pain, but instead she shuts her eyes so hard they start to sting.

***

Keene sits with Methuselah, thawed apple slice in hand.

Emma's watching from the hallway.

"We lament our lost time," he says. "And I wonder what our friend here has done for forty years."

She starts toward him, head down, hiding her eyes.

"What good is time, without anything worth doing?" he asks.

"You would have made a good father, you know."

He looks up, but she's still hiding her eyes.

"No," he says. "Not like you. One can worry too much about not seeing the whole picture. I've spent my life trying to understand things as they happen until it's too late to change them. There's something to be said for getting things done."

She sits, smiles with red eyes. "I guess that just means they would love you more."

He hands her the apple slice, watches Methuselah sniff the air. "How is she?"

"In pain," she says, feeding the mouse.

He nods.

"We should've stayed below, Keene. Gotten what we deserved. All of this would have happened without us."

"Would that have made it better?"

"All we've done is give her a false sense of hope."

"I like to think that if we're alone, we've lost nothing, and can perhaps find peace. And if we're not, it's an opportunity to start being honest, at least go forward with dignity. We have an obligation to make the best of whatever she wants."

"She wants something she can't have."

"Well then, she should never question whether she's human."

"It's a question I'm tired of," Emma says. "Maybe if the people that got us into this mess asked that question, we wouldn't be here. What kind of world is it where Lydia is suffering over that question, but a man from GenAssist blows his brains out because too many people are healthy, and is still given a proper funeral?"

Keene shakes his head. "The only one we ever knew."

"What do you think caused the disease?"

"I don't know."

"Do you really think it was an evolutionary response?"

"I don't know, but I think it's telling that if all that death was at our own hands, I find it murderous, and if it was an act of nature, I'm inclined to perceive it as justice."

"What do you mean? That nature knows best?"

"No, but we know better. And it might be our refusal to behave accordingly that's made greed our own ingrained population-thinner. Perhaps this was the only way for us to go forward. To stop worrying about whether our progress made us less human when people capable of producing plagues to inhibit the equal distribution of progress were still in the gene pool."

"I don't think that's very scientific," Emma says. "But I think that's what you would call poetic justice."

"Indiscriminate. But so were we."

"If you're right, maybe that isn't the only world we'll ever know. If we're being given a new start, I'll fight for better."

***

Lydia awakens to a low buzzing tone, the light above her now blinking a dull blue.

MAIA's voice comes from everywhere, "Begin making your way to the attachment pod. Descent will begin in twenty minutes."

She tries to picture waves breaking on the beach, but can only picture Caligatha, its looming city of stone hanging over the empty sand.

"All passengers must be secured in their cabins."

She tries to picture only her own footsteps behind her on the beach, but billboards stare back. The sand is pristine.

Her heart begins racing, and she focuses on her breathing, but then Keene is at her doorway.

"Come on. It's your hour."

She closes her eyes as he touches her shoulder, and in a soothing voice he says, "Follow me."

She rises in silence.

"The entire sleeping quarters detach," Keene's saying, "but the three of us are going this way," and he heads to the end of the hall, opens the last door.

It isn't another cabin, but a larger room with four chairs facing forward, screens running the entire perimeter. Emma is sitting, her back to them.

Keene walks to the chair nearest Emma, picks a box off the seat. "I don't believe you've met," he says, handing Lydia the box, then sits.

Lydia takes a seat behind him, peering through slits in the box. A little white mouse looks up, black eyes glinting. Only the third living, wide awake thing she's seen in her entire life.

"Ten minutes," MAIA is saying.

They sit in silence, Emma occasionally reaching forward to touch a screen.

"His name is Methuselah," Keene says. Lydia watches his pink nose sniff the air.

"Five minutes."

"You'd better set him next to you," he tells her, and she places the box on the empty seat. Jericho's seat. "He's spent forty years in our green room. It's time you gave him a better home."

She feels something wrap around her feet, then her waist, and looking at Jericho's seat she watches an amorphous material fluidly wrap around the box and tighten.

"We'll be fine," Emma says, but Lydia knows it's a lie, and Emma knows she's lying.

"One minute."

At this, there's a faint vibration coursing through everything. She can feel it in every limb, in her head.

She realizes she won't land near anything like Caligatha, no beach, no water, no buildings she'll recognize. MAIA's talking but she thinks of the places she's never been, forests and valleys and tundra and marshes.

Then there's a sensation like falling in a dream, except when she clenches her fingers into the armrest it doesn't go away, keeps pulling her down from inside.

Ice runs through her veins and she doesn't realize she's talking until she's been doing it for a while, saying "I'm sorry," over and over.

She's going to get all of them killed, there's no way there could be anything good for them below, and all of this is over her. She thinks of Emma crying outside her cabin, her saying she doesn't care over and over.

"It'll be okay," Keene soothes, and he's talking about landing safely and there's going to be people below, good people, and she's going to have a new life, the life she deserves, except that isn't what she wants at all.

She doesn't know how long it goes on, minutes or hours, but just as she's gotten used to the falling and can breathe, looking at the screens and realizing Emma's watching her heart-rate and an endless array of numbers about her, there's a sudden jolt. She's weightless.

***

Lydia comes to crashing backwards, thinking in reverse. Her forehead sticky, pulling her hands away, red. Blood. It falls from her fingertips, dripping up to the ceiling.

Then she remembers the giant rock formation, two bright white scissor arms sticking out of the flesh-colored ground ahead.

Then how the screen surrounding them changed, revealing so many colors pooled together like clouds of white and brown with little green patches.

Emma had been yelling, yelling at MAIA. They hadn't ejected, were going to crash, and she remembers trying to break free from the seat as Emma struggled to land somewhere flat.

She feels her eyelids close, a heaviness pumping through her entire body, but Keene is yelling at her.

He's below her, reaching his arm out, and she realizes she's upside down, crushed between her seat and the wall.

Squirming, pushing with all her strength, the seat falls back and Keene grabs her arm. She isn't crushed.

Everything falls in a painful mess, the seat following her, hitting her head, her falling on top of Keene, until she lands on hard rock below.

Ten feet above, stuck between giant bone white rock, the orbiter hangs, blinding in the reflected sun. The seat stuck above her head, wedged in the open hatch.

Her whole body aching, skin burning, she tries to sit up. Keene is beside her, his arm twisted at an impossible angle. Emma is a few feet away, on her knees, disoriented.

All around her, a world of baking clay, rolling dust and waves of heat. Everything spins and twists.

She tries to find a comfortable position and sit still, but she shakes all over until her body forces her onto her side and she vomits hard.

The sensation of her baking skin, the acid in her mouth and nose.

Then something explodes above, like a gunshot, and she's afraid the suspended orbiter is going to come crashing down, feels her arms and legs flailing.

Keene is yelling something, but a giant white insect body descends over her and she screams, flailing harder but getting nowhere.

It extends long, spindly legs around her, down to the ground, its torso close enough to touch. A blank white face, like a mask, stares down, expressionless. Where the eyes and mouth should be there's round protrusions, glowing red. The torso slides open, in half, and a series of bright flashes envelop her body. Thin wires whip out of the legs, grabbing her arms, piercing her wrist.

Then everything retracts and it stands erect. A group of half-limbs flanking each side twist around, begin blowing air and throwing up dust around her until the thing is floating again, turning its head to Keene.

Now she sees a second one hovering over Emma, striking her with its series of intense flashes. The process repeats for Keene, so much dust in the air now she can barely see anyone, and then they ascend higher, above the dust and turning their heads across the horizon.

Emma and Keene are standing up, but she feels an onset of nausea again, waits to throw up.

"We're okay," Keene says, but Emma starts yelling, limping forward, faster and faster.

More gunshot sounds, except these sound like they're real gunshots, and Emma is yelling ahead with cupped hands, "It's a medic!" In front of Emma, shots are reflecting off one of the hovering white bodies with long legs. It's struck in the face, the expressionless mask falling to its chin.

The other has made its way much farther by now, performing its lightshow over a just-discernable body until a shot makes it fall.

Then, through the dust, Lydia watches something shoot through Emma's body, a thick black line spiraling out behind her and splashing loud and wet on the rock below.

Screams are coming from all directions. Time seems frozen, Emma's body flowing gracefully, following the blood trail and falling back. Keene is running through the dust.

Through a gap in the dense white, Lydia catches an overturned vehicle on a stretch of road in the distance, just beyond the source of the gunshots, but then Keene's yelling out, collapsing violently as a chunk of his neck explodes in a burst of black. Lydia feels the spray, cool against her hot face.

A red laser sight pierces the dust, and two figures emerge, standing over the slowly writhing bodies.

"Holy shit," one says, steadying the butt of a rifle against his shoulder, aiming erratically back and forth between Keene and Emma, bright red line shaking over their faces.

Keene gurgles more black, pooling around his neck and running in dark lines across the rock, spreading thin fingers towards Lydia.

"They don't make none of this anymore," the other says.

Emma lurches up, and another shot, another burst of black. She's screaming, screaming, screaming and it doesn't end, doesn't change, inhuman, one long and extended note, slowly getting quieter and quieter until it's gone.

Then they see her. She throws her hands over her face, red light shining between her fingers.

"Don't move! Don't move!" one of them yells.

"Ah, shit, what the fuck *is* that?" the other says.

Peering between her fingers, she sees them look up at the orbiter.

"Okay," the one without a rifle says. "Okay. Watch her." He paces away, screaming now. "*Crane! Fuck!* They've got fucking medbots and droids."

He continues walking off, rambling in anger.

"What the *hell*, man?" the other says, shaking his laser sight across her face.

She looks over at Keene, starts crawling towards him. He struggles to turn his ravaged neck as she approaches.

"Lydia," he manages, choking. His blood is so thick, pure black, pooled under her palms.

"You're..." she begins.

He tries to nod. "You are," he manages, slow. "Human."

"Keene," she sobs, "You're the most human person I know."

"Emma."

Her body is still.

"What did they do to you?" She demands.

"You are," he repeats. "I passed." A gush of black. "The test. A year... as professor...but..." He struggles to look at Emma, moves his arm towards her slowly. "The real test," and he closes his eyes, taking his time, "is the same...for flesh." The black stops running from his neck. "Regrets."

"No, Keene," she says softly.

"Go." His lips unmoving. "And."

Behind her the men are talking, and in the thinning dust she can see more approaching, more men with laser sights relaxed and shining on the dirt.

Before she realizes what she's doing, she's at the foot of the rock, scrambling up, sliding, struggling to overcome her defeated muscles until she's reached the hatch. Her abdomen feels gutted as she exhausts the last of her strength hoisting herself up with slippery arms. She makes it in just as the yelling starts below.

"This is not where they were supposed to land!" someone yells. "And you didn't say a fucking thing about droids or medbots!"

"We can't lose our cool over one crushed truck!" a voice hollers.

"Perez is fucking dead and military bots are fucking crawling out with flashing lights, what do you expect, Crane? It looks like a *goddam* ambush."

She steals a last look back, but the men are still arguing amongst themselves.

"Anything should have been expected!"

One hits another hard across the face, and then the scuffle ends as they all look up at her.

But now she's on her knees, slick on the floor with her and Keene's blood.

"MAIA," she's begging, "We have to go. We have to go back."

"There's insufficient fuel for a second return," MAIA calmly tells her.

"Just *go*," she screams.

"Are you sure you want to return to orbit and–"

No, no she doesn't know what she's doing but this isn't the lonely beach, the real end of the world, there's only more death.

"Get me the fuck out of here," she sobs.

"Twenty minutes are required for cool-down"

"Okay," she says breathlessly. "Okay."

There's a rending, mechanical sound behind her.

"To begin preparation for ascension, the rear escape pod hatch must be sealed. Check for and clear any blockage."

The seat. She scrambles over, pushing against it with her weary muscles, but it won't budge. Shoving as hard as she can, she finally stands over it, peering at the rock below, looking for leverage as she places all her weight on it. It gives way, her arms flailing for anything to hold onto, but they only whip back and she's falling down, landing with the seat on the rock.

Above her, the hatch door slips into place.

She's surrounded by rifles.

"Who are you?" a man without a rifle asks her, adjusting a pair of dark, broken sunglasses. The man who was hit during the argument. He's younger than the others, dressed in a simple plaid shirt and jeans rather than covered in equipment.

She's too hurt to say anything.

"Alright," he says, "Bring the trucks around. Let's load all this up. Get to work opening the hatch, quick. We don't have time to waste. This place is gonna be crawling any minute."

As the men scatter, she watches the blood-stained ground.

The youngest man kneels down, takes off his sunglasses and stares her in the face.

"Where you from, lady? Anything in there I should know about?" he nods to the orbiter.

She watches a lone red ant stop at the edge of Keene's black blood. Flatbed trucks are pulling up around them.

"Look," he says. "We don't have time for a friendly chat. Now, I can tell you're injured pretty bad. You need medical help, and a place to stay. If I'm right, we can offer you temporary refuge. But try anything funny and you'll end up like them."

He nods at his men, approaching Keene and Emma's bodies cautiously, prodding them with the barrels of their rifles, then hoisting their limp forms into the trucks.

Several men are struggling with the giant white insect-like bodies, hauling them in one per truck.

He smiles, gives her a hand.

The orbiter begins wailing, and his eyes widen.

"No," he mouths.

His hand grabs hers, hard, and as abruptly as she fell to Earth, she's evacuated onto a truck.

"*Where is it going?*" he demands, his voice and eyes wild.

"Away," is all she manages.

He surveys the orbiter, unable to sit still, as though about to leap back out and pin it down himself.

He starts to speak as the truck revs, but collapses in disappointment and slams his hand on the flatbed.

So this is it. A prisoner once again.

***

Lydia and the man in plaid, who the others have called Crane, ride across from each other in the bed of the truck, bumping and speeding along, leaving a haze on the dirty asphalt behind them amongst the dead brush and trash-littered desert.

He's given her a surgical mask to keep over her face. It itches, and her trapped breath makes her all the more hot.

Beside her, a woman in fatigues named Mae stares icily at Crane, unspeaking.

He sits with one arm on a rifle longer than the other men had, with all kinds of intricate instruments and a hazy blue screen reflecting everything they pass. It must be some kind of sniper. The other arm holds a flask at his chest.

He repeats the same routine every few minutes: looks into the cab nervously, gulps from the flask, adjusts his sunglasses, and says something different.

First, "That was some interesting stuff we picked up back there." Then, "So, are you gonna tell me where you're from?" Then, "We're staying on 15 for now, but I can't let you see where we go when we hit the city."

Finally, he takes his sunglasses off again, squinting in the hot sun. "I'm sorry about your friends."

In the distance, just a tiny dot by now, Lydia watches the orbiter righting itself from its wedged gliding position, standing upright with a large plume billowing around its base. She catches him watching it too, and he mouths *God damn it* and breathes deeply.

"Stop," Crane yells to the driver, knocking on the truck's window.

They slow, watching the orbiter rise.

"Lydia," she says, dismissive. Her voice muffled by the mask.

"Alright," he says, returning his attention to her. "Got a place that you come from, Lydia?"

All she can think about is Emma's sickening scream, unending, one long and gut-wrenching sound of terror, slipping slowly into silence.

"Realm," she says.

"Realm?" He pretends to laugh. "No one's used that in forever."

She can only see the black gushing from Keene's neck in a heartbeat rhythm.

"Are you trying to tell me you're not infected?"

She looks him in the face.

"Bullshit," he says. "Everyone's been infected for decades. Are you trying to tell me you rammed us with a fuckin' time machine back there?"

Lydia says nothing. He's playing games with her. He knows more than he's letting on. He knows more than even she does. *Everyone* knows more than she does.

She watches the tiny dot lifting off. Just a faint white streak cutting through the sunrise, through layers of blood and honey, through bruised and then violet sky.

She feels a tinge of panic, thinking of Methuselah, but tells herself it was just a mouse. Just a mouse.

She's lost so much, what does the mouse matter?

But they're the same. Someone's insignificant stray pet.

The orbiter enters the atmosphere between swaths of sky.

Crane tenses again, holding back some inner fireball, then chugs the flask and puts his sunglasses back on. He knocks on the window again.

"No luck," he says, apparently having hoped it'd crash.

"What do you want?" she asks as the truck begins moving again, but he doesn't answer.

They drive a while in silence. The woman, Mae, tells Crane "Perez is dead," and "I hope it was worth it." But Crane says nothing.

"How many are there?" she finally asks.

"How many what?"

"How many survived?"

He leans forward. "What? Survived what? You're not talking about the disease?"

"Vesper Syndrome."

"You're delusional." Then he looks at the other flatbeds, at the bodies. "It doesn't make any sense. You come flying out of nowhere in a strange aircraft with out-of-production bots and droids and don't know anything about the last four decades?"

He's still acting, maybe just for her, maybe for everyone else too. She refuses to play along.

"It doesn't make sense to me either."

"Come on," he says. "Am I wasting my time here?" He raises a brow. "Was there anyone else on board?"

Nothing but endless desert passes in every direction. Caligatha is long, long gone.

"Jericho Amara."

He tilts his head, then pretends to laugh, still not truly amused. But then he stops, appears to realize something. He takes his sunglasses off again, stares at her.

"Holy shit," he says, backing up. "Lydia, you're dead."

"Something like that."

"I knew you looked familiar. You've been dead my *whole life*. You've gotta start giving me some answers."

She starts shaking at the word *dead*.

"Jericho cloned her, planted memories in her–in my–head, and we've been sleeping in space for *my* whole life."

He relaxes his brow, exchanging glances with Mae, who remains silent.

"It's a little complicated," she says. "I just found out about it myself. Sorry to waste your time."

"Wait, wait." He drinks from the flask. Calculating. Finding himself on the other end of the game now. "So Jericho is alive?"

He looks to the horizon again, and she follows his gaze. The streak in the distance has dissipated Gone.

Is Jericho alive?

"No."

"Just you?"

She looks at the bodies in the other trucks. "Now it is."

"Shit," he says, leaning back. "You might not be infected yet. When we get to the refuge, you need to clean up immediately. I can keep you that way."

She shrugs, adjusts the surgical mask. "Really? I thought you just didn't like my face."

"Lydia, if I can trust you, you might be able to help us." He watches her for a reaction, then asks why they came back.

"I never asked to *go*," she says.

"But what was the catalyst?"

"They thought someone sent a signal out. They thought there was a cure."

"No," he says.

She shrugs again.

"You sent the signal," she says.

"No. The Republic has been seeking you. We were in the right place at the right time."

She doesn't know what it means. Doesn't care.

"You need rest, and we're almost to the refuge now. I hope we can trust each other."

He puts his sunglasses back on, bottom-ups the flask.

"I'll be damned," he says.

He's right. Her eyelids grow heavy as they continue thumping along, a cityscape appearing in the distance. Nothing like Caligatha, this one is made of steel and glass and concrete.

"You never answered me," she says, struggling to hold her head up. "How many are alive?"

He considers this for a moment. "Here in the States... It's impossible to know. Eh, thirty or forty mil?"

All that wondering if somebody, anybody was alive. Anyone at all.

"You sent the signal," she tells him, closing her eyes.

He's quiet for a long time, and she begins to drift off.

Maybe to himself, he says, "There isn't a cure, but we have medicines to keep the side effects at bay."

"Wasteland," she says absently.

He laughs. "Ain't it always?"

She opens her eyes one last time, catching him forlornly staring at the sky, at his disappeared prize, at the only place she's ever known.

23

Refuge

    She's blindfolded once they reach the city. Crane gingerly tells her he has no choice, they can't risk the refuge being discovered, and rips his plaid sleeve off and ties it around her eyes. She remembers passing battered signposts along the way, but had been too tired to read them.
    They continue driving, stop-and-go, finally pulling into what sounds like gravel with a wide swing. But he still won't remove her blindfold, leads her through the stony path.
    There's the sound of old metal groaning, chains banging together, and he continues leading her onto what feels like tile, and then the metal groaning again.
    "I'm sorry this is such a process," he says, removing her blindfold. "Keep that mask over your face."
    All around her are beds, perhaps a hundred, row after row, some with machines beside them and some little more than broken cots. Children of all ages are curled under white sheets, some awake and sitting up. Many of them are missing arms or have many different types of prosthetics, mostly cheap metal appendages that barely resemble functional hands. Sunlight pours through high vertical windows above a metal catwalk connecting two rooms and glares off the seamless floor below.
    Behind her, the men are carrying Keene and Emma and the hulking insectoid bodies. There's a receiving door shuttering closed, chains still clanking.

"This used to be a slaughterhouse," Crane tells her. "Now it's the opposite. That's all you need to know for now."

Walking across the catwalk and to a long stairwell is a figure, entirely white.

"This is Eva," Crane tells her. "While you're here, you'll do as she or I say, and whenever you leave you don't mention any of this."

"Well, well," Eva says, descending the stairs. "What have we here?"

Everything about her is white. Her hair, the white cut off blouse under her white apron. Especially her face. Caked in layers of white makeup, only her pink lips and the shadow of her eyes showing through, there's almost an angelic appearance to it except there's something not right, something disfigured, asymmetrical. As she approaches, Lydia sees she's not only covered in white, but her eyes are the lightest albino blue-purple, and there's an imbalance in her jaw and cheek bone, like she's suffered a gunshot wound to the face. She's hidden her disfigurement from the children with an exaggeration of her albinism.

Eva looks her over, then moves onto the white insect bodies, studies them, running her hands over the gunshots on the most damaged one. She pulls the face dangling from its chin.

"You have refuge here, if you want it," she says, then walks to the nearest child's bed, placing the face over her own. "Boo!"

The child, only about five and missing a hand, giggles and throws the sheets over her head, pretending to be frightened.

Eva turns back to Lydia. "I have a lot of questions, and so do you. But first you should get clean. Get some serum in you so you don't have to walk around with that awful mask on your face."

"Come on," Crane says, motioning for her to follow him up the stairs.

"In return," Eva calls, "We'll be keeping your MeDX Medics. As you can see, they'll be put to good use."

Crane shows her the rooms on the second floor. The first four rooms are sleeping quarters, then a closet-sized lavatory, then an armory.

He lets her shower privately in the lavatory, little more than a rigged, pressureless hose and drain in the corner. In the dim lighting from an ancient incandescent bulb above, Lydia watches the endless blood wash away.

He waits outside with an alcohol-dipped cotton ball and a little syringe and says, "I hope you trust us."

"What do you want?" she asks.

He shrugs, rubs the alcohol on her forearm and expertly pricks a vein.

"You're tired," is all he says, then shows her to her quarters. "The serum is a mix of things. In the worst-case scenario, it will stifle the effects for several weeks. In the best-case scenario, you might have resistance. But I haven't been able to do a trial until now. With your permission, I'd like to run some blood tests when you're rested." He stares into her room. "Sleep well."

She looks around at the metal walls, the bare mattress in the corner.

"Who are you?" she asks.

"Doctors of sorts. Get some sleep."

He closes the door, and she moves to the bed. Every muscle aches as she lies down.

Everything is a prison. She only moves from cell to cell.

***

She can't sleep. It might be hours, but she lies staring into the dim, bland room, listening to faint chatter from the children below.

Every time she closes her eyes, she sees something horrible.

Keene's neck exploding. The feral children in Jericho's nightmare.

Eventually there's arguing outside her room between Crane and Eva, and she pushes up through the pain, places her ear to the door.

"Because it's not safe," Eva is saying. "You're always making promises we can't fulfill."

"Cassandra," Crane is pleading, even though it's certainly Eva's voice he's talking to, "Just give me until I run tests. I finally have someone that might really be uninfected."

"Someone that's fallen out of the sky in a billion dollar satellite. Someone associated, or claiming to be associated, with Amano, who had ties to every corporation that has us by the throat."

"You saw the data on the droids' memory as clearly as I did. We agreed on this."

"Not on keeping her. We were supposed to gut the orbiter for any leads. There was no plan for sheltering anyone long-term. This is the exact opposite of our plan."

"It's only one person. And now we have a second set of droids to decode."

"What are we going to tell everyone else about this, Crane? Eric is already tired of the secrecy. We have to straighten this out tonight, or getting punched is just the beginning. We'll have a mutiny on our hands by morning."

Lydia pulls away from the door, lays on her bed and weeps.

Everywhere she goes, she's a prisoner and bringer of death.

Those lonely beaches she'd longed for seem so impossibly far. Never had she pictured barren deserts or slaughterhouses refashioned into infirmaries. And the people, too–at worst she'd expected everyone to be obliterated, gone, forgotten to the world and forever unknown to her. But all those mangled children, she'd never expected that.

She curls into a ball just as there's a tap at her door.

It creaks, and in walks Crane.

"Just wanted to see how you're doing."

"I can't sleep," she says. "I don't want this."

"I understand," he says and sits. "Listen, for right now you need to stick to a very specific story, no matter how you feel. It's a simple story. You wouldn't be here if you didn't run us off the road. We were in the middle of intercepting a shipment of medicine to a corporate compound. We couldn't risk anything, and brought you back." He pulls out another flask, hands it to her. "We'll get to the real story after you've had time to rest."

"Fuck it," she says, grabs his flask and takes a burning gulp.

"You should know," he says, "I don't want you to be too afraid or think too much of the world outside just yet, but life is always shit, and you've been through a lot. There are a lot of people that won't believe what you've been through, either. You're always going to encounter assholes who think everything they're up against is the worst thing in the world."

She tries to swallow away the burning, tasteless sensation. "I just want to be alone. I don't care if anyone believes me."

Crane takes the flask back, swallows. "That's not what you really want. If you really wanted that you wouldn't be here. You wouldn't've come back."

"Does it look like I want to be here?"

Crane snickers and gulps again, tosses the flask on the bed. "No one wants to be anywhere. That's how your dreamworld came to be, sweetheart. Jerk-offs spending their paychecks to be an anthropomorphic rabbit or pig or some shit for a day, to fuck avatars of little kids. Being *anything* is overrated, being *anything* gets old. The first thing that gets old is being a quality human."

He stands. "That's yours," he says, nodding at the flask. "When was the last time you felt happy?"

He's heading to the door, means for her to mull it over, but without thinking she says, "When I thought I was giving my father a last good memory. Making up for all the times I was obsessed with making him happy, but not really doing that at all. I was really obsessed with paying our rent and his medical bills. On my last day, I took him to all the places that made him happy to be a father, and me happy to be his daughter. But all of that turned out to be a lie, so what good was it?"

Crane backtracks, picks up the flask, shakes it at her knowingly and swallows. "Did it? Who were you lying to?"

And then he's gone.

***

Lydia spends her days helping Eva administer serum to the children, and teaches them how to adjust to their new appendages. There's feeding schedules, and counseling sessions for which no one is qualified. Fights break out, and the kids sneak in drugs and alcohol. Sometimes they find a malnourished Expectant Mother Unit, and Eva confiscates it in anger, and the scary organic doll is never seen again.

The youngest ones cry and scream in the middle of the night. Some come and go, only dropped off by their desperate and scavenging parents. Some are new. Some never return.

She's already been infected.

Crane's always leaving for the "lab," or he and his officers leave with their combat rifles strapped to their back, returning with more serum or medical devices or food. Sometimes they're terribly injured by gunshots. Or the carnivorous wildlife. The animals are a lot more confrontational now that they've digested Jericho's artificial immune system.

"It's a real shit show," Crane told her. "The best laid plans, *etcetera, etcetera*."

They say one day they might be able to repair Keene and Emma, but their sticky black bodies were locked up in storage in the second building. They're sorry about all that.

Sometimes she can hear Crane and Eva arguing, or having sex, or Eva crying. Except in all those moments Eva is always Cassandra. Afterward, almost every night, Crane stops by Lydia's room and fills her own personal flask, a gift for working so hard and not selling them out.

The bridge of truth always leads to another lie.

At night, she still can't sleep well. When she does rest, she no longer dreams of empty beaches, but the nightmares she's seen during the day.

When she wakes, covered in hot sweat, she drinks from the flask, mindful to leave enough for daytime, and thinks of the world far above. The seventy passengers of permanent dream.

No matter how many children's eyes she stares into, telling them the feeling of their missing fingers will transfer to the scrap metal at their wrists, that they'll be able to hold crayons and draw scary monsters, and no matter how often they remind her that it's a scary world and they don't know what crayons are and they need to hold guns–still, sometimes she panics at the thought of the broken paradise above. Sometimes she panics, wants to burst through her ceiling and rip those passengers of dream who've abandoned their children out of eternal sleep, out of those cramped little cabins.

She wonders in those moments why the scariest things she's seen are the things that don't exist, then she sips her flask some more, and thinks it must have always been so.

She doesn't wonder anymore if she's human. She knows she's not happy, and she's drinking too much. Her greatest longing remains not so much freedom as to simply step out into the wilderness and see the sun, even have those moments on the beach where no one has ever existed, even her, her own footprints disappearing in the sand.

She knows Eva doesn't trust her, and the kids don't like her very much. She has no maternal instincts. And it'll only be a matter of time before Crane tries collect his interest on all that alcohol.

Still. The only time she feels real terror is when she remembers worlds far worse.

Those scary words.

Panacea. Elysium. Harmony. Rapture.

The grotesque doesn't scare her anymore. Not the tortured clay people shaped out of dream. Not the feral children.

It's the seventy sleepers, drifting eternally like the leftover embers of a great fire.

In those moments, she sips her warm moonshine, and remembers an old mantra.

They're not really there. They're not really there.

Worlds come and go with the sun, Crane tells her. Everyone thinks they're living in end times. Everyone thinks their life is meaningless.

It makes vanity easy.

In this story there is no yesterday, no tomorrow.

There's no end, no destination. Just eternal transition, he tells her.

There's no linear time.

But there is a beginning and it's every place, every time all at once.

The story's just getting started.

Lightning Source UK Ltd.
Milton Keynes UK
UKHW021145090120
356646UK00012B/1261/P